advance p

the nowhere p...

"A made-in-Halifax *Lives of Girls and Women*, Susan LeBlanc's *The Nowhere Places* is the novel I've been longing to read most if not all of my adult life. This powerful debut is a profoundly moving story about daring to be different in the small, white-washed city my generation knew growing up—the Halifax of the 1970s as riven by entrenched rivalries as it was (and still is) sustained by tightly-knit families and communities. A city where the boundaries between its working-class North and affluent South End seemed impenetrable, a city where those of modest means lived in quiet desperation chafing against the desire for more. Against this milieu, a time and place as stifling as it was nurturing, LeBlanc's exquisitely drawn girls and women strive for selfhood, dare to make lives that are fully their own. Just as Alice Munro's book was a revelation back in those days, so too is LeBlanc's: I cannot think of a more vivid, truthful portrait of ourselves or of this era and place. Gutting, uplifting, propulsive, *The Nowhere Places* is a triumph. I love this book."
CAROL BRUNEAU, author of *Threshold* and *Brighten the Corner Where You Are*

"In a loving and clear-eyed depiction of North End Halifax at the turn of the 1980s, Susan LeBlanc's *The Nowhere Places* immerses us in a time and setting that feels both minutely and beautifully particular, yet deeply relatable and free from the kitsch and sentimentality of nostalgia. LeBlanc writes her characters—the sensitive, teenaged Lulu, the weary single

mother June, and a myriad of memorable, sharply drawn secondary characters—with nuance, compassion, and a telescopic view of the world as it was then that is grounded in the one we know now. LeBlanc's hilariously funny yet heartbreakingly sad story reflects the tenderness and grit of David Adams Richards's *Nights Below Station Street* or Heather O'Neill's *Lullabies for Little Criminals*. It offers a stirring and deeply satisfying story of a community that will keep you turning the page."
BECCA BABCOCK, author of *Some There Are Fearless*

"Susan LeBlanc has given us a portrait of North End Halifax that is both graceful and gritty. This gentle, understated novel draws us intimately into the lives of ordinary people, with all the love, worries, triumphs, and losses of ordinary lives. I found myself caring very much about them all, especially loving their courage as they try, over and over again, to do the right thing."
ANNE BISHOP, author of *Under the Bridge*

"*The Nowhere Places* explores the consequences of secrets held close to the heart—the guilt, the shame, and even the regret when those closely held secrets are eventually exposed. Told with compassion and a deep understanding of what motivates her characters, LeBlanc eases the reader through the ripple effect of those touched by the lives of others. A moving portrayal of the courage and the struggle to find one's own place in the world, no matter what age. A story that tugs gently at the heart."
LAURA BEST, author of *Good Mothers Don't*

the nowhere places

susan leblanc

Author's Note on Language

In this fictional story set in Halifax in 1979 and 1980, the characters use words, including labels for others, authentic to the time but which we now know are offensive. I have used this language with care and to help tell a story that genuinely represents its time, with all its biases and prejudices. Language evolves, as does our understanding of it, and seeing how it changes can help us see how our culture itself has changed; our responsibility to write thoughtfully, however, remains the same.

the nowhere places

susan leblanc

Vagrant
PRESS

Vagrant Press is an imprint of
Nimbus Publishing Limited
3660 Strawberry Hill St, Halifax, NS, B3K 5A9
(902) 455-4286 nimbus.ca

Nimbus Publishing is based in Kjipuktuk, Mi'kma'ki, the traditional territory of the Mi'kmaq People.

Printed and bound in Canada

This story is a work of fiction. Names, characters, incidents, and places, including organizations and institutions, either are the product of the author's imagination or are used fictitiously.

Editor: Penelope Jackson
Editor for the press: Whitney Moran
Cover design: Whitney Moran
Cover image: hand-tinted postcard of North End Halifax, from the collection of Dan Soucoup
NB1727

Library and Archives Canada Cataloguing in Publication

Title: The nowhere places / Susan LeBlanc.
Names: LeBlanc, Susan, author.
Identifiers: Canadiana (print) 20240400879 | Canadiana (ebook) 20240412184 |
ISBN 9781774713280
   (softcover) | ISBN 9781774713297 (EPUB)
Subjects: LCGFT: Novels.
Classification: LCC PS8623.E3558 N69 2024 | DDC C813/.6—dc23

Nimbus Publishing acknowledges the financial support for its publishing activities from the Government of Canada, the Canada Council for the Arts, and from the Province of Nova Scotia. We are pleased to work in partnership with the Province of Nova Scotia to develop and promote our creative industries for the benefit of all Nova Scotians.

To my late mother, Carole (Borden) LeBlanc,
a proud North Ender

Prologue

The No. 9 bus veers off the busy road and pulls up to a long building with lots of cars and buses in front of it.

"Shopping centre," the driver calls out, and people start getting off.

Gerald stays on the ripped bench seat, squeezed against the dirty window. He looks up at the bus driver, who's eyeing him in the rear-view mirror.

"End of the line," the driver says. "You gotta get off."

Gerald follows the people down the steps, then stops. The last step to outside looks pretty high off the ground. He doesn't like to be high up. He won't budge.

"Move it," says a woman. She's right behind him; she smells flowery like Nana.

He waggles his foot, reaching for the pavement. He lands funny and his ankle kind of twists. Pain shoots up his ankle and calf.

He stands, unsure. People scurry by, getting on and off buses. He doesn't know this place. There are glass doors that must go into the mall, but he doesn't want to. Someone bumps into him and keeps on going.

"Watch it, buddy," the man calls over his shoulder.

He looks down and he's still holding the transfer the driver gave him. Gerald inches toward the sole bus left at the curb, but the door's closed and on the front it says "Out of Service." He knows what that means.

He wants to go back home. He won't be finding his father, the cowboy, in the wild, wild west today. He walks the wide stretch of pavement that leads to the end of the building and peeks around the corner. A hill slopes to another parking lot, with a line of bushes and train tracks behind. Maybe the train goes to the North End; he hears train whistles when he walks around home.

Two guys with their hoods up arrive and stop a ways from him. They pass a stinky cigarette back and forth. One looks over.

"What you lookin' at, retard?" the guy says. They're mean boys, like Danny and Mikey.

Gerald starts down the hill. He limps and it seems to take a long time to reach the far edge of the parking lot. He stops and stares at the ditch between him and the train tracks. No sign of a train. But he gets an idea, to walk the tracks home, like a boy did on TV.

He just needs to get into the ditch and climb up the other side and onto the tracks. He gets on a knee and dangles his leg, the one that doesn't hurt, searching for the ground. But the ditch is deeper than he thought; he loses his balance and tumbles in. He lies there, the pain from his ankle really bad now, and whimpers.

After a while he stops crying and wipes his face with his sleeve. *Don't be a sook.* He spies something farther down the ditch behind a bush, which is still mostly bare because it's spring. He has to crawl, over dirt and rocks and garbage, chip bags and pop bottles and beer boxes, and when he gets to it, it's just a big piece of cardboard. But it's thick and it's folded in a point like a teepee. He shimmies inside on his stomach.

It's okay in there, like a secret hiding place. The cardboard's dry and smells like books. He curls up and his stomach growls, and he remembers the chocolate bar and Canada Dry he bought before he decided, just like that, to get on the bus. Telling the driver he wanted to go west. He eats and drinks, pulls a cowboy comic book out of his jacket pocket.

June

When Frank's father opened his barbershop in the 1930s, he picked a busy street in North End Halifax. The spot sat between a five and dime and a diner, and he set it up with a striped barber pole and two spinning chairs. He did a good trade for decades. Never dreamed of cutting women's hair, but when Frank took it over in the early sixties he saw the potential. That's when he hired June Green.

Fifteen years later she still draws customers, older women who like the routine of a weekly set, or neighbourhood housewives looking for a bargain. So Frank puts up with her crankiness. On this May afternoon, when June's mother calls, he waves the receiver at her and knows she'll complain about the interruption.

"Not now," she mumbles, bobby pins clasped between her lips. She removes one and secures a pin curl on Doll's head. Trying to make something special out of lank, white hair. Frank lets the phone clatter on the wooden counter.

"It's your mum. Sounds important." He returns to his customer: a weekly shave (needed) and trim (not needed).

June groans. Mom's getting worse, ignoring the rules they've lived by for years like no calls at work. She squeezes Doll's bony shoulder.

"I'll be right back, honey," June says. Doll smiles at her in the mirror.

"Yes, Mom?"

"June, he's missing," her mother says, her voice high and strained. "I don't know what to do. I haven't seen him in hours."

"Who? The cat?"

"No, Gerald. He's not here and he's not up at Farrell's—I called. I fell asleep. June, you better get home."

"For god's sake, you're not thinking straight. He's not missing."

"He is! He is. You never listen to me." Mom stifles a sob. The line goes dead and June shivers.

"Mom?"

June frowns and returns the receiver to the cradle on the wall, the beige corkscrew cord touching the floor. She turns and everyone—Frank, his lonely regular, and Doll the spinster—is looking at her. Don't be a bitch to your mother, they're thinking. She can tell.

"Frank, I don't know, I think I need to go." Her hand goes to the base of her throat. "It's Gerald."

"Go," he says, waving her out. "Get home." He nods and she knows he doesn't mind. He turns to June's customer.

"I'll fix Miss Dolly up, right?" Frank is useless at pin curls and sets. Doll manages a smile.

June hangs her pink smock on the hook and pulls on her raincoat. Rummages for her purse behind the dryer chair with the dome hood. Gerald goes nowhere except to the druggist's or Buppy's. He likes to dilly dally though. That's probably it.

"Call you later, Frank." June opens the glass door and looks back for a second. "Sorry, Doll."

She has ten blocks to cover to get home. She walks at a good clip, grateful for her comfortable work shoes. The cloudy spring day feels like rain. June needs a smoke but doesn't want to pause to light one, knows she doesn't have the breath to walk fast and smoke at the same time. She's heading toward the far north end of the city, past flat-faced wooden houses built to the sidewalk's edge and with few adornments. There's the yeasty smell of the brewery, where Dad worked until he dropped dead in the bottling section.

This can't be real. Gerald has never given her any trouble. Not on purpose.

She gains on the Hydrostone, neat streets of cement row houses built after the Explosion, fronted by grassy, treed boulevards and backed by lanes good for hiding clotheslines and cars. Gerald knows he's not allowed past the row of old shop fronts that marks the south end of this neighbourhood.

By the time she reaches their street in the Hydrostone, June is half-running, sweating and out of breath. It's Mom's fault for getting her worked up. Five houses down and Mom waits inside the screen door, hugging a baggy cardigan to herself. Her milky eyes are wide.

Margie Green opens the squeaky door for her daughter. Gerald's ginger cat slips past and dashes outside.

"Mom, this is crazy. Where is he?"

"I don't know. I told you."

June drops her purse, hurries upstairs, and opens the door to Gerald's bedroom. It smells sour. A grey blanket lies in a tangle on his single bed. A transistor radio shares the top of the battered dresser—drawers open and clothes trailing— with stacks of comic books, a half-peeled orange, and his Red Sox cap.

She stumbles down the stairs, brushes past her mother, and enters the kitchen to look out back. Mom has hung a line of wash. June looks right, toward the car that's been up on blocks forever, and left toward Crazy Lady's cat colony, where at least four cats recline. No one in the laneway.

She thinks of the cellar. Gerald's scared of it and must be yelled at to fetch potatoes down there for his grandmother.

"Dark as the inside of a cow," Mom always says. June edges down the steep steps and squints. Spiderwebs, the stubborn wet patch in the middle, a ripped box of Christmas ornaments, a fifty-pound burlap sack of potatoes, almost empty.

"Gerald?"

Her mother stands frozen in the front hall.

"When did you last see him?" June says. She's aware of a catch in her voice and her heart beating through her blouse. Sweat colouring the polyester under her arms. Margie swallows.

"It was just before dinner. He wanted to go to the drugstore for his treats. I said wait, wait 'til after, but he went. Mr. Farrell said they saw him there."

That was about noon, over three hours ago, June calculates. He's never gone this long. "I'm going to look for him," she says. "You stay here."

Back outside, the world is fuzzy and changed. The boulevard's empty. She turns right at the sidewalk, eyeing the spaces between the strings of townhouses; forgets to envy the clump of daffodils and red tulips bobbing in the Beatons' postage-stamp front yard. A woman with a baby carriage turns the corner and wheels toward her. It twigs a memory of eight-year-old Gerald peering into a carriage and the young mother screaming at him to get away from her baby. June told her where to go.

She hurries up to the house three down from theirs, and knocks. Two elderly sisters, Archina and Dougelda—whose parents must have wanted boys—live here and don't miss a trick. The sisters answer the door together, as is their way, but when June asks after Gerald they shake their heads. As she retreats they watch through the front window.

June pivots at the corner and attacks the other streets, calling his name until she's hoarse. She checks the narrow rear lanes, just back stoops, clotheslines, and garbage cans. She should go up to the drugstore and the diner, but first she'll run home. Maybe he's back.

She's furious at Gerald for pulling this stunt. And at her mother for letting it happen. He would never get lost; he's twenty-eight and he's been walking these streets most of his life. Jesus, maybe he's hurt. Because he'd never run away. And surely no one would pick him up.

Lulu

ulu Dawes walks to work, pondering sin. She's free to sin now because her grade nine class completed their ninth first Friday a few weeks ago. Sister dragged her class to morning Mass on the first Friday of nine straight months, starting in September. Apparently, God has this deal that if you go to church for nine first Fridays in a row, he lets you into heaven. All sins forgiven, no questions asked.

The kids joked about it, but Sister took it seriously. She seemed relieved when they got in all nine, despite snowstorms threatening to cancel school, and that time a boy puked just as they were leaving for Mass. But they made it to May.

So as Lulu heads to her part-time shift at the drugstore, she wonders which sins she should commit. Don't honour thy father and thy mother? Despite their fighting, she's respectful. Murder: never. Swearing: yes, why not? Coveting: she covets her classmate's perfect Farrah Fawcett sausage curls. Sex: you need a boy for that, but at fourteen Lulu hasn't even kissed one.

She enters Farrell's, absorbing the sound of the bell and the soothing aroma of sweets and medicine. The front counter's empty; Miriam the full-time woman had an appointment so Lulu was called in on a Tuesday. As she goes back to hang her jacket, Mr. Farrell the pharmacist is talking on the phone.

"Try not to worry, June. I'm sure he'll turn up any minute. Of course we'll call if we see him again." Jim Farrell stops to listen. "Yes, that's not a bad idea. Good to let them know. Bet he'll walk in the door before they arrive. Take care now."

Farrell shakes his head, opens a cupboard, and surveys the large bottles of pills. Lulu approaches the pharmacy counter. She's been here six months and he still makes her nervous. He turns in his white smock jacket with stand-up collar that reminds her of the parish priests. Farrell says he hears just as many confessions.

"Gerald Green is missing," he says. "It's probably nothing, but if you see him on the street let me know right away. His mother and grandmother are frantic."

Lulu nods though a nod doesn't seem right. Gerald seems to have the most boring life of anyone in the neighbourhood. She has stood at the front counter and watched him wave at cars at the intersection—he just waves at cars. When he heads home, he crosses at the same spot every time and cuts across the playground, every time, avoiding the German shepherd tied at the blue house. He seems to talk to no one.

"Oh, and Liz is coming in at four to help with drug inventory," Farrell calls.

Liz. Who Lulu dreams of becoming—a university student, sharp, confident, pretty. Sometimes she brings her textbooks to work on Saturdays, thick books on politics and history, and immerses herself while Lulu tends the cash. Then they order toasted sandwiches from Buppy's Snack Bar across the street, and Liz goes on about school and dates. Once Lulu saw her and a guy making out on a blanket in the little park next to the church, right under the nose of the Virgin Mary.

But at this moment, Lulu's head swims with Gerald. She returns to the front shop and takes her post by the ancient brass cash register. Miriam has said Gerald was "born out of wedlock" and has caused his mother nothing but heartbreak.

"That poor woman. She's had no life," Miriam told Lulu, who pictured Gerald, too shy to catch her gaze, and wondered if he was ashamed.

She rests her fingers on the round keys of the cash register. It's an old-fashioned brass beauty Farrell's been too cheap to replace; inside the glass window, tabs pop up that say "50 cents" and "$5."

The bell over the door chimes and a curly-haired man enters. He wears a tan corduroy blazer and an open-collared shirt in orange swirls, bell-bottom slacks. He smells good as he passes and kind of looks like Tom Jones. Lulu's mother and aunt, even Gran, love to put Tom on the record player after supper and swish around the front room. Imagining partners.

The man looks impatient scanning the shelves. He can't find what he's looking for. He glances at her, steps forward, and clears his throat.

"Um, is the druggist in?"

She can feel colour rise in her face as she walks quickstep to the back. She can guess what he wants. She sticks her head into Farrell's dim office and tells him he's needed. The men speak in low tones and Farrell brings the customer a small paper bag.

A price is marked on the bag in pen. The man pays and leaves, and through the long glass windows she sees him slip into a car with a woman in the passenger seat.

Condoms. Liz says Farrell won't display them on the shelves because it embarrasses the nuns who walk down arm-in-arm from the convent. And the paper bag, meant to protect her, she imagines. Silly.

She starts tidying the cigarettes and pouches of tobacco displayed behind the counter. Thou shalt not steal. People steal all the time here. Last week she watched an old lady sneak a bottle of cough syrup into her purse. Lulu didn't say a word.

Gerald always pays for his things, shoving them across the counter with his head lowered. He likes comic books and has a sweet tooth. Lulu talks to him extra nice but he never answers. Then he leaves and waves at strangers in cars. Bizarre. And to think he's missing.

The bell over the door tinkles again. Liz rushes in, all curly brown hair and long denim legs. Lulu's eyes go to the wall clock—ten minutes past four. Liz is forever late.

"Whew, made it just in time," the older girl says, flinging her bulky patchwork bag onto the counter. "My bus was late." She removes her cardigan and jams it behind the counter. She stands and she and Lulu are close. Liz smiles.

"How're things, kiddo?"

Lulu, for once, has something exciting to tell her.

"Gerald Green is missing."

Liz frowns. "Who?" She circles to the front of the counter and studies the candy on the low shelves.

"You know, the slow guy who comes in all the time. He picks up pills for his nanny. He always buys ginger ale."

"Oh yeah, him. Missing?" Liz offers a bite of chocolate bar to Lulu, who shakes her head no. "Where would he ever go?"

"His mother's frantic."

"I bet. Hey, you working Saturday? I can't come in 'til noon so you'll have to open."

"Yeah sure, if Farrell will let me."

"It'll be fine." Liz leans on the counter and bites into the chocolate. "Man, I shouldn't be here. I'm taking two killer courses this spring."

Lulu begins to feel uneasy on Liz's part because Farrell must be waiting for her in the back. Out the picture window, three high school guys stroll toward Buppy's. She knows who they are. The leader is Danny, tall and skinny, stringy blond hair shielding his eyes. He leans against the brick wall and cups his hands, trying to light a smoke. His best friend, Mikey, is stocky and fidgety, a ball cap perched atop long, dark hair. He pushes the third and smallest guy, Banger—she thinks he's Danny's cousin—and the two begin a back-and-forth, joking around. Mikey does something slick with his foot and Banger falls. Danny laughs and Mikey looks pleased.

One day last winter, when she was arriving for work, she saw them harassing Gerald. As he left the diner with a brown paper bag, the gang started in on him.

"Hey Ger, how's it hangin?...Ger Bear...Hey, dumb-dumb." Danny flicked his butt on the ground and put him in a headlock. Gerald struggled, his backside squirming. His bag fell to the sidewalk and split, and a dark gravy stain began to bleed on the paper. Finally Danny released Gerald, who stumbled and fell onto a knee. The boys laughed. Gerald stood, pants wet with slush, grabbed his food, and hurried away, glancing over his shoulder. He looked terrified.

Danny looked over and saw Lulu watching. He smirked.

June

Soupy fog muffles the evening birdsong and obscures the trees on the boulevard, cloaking their feet and erasing their upper branches. The city feels heavy. Though there's still daylight, someone across the way has switched on a lamp that glows through sheer curtains. Tulips close in upon themselves for the night. A foghorn bleats.

June sits on the front steps with her umpteenth cigarette. She's seething. Cops are useless. Two just left in their cruiser and said they'd keep an eye out, but it was too early to call Gerald missing. He's a grown man, they said, he can go where he likes. June tried to explain that he may be twenty-eight years old, maybe even looks like a man, but he's more like a boy. She pleaded. They said if anything turned up, they'd let her know.

Her stomach's in knots. She walked and searched for two hours, as far as the old prison field, past the church and school, into Farrell's, through the streets of simple wooden prefabs built after the war. She wishes she could cry.

But she seemed to cry all her tears years ago after it happened and she had to go away to have the baby. Then Dad died. Her guilt was immense: she'd caused his death by disgracing the family. A crone on the street had called her a whore. June didn't break out of it for almost two years; she wasn't cut out for this, a baby at seventeen. But Gerald began toddling around and needed her.

"Gerald go, go," he would shriek. She once chased him down this sidewalk after he escaped bare buff from the bath, laughing with joy. Wrapped the little squiggler in a towel and carried him inside. She had to discourage his antics—people looked at him funny as it was. She had to grow a tougher skin. A suit of armour, really.

A robin pecks at the sparse grass near June's feet. This time of day has always been her favourite. She looks forward to coming home to Gerald and Mom, putting her aching feet into slippers, and curling up on the chesterfield to eat supper—macaroni or frozen fish sticks—on trays in front of the TV. When Gerald was little, she'd bathe him after and they'd cuddle on his bed. He'd melt into her, hair wet and smelling of Ivory soap, anxious for his stories.

The screen door squeaks.

"June Rose, you'll catch your death of cold in this damp. Come in for a cup of tea."

June takes a deep drag of her cigarette.

"Barry's on his way from the dockyard," Margie says. "He's gonna help you look."

Big brother, how much help will he be? His whole life a screw-up: losing jobs over laziness and booze, scarce when June and Mom needed him, gambling away the down payment he and Sheila had saved for a house. June didn't blame Sheila when she left him.

Within minutes, Barry's car rumbles around the corner and pulls to the curb, rock and roll pulsing through the open window. It dies with the motor. He hefts himself out, heavy gut and hair pushing past his collar.

"So, no sign?" he says.

"What do you think?" June says. Barry ignores her snarkiness.

"Jeez, it doesn't make sense. He's a good kid." He looks at his mother, who motions toward June.

"C'mon then, Sis, let's go find him."

They drive over the same ground June covered earlier, streets and corners they grew up on. She doubts Gerald has been in half these places. Before she can protest, Barry swings into the parking lot of the Frugal Mart, still open for a bit.

"Maybe they seen him," he says.

It's a small neighbourhood market, here forever. Signs in the windows advertise the week's specials: bologna, catsup, oranges. The smell of oranges always returns June to her days at the Mart, where stock boys would open crates of Christmas oranges, currants, and sultanas from faraway places and scrape away the maggots before piling the fruits out front. That crowded stockroom, the smell of overripe fruit, the hum of the large freezers. That day, as Connelly pinned her against the cartons, she smelled spilled vanilla.

"You ask. I'll stay here," she says.

"What's wrong with ya? You worked here, for Christ's sake."

She unwraps a stick of gum and shoves it into her mouth. Barry shrugs and gets out, slams the heavy door.

June hasn't been in there in years, telling Mom she has bad memories of the place. It's the truth. But not all of it.

Lulu

Lulu smells the fishcakes and baked beans from the porch, and enters her grandmother's house, smiling. It's noisy and overheated and smells delicious, just how she likes it.

She passes through the front room, where the television blares for no one, and into the kitchen. Gran's Heinz 57 sniffs Lulu's crotch. She brushes the dog away and takes in the familiar room: old fridge and stove, rough cupboards, chrome table and chairs under the window. She has spent so much of her life here. It's her favourite place in the world—safe, warm, and always a whiff of bleach.

"There she is," Gran says, standing spatula in hand at the stove. "Did they work you hard?"

"No," she says, burying her face in Gran's grey curls, needing her scent. Lulu's mother, Viv, leans against the counter, smiling and raising a cigarette to her lips. She telephoned Lulu to join them after the store closed at six.

Lulu's father, Jack, and Aunt Brenda sit at the table. Brenda is always on a diet and hasn't touched her food. Jack shovels beans into his mouth.

"Well don't let old man Farrell take advantage of ya," he says. He holds out his plate. "Gran, got any more?"

"Hold your horses. Let me get Lulu settled." Gran dishes out a generous portion.

Lulu takes her plate and settles next to Brenda. Brenda will put herself on a diet of boiled eggs and grapefruit, or cabbage soup, or she'll pop caramel-like cubes that are supposed to fill you up and make you skinny. Lulu feels a bit bad for Brenda, who's always compared to her older sister. Viv got the tall figure and thick auburn hair. Brenda got dirt-coloured hair and a knack for putting on weight. Like Lulu.

"Hi, Brenda."

"Hi, kid. So that strange boy who hangs around the store has gone AWOL, huh?"

"Yeah, it looks like it." Mom must have told them.

"Well whaddaya expect? He's only half there," says Dad.

"Jack, don't be like that," says Viv, swatting away her cigarette smoke.

"Well it's true." He gestures with his left arm. "He's the freak bastard of the neighbourhood."

Lulu counts four stubby beer bottles in front of him. She hates him like this.

"He's just left to wander, creeping people out," says Brenda.

"No he doesn't," Lulu says.

"He's harmless," says Gran. "That boy grew up without a father, raised by his grandmother, poor Margie."

Lulu has heard this story before, one of many neighbourhood tales told on rotation.

Gran pours boiling water into the teapot.

"It never came out who Gerald's father was," says Brenda. Viv gives her a look. Brenda loves gossip.

"June was seeing a boy but he swore it wasn't him," Gran says, setting down a package of ginger snaps. "In those days a teenage pregnancy was shameful. Still is, I suppose." She sits with an "oomph," probably the first time she's sat all day.

"You remember, Vivian, they sent her away but she came home with the baby," she continues. "He was born funny and nobody wanted him."

Jack drains his beer. "The boyfriend served with my buddy in the navy. He got the hell out of town after she got knocked up."

Lulu tries to imagine getting pregnant in high school. She'd be mortified, walking the halls with a big belly. And she'd have no clue how to look after a baby. It seems like the worst thing that could ever happen, your life ruined.

"So, Lulu got an award in school," Viv says, smiling.

"Is that right, Loretta? I didn't know you were a smart one."

She hates it when Brenda uses her real name. Named after her other grandmother.

"Tell them, Lu," Viv says.

Lulu wishes they'd stop looking at her. "It was Janet and me, together. We did a project on trees and it came second in a city contest. We got certificates."

"Well, isn't that wonderful," says Gran. "I always said you'd go far."

Jack opens the fridge. "Gran, you got any more beer?"

Viv sighs. "You've had enough," she says. "It's a work night."

"Come on, it's just beer," he says.

"Just beer."

Jack and Viv eye each other and Lulu's stomach flutters. Another argument, which will carry over when they get home. Gran stands and begins filling the sink with sudsy water. Viv pecks her mother on the cheek and heads for the front door.

Lulu follows her father out. She'd rather stay. She has spent so many evenings here, fleeing the dark cloud in the apartment; doesn't plan it, just finds herself walking over. Gran doesn't ask questions. They slump in front of the TV with the dog and Lulu eats Oreo after Oreo.

It's drizzling. It's just a short drive home, but Lulu's glad for the car tonight. The windshield wipers squeak and thump. From the back seat she watches Dad glancing at Viv, who looks out her side window. It drives him insane when she stops talking.

The tension roils Lulu's stomach. They drive past the drugstore and she remembers Gerald, out there somewhere in the rain. Hopefully he's home now. She enjoys his visits to the store. Crusty Mr. Farrell, the customer they call the Pervert, sick people with sad stories, even her worry about home—it all evaporates as she watches Gerald twirl the rack of comic books again and again, and spend forever choosing candy. He's in no hurry.

The glass of the car window cools her forehead. She misses Jimmy, her older brother working up in Ontario. When he left last year she blamed her parents. He was escaping their bickering, she was sure of it. He's the only other person who understands.

The three of them enter the apartment in silence and Lulu goes straight to her room. She puts on a record and lies on her twin bed under the magazine posters of David Cassidy and Michael Jackson.

In the morning she'll tell Janet about Gerald. The two girls love mysteries, first devouring Nancy Drews and then paperback Agatha Christies that Janet bums from her mother. They've dreamed of something exciting happening around here, a true case they can sink their teeth into.

They've grown up together: jumping double Dutch, slurping Popsicles on hot afternoons, laughing until it hurt. Lulu loves Janet's house, craziness and a slew of kids. Janet's mom pierced their ears in their kitchen, applied ice cubes and shoved a hot needle through. They cried together that night.

But lately, Janet's been less interested in books and more obsessed with boys. Lulu thought it was just talk, but recently Janet boasted she'd hung out with some guys and girls at the playground one night. They'd passed around a joint. Lulu was shaken. They'd always told each other everything. And Janet hadn't invited her.

She worries Janet considers her boring, a baby. Lulu couldn't even get eyeshadow right so she stopped trying.

"Don't you want to look sexy?" Janet had said.

Yesterday at recess, Janet huddled with a couple of girls from another class. Lulu and Janet are in the "smart class," but these girls have been assigned to a group that's not expected to be smart, where it gets loud and the teacher can be heard shouting across the hallway. The girls smoke, they swear, they dare to sass the nuns. One got suspended for it. They've got an air of girls who could beat you up at will. Janet, in her Anne of Green Gables red braids, trying to fit in.

Lulu looks at her shelf. She owns few books, just some Bobbsey Twins and Nancy Drews, and the hardcover about birds she was awarded in grade four for being Top Girl. The teacher placed it in Lulu's hands with a smile, saying, "I thought you'd enjoy the illustrations."

The paper dust jacket is decorated with a watercolour painting of birds. Truth is, the book intimidates Lulu; she's only read a few pages. Yet she's been able to look at it and know someone thinks she's smart. That she might be the sort of person who enjoys illustrations.

But these days getting good grades is not cool. Acting out in class, meeting boys in the dark at the playground—these are the things girls try to hold over each other. Janet's been drawn into it. Lulu feels her best friend slipping away.

So, she works out a plan. Yes, she's worried about Gerald. It's a mystery, one that needs solving. And she knows who to recruit to help her do it.

June

Rain trickles down the dark front window and drips off bare branches. June flinches and imagines each drop hitting Gerald, vulnerable, freezing, scared. She just got off the phone with Trudy, who wanted to rush over, but June said wait until morning. She can't talk anymore.

Barry and Mom whisper in the kitchen. Let them. Everyone's talking. Barry told her it's all over the neighbourhood. Gossip infuriates June, but Barry said it's a good thing: the more people who know, the better.

After supper he called the cops demanding some action, so two showed up. They wanted a description of Gerald and a snapshot. June was embarrassed because she had trouble finding one. They used to own a camera but it broke. Finally she found a photo taken when Gerald was about sixteen. It had been a family reunion down on the Shore, and he wore a big grin and someone's stained fishing hat, lures hanging from the brim. He'd just run in the three-legged races. He called it the best day.

The police asked if Gerald talks to strangers or sneaks off to places that are forbidden. No and no. Does he have friends? Acquaintances? A girlfriend? June was rattled.

"He's more like a child," she said. They asked to see his room and the younger cop said he followed the Red Sox too. They said they'd keep her "in the loop."

June sinks into the brown flowered armchair. She thought the officers looked at her funny when she said Gerald has no friends or acquaintances.

"How does he spend his days?" the older cop asked.

June paused.

"You're his mother, you must know," he said. *You're his mother for Christ's sake, don't you know your own son?*

He walks. He does simple errands for his grandmother. He buys treats at Farrell's and waves at cars up at the intersection, like a fool. He watches TV with Mom. He feeds Kitty. He takes the garbage outside. After supper, he lies on his bed and listens to baseball on the radio. Reads comic books. No, officer, he doesn't have any friends.

Barry enters the front room. "I'm gonna stay the night. I'm good here on the chesterfield," he says.

Mom follows and settles into her rocker recliner. "Poor little Gerald. When Wes gets home, he'll know what to do," she says, rocking rocking rocking. June wants to scream.

"You know your father's full name is Westminster, don't you?" Mom says. "His mother was English, a pretty girl from Southampton."

They've heard this story a thousand times. But people stopped talking about Wes in the present tense a long time ago.

"Mom, he's gone. Died years ago," says Barry.

"Gerald's dead?" She stops rocking and clutches her chest.

"No, Dad's gone, Mom. Gerald is…he's okay. We just need to find him." June tries to believe this.

"Yes of course, your father, bless his soul. I get muddled. Barry, why don't you stay the night, dear?"

"We already decided that."

June has had enough. She rises, can barely make it up the stairs. Instead of removing clothes she adds them—thick socks and a sweater—and crawls under the covers. The mattress sags in the middle and she doesn't fight it tonight. She lets herself slide into the hollow.

She's done in but can't sleep. *Where can he be?* So gentle and kind. Last week they were sitting in the front room and Kitty jumped on his lap. Gerald stroked the cat and it curled up.

"He's happy," he said. June asked how he knew. He placed her hand on the cat's side and June felt a faint vibration of purring. "See? That means he's happy."

She thinks she should pray. *Hail Mary, full of grace, the Lord is with thee.* She can't find the next line.

The faces begin to appear. It's the faded print on the wall, the only decoration in the room, cherry blossoms in peach and grey. She identified the faces ages ago: the bald man in the lower corner, slightly menacing. A couple of cherubs reclining in the blossoms. The biggest is the floating baby, just his hairless head, shadowed eyes serious, a tiny hand held to his face. But tonight the baby accuses her. Bad, bad, bad. Bad mother. You lost me. You are my only friend. And you let me down.

Lulu

Like many schools in Halifax, the one Lulu attends is named after a Catholic saint. It's built in the shape of a squared-off C, with a flat roof and white wooden siding. Tall windows protected by thick screens run down the wings. Older students, those in junior high, gather in the paved courtyard in the middle of the C. The elementary school kids are kept on another side.

On this morning, older boys kick a ball across the patchy sports field while little kids bop up and down the length of a hopscotch. Their spring jackets in optimistic colours pop against the grey sky.

Lulu scans the grounds, looking for Janet. Next year she'll be in high school and won't have to go to school with babies. She spots her against the building with one of the tough girls. Lulu takes a deep breath and goes to them.

"Hey, what's up?" Janet says.

"Can we talk?" says Lulu. "Just the two of us."

Tough Girl glares at her. Janet scrunches her face into a question mark.

"I just, we need to talk," Lulu says.

Tough Girl gives Lulu the finger, then saunters off. Janet crosses her arms.

"I need to tell you something. It's a mystery. A real-life mystery in the North End," says Lulu.

"You mean the guy who's missing?"

Lulu's shoulders sag. "Yeah, how did you know?"

"It's going around."

"I know him, sort of. Gerald," Lulu says. "He comes into the store. I think I might know who took him. Or beat him. Or whatever."

Janet's eyes widen. "Who?"

Lulu pauses. What if she's wrong? She steps closer and they each lean a shoulder against the building.

"You can't tell a soul," she says. "It's that bunch of high school guys who hang on the corner—Danny, Mikey, and Banger. I saw them beating Gerald up last winter." Maybe a slight exaggeration. "They bully him."

Janet's silent for a moment. "What're you going to do?"

"I don't know. I was thinking we should be sure, maybe investigate them before we tell anyone our theory."

"You should tell the police."

"But what if I'm wrong? I don't want them mad at me. They're criminals—that's what Liz says."

Janet strokes a braid and gets that faraway look.

"Miss Marple's an amateur detective too," Lulu says. She knows she's grasping. "We could spy on them."

The bell rings and they file into school. Miss T. stands at their classroom door smiling. Lulu and Janet think she's a dead ringer for Ali MacGraw in *Love Story*. They told her and she laughed her musical laugh. She wears long, gauzy skirts, in contrast to the stiff habits some of the teaching nuns wear. She studied art in college. Her fiancé has a beard and picks her up in a beat-up Datsun. She's perfect.

Miss T. wishes the class good morning and asks, as usual, if anyone has a conversation starter. Janet looks at Lulu, two rows over, and Lulu catches her breath because she knows what Janet's about to do. Janet raises her hand and the teacher calls on her.

"Miss T., I have some news. There's been a disappearance in the neighbourhood. It's Gerald—I don't know his last name—but he's mentally retarded and went missing yesterday. He's a grown-up."

The teacher looks startled. "Oh no, I hadn't heard this." Other students shoot up their hands.

"It's Gerald Green, Miss, he lives near me in the Hydrostone," a boy yells.

Then many people are talking at once. It seems about half the class knew and half did not. A couple of boys argue over whether the police have found his body already.

"Settle down, everyone." Miss T. has to raise her voice. It takes about half a minute but the students go quiet.

"Thank you, Janet, for bringing this to our attention." She perches on the edge of her desk. "Of course you're all concerned. I'm sure the police will find him soon. Let's send him good thoughts. Now let's pull out our math books, while our minds are fresh, and tackle that new chapter."

At recess, Lulu asks Janet why she brought it up. "Because a good detective never knows when she might find valuable clues," Janet says. "A lot of kids already knew. Maybe someone saw something."

Before the school day ends, Miss T. talks to them again about Gerald. She says she thought about it over lunch and wants to discuss personal safety. She speaks about travelling in pairs or groups, and never accepting rides from strangers. She says they should let an adult know where they're headed, in case they get injured or lost. She says it's important to tell your parents if you have a strange encounter with someone. And she says people like Gerald are among the vulnerable in our society, so we need to look out for them.

From across the classroom, Janet gives Lulu a thumbs up.

June

June leans against the sink to fill the kettle; she can barely stand. Last night she didn't want to sleep—she wanted to lie there and will him home, figure out where he's hiding, listen for the slightest noise at the door. Around three she walked the block in her housecoat, softly calling his name. Near dawn she fell asleep, and hated herself for it after.

She's not dressed, and her dark blond hair—pitiful hair for a hairdresser—lies matted against the back of her scalp. The rain has weakened to a mist, but the kitchen remains gloomy. The sodden cat stares from the back porch door, scratching at the glass. June ignores him and grabs the tea tin. Margie shuffles in wearing a sweater over her nightgown, socks and slippers.

"Not working today?" Mom says. She hums "Moon River," digging out bread and jam. She must have forgotten.

June has thought of nothing else, not for one second. She dreamed of him last night. He was crying but when she ran to him it wasn't lost Gerald, it was Gerald from the day of the picnic. Eight years ago, the day she knew it was over with Lorne.

Lorne, a carpenter who had entered the barbershop one day looking for a trim, was her only serious relationship. He was lean with thick, sandy hair, sleepy brown eyes, and a big laugh. Together for over a year, they went to movies and the drive-in; he taught her to fish trout and cook it over an open fire. At Christmas he gave her an inlaid wooden jewellery box he had spent weeks on. He made her feel beautiful and safe.

Yet June sensed he'd rather not get Gerald as part of the package. Gerald may have felt it too, and the two men in her life circled each other. She kept trying to nudge them together.

That summer day, Lorne, June, and Gerald shared a picnic at a lakeside park. Lorne got Gerald horsing around on the grass and Gerald let loose and began to enjoy it, June could see that. Lorne pinned him down, tickling him. Then Lorne let out a godawful cry, rolled over, and cupped his left eye.

"My eye, my eye," he screamed. He writhed in agony. "You fucking retard!" Gerald sat up and cried.

The doctor at the hospital said Gerald must have scratched Lorne's cornea with a fingernail, an incredibly painful injury. Lorne was sent home with a temporary eye patch and eyedrops.

Over the next two weeks June helped with the drops but she couldn't get over it. Lorne's reaction had been like a slap to her face. The anger, the hatred. That's how he truly felt about Gerald. He could never love him as a son.

Once Lorne muttered, "Sorry, I didn't know what I was saying," but that changed nothing. When his eye healed, she broke it off. Months later she heard he'd moved out west to build houses.

Someone knocks at the door. She tightens the belt of her housecoat and goes into the hallway. Another rap. Hold on already.

It's a woman with shiny silver hair cut in a bob. She wears a casual jacket, maybe a man's jacket, over khakis and chunky shoes.

"Hello, Mrs. Green? I'm Evelyn Winthrop. I'm a friend of Gerald. I heard he's gone missing and was just so upset. I wanted to come down and express my support." She smiles a little, clutches her purse.

June shakes her head. "I never heard of you."

"That's entirely possible. We both know he's a man of few words." The woman leans in. "Have the police had any success?"

June wonders if she's just a psycho who loves other people's problems.

"Who's there?" Margie appears and smiles at the stranger. "Oh, hello."

"Hello. You must be Gerald's grandmother. I'm his friend, Evelyn Winthrop." She reaches her hand to shake. June feels things moving away from her.

"Come in then, dear," says Margie. *Oh Jesus.*

"I'm sorry, I've caught you in the midst of breakfast." Evelyn steps into the hall.

"Don't be silly. Come have a cup of tea." Margie, hostess with the mostess. They enter the kitchen, which seems smaller with this woman in it.

"I've always admired these Hydrostones." Evelyn takes a seat.

Margie brings her a mug. It's one of the nice ones, with no chips, but Margie's brought her a fork instead of a spoon. Evelyn doesn't mention it. She pours herself tea and uses the fork to stir in some milk.

"So you know Gerald?" Margie asks, brushing toast crumbs off the table and onto the floor.

"Yes, he's been coming to see me for, what, five years now." Evelyn takes a sip.

June is stunned. She has a million questions but Evelyn speaks first.

"So please, tell me what's happened. I'm so worried about him."

Margie looks to June. "What's wrong with him then?"

"He's missing, remember? Since yesterday afternoon."

Margie shrinks back. "Oh my gracious. Oh yes, of course. The poor boy. We're all looking for him." Evelyn watches her and Margie continues. "He never goes far. Once, when he was little, he hid under the back steps half the day. But we found him, the little bugger."

"How do you know him?" June blurts.

Evelyn turns to her. "I live around the corner from the drugstore, and he'd walk by every day. I started saying hello—I'm out in the garden a lot. It took a long time but eventually he answered. He's a dear young man."

June doesn't like this busybody. "By the drugstore? Which house?"

"It's a little white house with black shutters. We're set back, so people often don't notice us. Big rhododendron that will be glorious soon. My Albert and I have lived there almost seven years."

"Winthrop, you say? You have any people around here?" Margie asks.

Evelyn shakes her head no. "We go down to an Anglican church. That's why we don't know many people." She looks into her mug. "Unfortunately, we never had children."

Still, she shouldn't have latched onto Gerald. Evelyn lays a hand on June's. It's dry and rough. June slips her hand out from underneath it.

"We just talk, that's all," Evelyn says. "I show him around my yard. Last year there were baby squirrels in the oak, and my, didn't he enjoy that. He likes my ginger cookies, too."

June feels a hot flash of jealousy. This stranger, baking GD cookies for her kid. "He never mentioned you, so he can't know you too good."

Margie frowns at her, turns to Evelyn. "Well isn't that something, that you made a friend of Gerald. The boy hardly knows a soul. Now that you say it, I remember him talking a blue streak about squirrels."

"That's nice," Evelyn says. "So I'm wondering what I can do to help. What are the authorities doing?"

"The cops are looking," says June. "We've all been up and

down the streets, everywhere. We have lots of help." She remembers Barry stayed over.

"We don't know, maybe he hurt himself, maybe he's mixed up." Margie starts to tear up.

Evelyn places a hand on her shoulder. "I can't imagine being in your place. But if there's anything I can do?" She looks to June, who turns her head away.

"Well, I must get going." Evelyn rises and they follow her to the front door.

"Nice of you to come by, dear," Margie says.

Evelyn smiles and they watch her go. She's a fast walker.

"Well who would've thought?" says Margie. "Gerald has a friend."

In the front room, Barry's blanket lies abandoned on the chesterfield. June returns to the kitchen and recognizes Trudy's red headscarf approaching down the back lane. The thought of talking again almost brings June to her knees, and she collapses onto a chair. Trudy comes in without knocking. She and June have been friends since age six, there were never any formalities.

"You look like shit," Trudy says.

"Didn't sleep."

Trudy grabs a mug from the cupboard. She knows where everything is. In junior high they botched fudge here, getting nothing but sweet slop. Another day they tried to make tea biscuits as they'd been taught in home ec, but the biscuits blew up in the oven. The girls rolled on the floor laughing. They stole butts from the overflowing ashtrays to smoke behind the school.

Trudy sits down. "What are the cops saying?"

June's warm. Her throat constricts, the tears want to come.

"Not much," she says. "They say they're looking but he's an adult and free to go where he wants."

They look into each other's eyes, Trudy's brown, June's blue.

"Okay, we're going to find him," Trudy says. "The poor guy must be hurt or something. You know how clumsy he is."

"I don't know, is he?" June hangs her head and runs a hand through her hair. "Where can he be, Trude? He must be so scared."

Trudy lays a hand on her wrist. "He can't be far, honey," she says. "Between all of us, we'll find him. Today. Martin's searching Fort Needham on foot."

June sits back in her chair. "It's my fault. I should keep a better eye on him."

"And how in hell are you gonna do that while you're working to support this house? Your mom's a good help, right?"

June shakes her head. "I told you she's been asking about Dad. He's been dead twenty-seven years, for god's sake."

"Remember what I told you about my grammy? They forget the important stuff but know the words to every Vera Lynn song."

Trudy gets up and dials the wall phone. June takes a jagged breath and Trudy gestures for her to go get dressed.

"Martin, when you heading out?"

At the top of the stairs June turns her head so she doesn't have to see his bedroom door. She knows what Trudy's thinking: this has been a screw-up since the start. June didn't want him. June got stuck with him. Gerald ruined June's life. He killed her relationship with Lorne—her best chance at marriage. Good riddance, Gerald.

In the bedroom shared by mother and daughter, Margie stands at the dresser in her nightgown, pawing through bras and nylons. She pulls out an old girdle and considers it. June asks what she's doing.

"I don't know," her mother says.

Farrell and Buppy

Over at the intersection, Buppy leaves his diner and lumbers across the street to the drugstore. It's early morning and Jim Farrell is up front counting the cash float for the register, getting ready for the day ahead. He looks up, goes and unlocks the door.

Buppy enters, greying, balding. Deep, dark pouches underline his eyes. His shirtsleeves are rolled up. Somehow his baggy beige pants, belted under his pot-belly, stay up. He smells of fried onions.

The two men have run their businesses across from each other for decades. They discuss the weather, the health or weaknesses of their trades, sports. Never politics.

"Jim, how ya doing? What's this about Gerald?"

"I know, it's a shock, isn't it?" Farrell says. He goes back and shuts the till.

"But what in hell happened? Where would he ever go?"

"I don't know. He was in here yesterday as usual. That's the last that was seen of him, far as anyone knows."

Buppy shakes his head. "Doesn't make sense, Jim, a kid like that. Gentle, like a kitten. He don't go too far, I know that, 'cause his mother and nan keep a hawk eye on him."

Farrell nods. Buppy points to the Rothmans and lays down some money. Farrell hands him a pack and Buppy lights a cigarette. The men watch the smoke curl from its pulsing red tip.

"You know, Jim, Gerald's been an inspiration to us," says Buppy. Farrell stares.

"We hold him up, you know? He's not all there, everybody knows that, but he's a good boy, helps his grandmother. He gets by. I got a grandson, Trevor, he's three now and he was born different too. Maybe not like Gerald, but I tell my daughter about him, to give her hope. More than anything, she wants it so Trevor can look after himself when he's grown."

"I didn't know, Bup."

"Yeah, he's an angel. He's our world. I imagine just like Gerald is to his mother."

Farrell fiddles with the books of matches on the counter.

"Well, I better get back to the coal mines," Buppy says.

Farrell sees him out the door.

"Keep me posted."

The druggist promises and locks up until opening time at nine.

June

June wades through the brush, stumbles over a rock. Ahead, Trudy climbs the grassy path, her red scarf flashing through the trees like a bird perhaps seen, perhaps not. June stops to catch her breath, feeling every ounce of the twenty pounds that have sneaked onto her middle.

She's in a thicket of tall mixed evergreens carpeted by bronze pine needles. It smells fresh. She hears the faint sound of a car passing at the bottom of the hill, but it's peaceful in here. A person could hide if they wanted. She creeps farther in. Some shorter trees have intertwined and cling to each other, edged by a thorny tangle that catches her sweater. She peers into the bushes.

"June?" calls Trudy.

June could stay here and rest against a tree. Forget.

"June, up here."

She backtracks and connects with the path, climbs another twenty feet and alights on the flat summit of Fort Needham, a grassy expanse with no sign of a fort that June knows of. A breeze lifts her hair and she pushes it from her eyes. She strains to pick out the roof of their house. Trudy waves and walks toward her husband, Martin, and a man June doesn't recognize.

June looks toward the new bridge that spans the harbour and connects to Dartmouth on the other side. Beyond is the harbour basin. As a kid she'd come up here with Dad, during the war, and count the warships anchored in the basin before they sailed in convoys to Europe. Dad told her about the 1917

Explosion at the Narrows, straight through the trees. He was young then, living out in the country, but people said the blast sent kids flying across this hill. It ripped people's clothes off, smashed windows, and blinded gawkers.

"Gerald! Gerald!" the men yell.

Trudy walks toward her. "Martin and his buddy are gonna keep looking. Why don't we go back to the house for tea?"

"But there's so many hiding spots, bushes, trees." *He never comes up here.*

"They'll look everywhere." Trudy slips her arm through June's.

June doesn't move. "What if he's lying with a broken ankle?"

"They'll cover it. They're military."

Military. Martin, the know-all. If he only knew about that car salesman Trudy took up with when he was at sea two years ago. Trudy was ga-ga. Then Martin's ship returned to port.

The women head toward the house, to the confused grandmother rattling around, maybe to Barry, who's been searching too. To the cat sitting outside Gerald's door.

When it's normal, when they're all home with Gerald up in his room and June and Mom downstairs, the house feels full. June can't see him but she can feel him. She can't feel him now.

Above all else, protect baby's head. The matron's words come back clear as day. Those months at the maternity home, scrubbing dishes and floors, shivering and sobbing under itchy blankets. Girls told nothing about the mystery of childbirth; those same girls screaming from down the hall when they found out. A nightmare June wishes she could erase. But the memories always resurface, eventually.

After giving birth, one girl asked matron when her baby's eyes would open, as if it was a kitten. The staff roared about it for days but the girls didn't laugh. Mothers for just moments before the title was snatched from them, not always wishing to give up their babies. Or, rarely, like June, boarding a bus home with a new bundle, terrified. *I will protect his head. I will protect his head*, she repeated all the way home.

Lulu

When Lulu received her record player two Christmases ago, Janet seemed jealous. She kept stroking the smoky plastic dome top that flipped back to reveal a turntable on a round black base. Two speakers like balls. The girls didn't know anyone else who had one.

The two friends sit cross-legged by the record player now, sipping cans of root beer. Lulu places the needle gently on her Elton John record and keeps the volume low. They need to plan their investigation.

"I'll take notes," says Janet, pulling out a scribbler. She writes and reads aloud, "'The Mysterious Disappearance of Gerald Green, of the Hydrostone, Halifax, Nova Scotia, Canada.'"

"There are three suspects," says Lulu, bolstered by the music and the sugar and having Janet here again. It's just an upstairs apartment in a four-unit building, which Mom gripes about but Dad says one day, for sure, we'll have our own house.

"Suspects: Danny, Mikey, Banger," Janet says. "Do we know Banger's real name? And what are their last names?"

Lulu considers. "It's Danny McMichael. Mikey...starts with an F. Banger, I don't know."

Janet records this, asks where they live.

Danny often heads toward the train tracks, and Lulu's pretty sure he lives in one of the little houses down there. Mikey lives in a squat apartment building up the street from the store. His mother comes in for her pills—she takes a lot. Banger might live near Danny.

Janet looks up from her notes. "You really want to spy on them?"

Lulu still struggles to speak to strangers at work. But finally, they have a daring plan and she came up with it. It's got Janet hooked.

"They might have Gerald hidden somewhere," Lulu says, only half-believing herself.

She can't imagine them keeping him at home. They discuss possible hiding places: the empty warehouse that keeps getting broken into, behind the McDonald's, the cluster of commercial buildings near the overpass to the bridge.

"What if they catch on to us?" Janet says, sitting back against Lulu's bed.

"So what? Nobody takes a couple of schoolgirls seriously. Look at Miss Marple, people always underestimate her and she's smart as a whip."

Lulu sips her pop. Miss Marple lives in a foreign world of rose-covered cottages and vicars.

"One thing we haven't discussed," Janet says, "is motive. What's their motive for taking him?"

Lulu has been sidestepping this because she doesn't know. They can't be looking for a ransom. They bully him but so what. Revenge is a common motive, but what has Gerald ever done to them? They have to list the motive as "Unknown."

They agree to start surveillance tonight, meeting outside Buppy's at six o'clock. Lulu's nervous now.

"Lulu?"

She goes into the hallway and Dad's home. He grins, revealing the gap in his upper teeth, but she thinks he's handsome, tall with a lock of brown hair at his forehead that won't lie flat. Crinkles around his eyes and mouth.

"Your mother home yet?"

"No." Lulu steps to the side. "Janet's here."

"Oh yeah. The contest," he says.

"Actually, we're working on the Gerald Green disappearance," Janet says.

Dad looks at her weird and heads for the kitchen. He's never interested in what Lulu's doing.

"Come on, let's finish up," Janet says. The record is skipping. Lulu switches if off and Janet gathers her things.

"Remember, six o'clock."

Lulu nods. The front door opens and Viv's heels click down the hardwood toward the kitchen. The footsteps stop.

"We need to talk," Viv says. Her voice is brittle.

"I should go," says Janet. She's seen it too. Lulu hurries her out but it starts before Janet leaves.

"What now?" says Dad.

"You didn't stay in Truro that night. I talked with Stan today at work."

"You're nuts," Dad says. "I was beat from driving all day. The car was on empty."

"Who is it, Jack?" Her mother's voice loses some of its power. "Who's it this time?"

Lulu shuts herself in her room. She doesn't need to hear. They seem to fight daily, over little things like cleaning the apartment, or they return to the same big issues: Dad's drinking. Mom's belief he's cheating on her. Money. They get nowhere. Lulu can't even have a friend over without the friend hearing. Their family secret exposed. She's so frustrated she could cry.

It reminds her of Pinky, the hamster she and Jimmy got the year she was eight and he was twelve. They didn't necessarily want a hamster, but they wanted *something*. They'd moved so much, Mom giddy each time about the fresh start. She'd twirl in the kitchen and describe the curtains she'd sew and how she'd fix up the apartment—while not putting too many holes in the walls.

"This is it, kids," she'd say. "No more moves."

Lulu was little but she remembers someone's mother saying to her, "You moved *again*?" She didn't count the apartments. The summer before grade two, they moved out of the neighbourhood on a whim; the family told them they were crazy. She hated her new school but by Easter had made a few friends. Then they moved back here. She and Jimmy couldn't control that or the promised family outings that got cancelled, nor the worries about money, the constant talk about money.

Maybe that's why Jimmy decided they needed a pet, specifically a dog. He wrote a Manifesto for a Family Dog; he'd been reading adventure books about heroic boys. He read his manifesto aloud and she and Mom and Dad sat on the chesterfield and clapped. But apparently all landlords banned dogs, and he lost his case. Jimmy wouldn't speak to them for a week.

One day their parents came home with a hamster, "one, to share," Dad said. It had golden fur and a pink nose and feet, and Lulu won the argument to name it. They were handed bags of shavings and food pellets but Dad hadn't bought the recommended cage. He dug out a wire container about the size of a shoebox and said it would do.

They had Pinky for two months. Jimmy and Lulu would kneel at his box in a corner of the living room and watch. When they took him out he'd slip out of their hands and scurry up their shirts and around their necks, tickling. Yet Pinky soon lost his appetite. His fur began to fall out. One morning, Jimmy let out a howl. Pinky wasn't moving.

"Yep," Dad confirmed. "It's a goner."

"This wouldn't have happened if you let us get a dog," Jimmy said, tears running down his face. That scared Lulu; her brother had vowed at age ten never to cry again.

The children took Pinky into the bathroom because that's where people went when someone got hurt, and looked at the tiny corpse in Jimmy's hand. Lulu was afraid to touch it.

Jimmy glanced at the toilet.

"We need to bury him," he said.

The back of their building was paved so they did it at Gran's. They held a funeral with a few friends; Jimmy made a coffin out of a cracker box and Lulu placed acorns and dried leaves on the grave—it was fall. A boy sang "Silent Night." Everyone cried.

Jimmy hardened after that. Come spring he demanded to play baseball like other boys, and said he'd snagged a paper route to help pay for it. Mom and Dad didn't argue, just scraped together money for his uniform and registration. Dad grew to love it and never missed a game over the years. It was their special bond. It was Jimmy's triumph, something he had wanted and achieved.

Lulu hasn't had a triumph yet. She doesn't even know what she wants.

June

Margie hums to the radio, somehow able to hear it while banging pots around the stove. Barry drinks a beer at the table, looking defeated. He spent all day searching for Gerald, burned an entire tank of gas.

Margie has made supper, baked pork chops with cream of mushroom soup smeared on top. They sit steaming on the counter. June wants to gag. She wants nothing, except for Gerald to walk through the door. She slams a cupboard.

"Why haven't we heard from the cops? What the hell have they been doing?" she says.

Her mother adds margarine to the potatoes she's mashing. "I think it was a policeman who called this afternoon," Margie says, not looking up.

June wheels around. "You think? What did he say?"

Barry holds up a hand. "Settle down. Mom, what did he say?"

Margie holds the masher midair. Blobs of potato fall to the floor. She looks from one child to the other. "He said…he said they'll keep looking."

"Jesus." June puts her hands on her head. "Why didn't you let me talk to him?"

"You fell asleep. You needed the rest." Margie sits.

"Let's call down there, see if we can talk to someone," Barry says, standing up. "June, what's the number? Who's the cop?"

"How the hell should I know." She enters the back porch and looks out, not focusing, pats her sweater pockets for cigarettes. "The cop was Cole or Colby or something," she says over her shoulder.

Shouldn't have gone, he shouldn't have gone. I shouldn't have gone to work. Shouldn't've.

June squints. A couple of people are poking around in the back lane. It's a silver-haired woman and a tall man with white hair and a dark moustache. Evelyn. That must be her Albert. Evelyn lifts the lid off a wooden garbage bin and peers inside. Across the lane, Albert spies through the slats of a neighbour's fence. They move a few feet and rummage again.

"And in local news," the radio says, "Halifax police ask for the public's help in locating a missing North End man. Gerald Green is five foot eight inches tall, with brown hair and brown eyes, last seen Tuesday wearing a navy blue jacket and dark pants. Anyone with information should contact Halifax police." The announcer moves on.

"Good lord, it's on the news," says Margie. "It must be true."

Barry hangs up. "They said the guys are patrolling. They'll call as soon as they know something."

June goes up to Gerald's room, she's been avoiding it. She plucks the shrivelled orange from the dresser and eases onto his bed, strokes the blanket. Comic books lie strewn on the floor—teenagers at Riverdale High, cowboys, a friendly ghost. All fantasy for him, even high school.

Comics helped him learn to read, though. Then he got stuck, stuck at age nine, the doctor said. He'd never mature mentally beyond that. Should never dream of becoming a fireman or an astronaut like other boys.

"At least you learned to read," the school principal said, patting Gerald on the shoulder. "Not many boys like you do that."

Then he ushered June and Gerald out of his office, Gerald pushed out of school after grade six. For weeks after, Gerald cried and said he missed the kids, though some of them could be rotten to him.

She looks out the window under the eaves, so long since she sat here. She and Barry shared the room growing up; it was tight but they got along, laughing and dancing to his records. Then he moved out and she got a part-time job at the Frugal Mart. She needed spending money for bus fare and school.

She was shy but they trained her to work the till. That's what the girls did; the boys stocked shelves. Mr. Connelly, the assistant manager, was sweet about it. He was patient, didn't get angry when she couldn't balance her cash or rang something in wrong. Driving over there yesterday brought so much of it back.

Connelly complimented her hairstyle, told the cashiers to wear lipstick "to look our best." Sandy, who worked the cash beside her, would roll her eyes when he walked by, but June didn't mind. He was older and married, perhaps thirty, sort of handsome with a strong jaw and dark, slicked-back hair.

After school she'd change into her uniform—a white cotton dress with a long zipper down the front, red pointed collar, and short sleeves with red cuffs. She'd stare in the mirror and cinch in the waist. Would Mom notice if she took it in? She was strict about hemlines and tight clothes.

Maybe Connelly smiled at her more than he smiled at the other girls. Maybe she held his gaze an extra second. She can't be sure. But his hand would brush hers as he delivered rolls of change or demonstrated how to void a sale.

She'd been fighting off her boyfriend for months; she wasn't that serious about him. But when Connelly touched her, something shot through her. He smelled of aftershave and spearmint gum. When he was hovering around June, Sandy would turn away.

"What?" June wanted to say. "He likes me, that's all."

So on the day he took it too far, on the day he took what he wanted, maybe it was inevitable. Maybe it was her fault.

She'd flirted with her blue eyes, which people called her best feature. She'd switched to a more daring lipstick and had been taking extra care curling her hair. Maybe she'd sent messages she couldn't follow up. She'd been playing games with an adult and she should've known.

He asked her to follow him into the stockroom. Unusual, but maybe she was doing something wrong and he didn't want to embarrass her in front of the others. It was a slow Monday night, just her and a cashier named Beth, so she locked her till and went.

Normally, she only went out back to hang her coat or use the bathroom; she'd hurry through if the guys were there, tossing boxes in a human chain, speaking a shorthand in loud voices that carried above the radio, the exterior doors thrown open and truck exhaust spilling in.

The stock boys were done for the day; later she realized Connelly had planned that. He walked around a corner and she followed, stood before him awaiting her reprimand. Instead he smiled and cupped her left elbow, pulled her toward him.

"You and me," he said, and dipped his head to kiss her.

She stumbled back, shocked. His hand moved to her shoulder and he used his body to push her into the stack of heavy cartons behind. She was five foot two and weighed a hundred and five pounds. She was pinned, could feel the corner of a box jabbing the small of her back. Boxes loomed overhead.

"Don't," she said. She had trouble finding her voice.

He said nothing, worked quickly to pull down her underwear and do what he wanted. Pain seared through her.

"Stop," she said, sobbing. "Stop."

"Shh," he said.

When he was done he backed up and kissed her hair. That almost bothered her more than the other. He tucked in his shirt, smoothed his hair, and left, whistling. The aftermath's hazy but she must have gone home. Walking the streets with his juice running down her thighs, blood in her underwear.

There was absolutely no way she was going to tell her parents. She skipped school the rest of the week and called in sick for her next three shifts. A flu, she told Mom.

But the thing is, the thing she can't forgive in herself, is she returned to work the next week. She didn't know what else to do. If she quit, wouldn't her coworkers suspect something? Beth had seen them go to the stockroom, perhaps saw June leave. Wouldn't people somehow know what Connelly had done to his pet cashier? What the two of them had done. She berated, hated herself. She'd been asking for it, that's what the stock boys would say.

And her parents. Dad would demand to know why she'd quit when she needed the money so badly. So, she returned. That first shift, she had to build herself up to walk in. She hadn't curled her hair, wore no lipstick. Hung up her coat and went right to her register. She tried to smile at customers, kept her head down, avoided his eyes. He seemed to avoid her too.

Somehow she kept working, but when her period didn't come the next month, a new worry began. Her breasts were tender and she felt sick in the mornings. She took scalding baths, having heard something about that working, then lay under the eaves and prayed. The Virgin Mary had come through before.

Yet she thickened and her skirts became uncomfortable. She held off as long as possible before quitting that summer of 1950. People were staring at the small bump in her uniform. She saw Connelly looking one day. She held his eyes and he wheeled around, headed for the meat department.

Dad was enraged—didn't she know jobs were hard to come by?—and so she spat it out, she was going to have a baby. No, it wasn't the Murphy boy she'd dated all school year.

"I swear, don't blame him," she said, sobbing. But she wouldn't name the father. Dad turned on her and was never the same. "What decent man will have you now?" he yelled.

She knew she was done with school and she'd never graduate grade twelve. She was sixteen and her life was over.

Lulu

The slim houses near the train tracks are painted garish colours: purple, lipstick red, cobalt blue. The paint peels in spots and one house has no front steps, leaving a four-foot drop for the unsuspecting. The house next to it has a stained bed-sheet stretched across its front window, a makeshift curtain.

"Maybe the colours cheer people up," Janet whispers. They're crouched behind a car across the street, sneakers muddied. It's been fifteen minutes and Lulu's thighs burn. They don't know which one is Danny's house, just that he maybe lives here. Lulu loses her balance and falls onto her side on the sopping ground. Surveillance.

She moves onto her knees. Her pants are soaked and she shivers. The wind's coming up. A bus whistles by, its back end passes, and that's when they see him.

Danny's leaving the blue house. He lopes down the rutted driveway, shrugging into a jean jacket. As he reaches the side-walk, the front door squeaks open. A skinny older woman sticks her head out. She has brassy hair and wears a quilted floral housecoat.

"Where you think you're goin'?" she says.

"Out." He doesn't look at her. He pulls a lighter from the patch pocket of his jacket, starts walking again.

"I wasn't done talkin' to you." She's on the step trying to send her words after him, but the wind is against her. Her words evaporate. The back of his jacket heading up the hill seems to infuriate her.

"Bastard! Don't come home then," she screeches. She slams the door, as much as a rickety metal door with a torn bug screen can be slammed.

The girls glance at each other. Janet waves her on to come.

Lulu feels exposed, leaving the cover of the car. "He'll see us," she whispers.

Janet starts walking. Danny has a good lead, in the direction of the intersection near the drugstore. He cuts across the street on the diagonal, avoiding the red light, turns a corner.

Lulu and Janet pause near the sub sandwich shop, then edge to the corner and make the turn. Danny walks half a block and enters an apartment building. Mikey's place.

They're in front of Buppy's and the aroma awakens Lulu's stomach. Inside the fogged-up windows, Buppy reaches across the red lunch counter and twirly mushroom-shaped stools and hands a paper bag to a customer. Viv, crying in her bedroom, didn't make supper tonight.

Janet pokes her arm. "There they are."

The two boys jog across the street, then slow to a walk. The girls follow again, staying on their side of the street until Danny and Mikey turn onto a side street of small wooden houses. Maple leaves still unfurled in a cold spring.

The guys head to the piddly ball field, where a strong Little Leaguer can clear the chain-link fence with a good connection of bat to ball. The surrounding houses have cracked windows to prove it. The boys climb the wooden bleachers, two at a time, and settle at the top. Mikey pulls out a bottle of beer and uses the metal fence behind as an opener.

The girls creep over to the ball field and, with no other option, hunch behind a mailbox outside the fence. Danny sees them right away.

"Hey," he shouts. "Stop tailing us, ya little weasels."

"Damn," Janet says.

"That's Lulu," yells Mikey, "from the drugstore." He stands. "You know they named you after the wrong character, right?" he calls to her. "From the comic. You should be called Tubby."

Lulu wants to sink into the earth. Danny doubles over in laughter, his golden hair touching the wood beneath his feet. A tear squirts from the corner of Lulu's eye.

"Come on," says Janet, sounding annoyed, "let's get out of here." She hurries across the street, but Lulu is frozen.

Danny scrambles down the bleachers and trots toward her, Mikey following. They wouldn't hit a girl, would they? Danny stops within arm's reach. She's always found him cute but up close he has pockmarks. She swallows.

"What're you girls up to?" he says.

"Nothing," says Lulu, her voice small.

"Why you spying on us?" he says. "I saw you by my house."

"We're not. We're just goofing around."

"Well goof the eff off," he says and laughs at his joke. Mikey grins.

"Lulu," calls Janet from across the street, "come on."

Lulu inches backwards. *Where's Gerald?* If she were brave she'd say it.

"C'mon," Mikey says, tugging Danny's jacket, "let's go drink beer."

Lulu turns and runs. *I'm a terrible runner. I look fat. They're chasing me.* The boys laugh. She flashes to Gerald running from them. The laughter, it sounds the same.

She reaches Janet, who looks unfazed. She didn't have to stare them down.

"Let's go," Janet says. She walks, her braids bouncing on her back.

Lulu's breathing returns to normal and she follows. Well, they'd get an F in surveillance.

Janet stops and turns. "They're not kidnappers," she says.

"How do you know? How are kidnappers supposed to act?"

"They're jerks. But they're not big criminals."

Lulu's disappointed. Janet's attention is already dwindling. But she's probably right. She looks over at the drugstore, closed now. Liz wouldn't take their crap.

"And they're not very bright," says Lulu. They giggle.

Janet pulls out her notebook and writes.

Lulu needs to salvage something. "Let's make posters. 'Missing person,'" she says. "We'll put them around the neighbourhood."

"Posters? The police already have the word out."

"Yeah but some people might not know. They might help someone remember."

Janet rolls her eyes. "Okay, I'll make some posters."

They agree to bring them to school tomorrow and hand them out after dismissal. Lulu heads home, glancing back every block. *Tubby*. She knows those old comic books. A rolypoly kid in a tiny sailor hat.

She climbs the steep staircase to their place. The hallway is quiet and dark but a circle of lamplight draws her to the kitchen.

Her mother sits at the small table working the crossword in the newspaper. Viv wears her kimono robe, deep blue silk with fluffy pink flowers all over it, a second-hand find that delighted her. Her hair's piled messily on her head and she has been painting her nails. The smell hits Lulu before she locates the ruby bottle beside the ashtray. The lip of Viv's teacup marked with a half-moon of pink lipstick.

"Hi, Mom."

Viv looks up. "Hi, honey, where were you?" She takes a final puff of her cigarette and stubs it out.

"With Janet."

"That's nice. She's nice."

Viv goes back to the crossword. She's good at them. She told Lulu she always longed to be a schoolteacher. As a girl she'd line up Brenda and other tots and "teach school." But teachers' college—let alone university, which was for rich people—seemed impossible. At least the way Mom went about things.

She and Dad married young, barely out of their teens, and they've fought since to stay out of debt. For years Dad struggled to find a steady job. When Lulu was small Viv went to night school, then landed a job as a receptionist in the nearby doctors' office. Her stories from there can be funny.

Lulu goes to the avocado green fridge and takes an inventory: eggs, milk, half a tin of Spam on a saucer, covered in plastic wrap. She closes the door.

"Where's Dad?" she asks without turning around.

There's a pause.

"Darts."

I almost got beaten up tonight. Lulu won't tell her. Things that happen out on the street rarely get brought inside.

Viv pours more tea. "You have any homework?"

"Yup, gonna do it now."

Lulu enters her room and feels under the bed for her leftover Bristol board. She sits on the floor with a black marker. Like a child with her crayons, trying to save the world. Draw a smiling sun in the corner and all will be well.

She uncaps the marker and holds it above the white cardboard, hesitant to begin. You can't erase marker. How should she describe Gerald? Do people know who he is? Do they even notice him? The plain-looking guy who waves at cars. That's all.

Bus Driver

The bus driver sits at his kitchen table slurping sweet, milky tea. "North End Man Missing." He notices the page-three headline, yawns, begins turning the page. Stops.

He reads: "Halifax police are asking for the public's help in locating a missing North End man. Gerald Green, 28, was last seen at Farrell's Drugstore at approximately noon Tuesday. He is 5 ft 8 inches tall and weighs 165 pounds, with brown hair and brown eyes. He was wearing a dark blue jacket and black pants." There's an odd picture of the guy wearing a fishing hat.

Holy shit, I remember him. He wasn't all there. Didn't know the fare.

The driver gets up and paces. *The kid wanted to go to the mall, didn't he? He said West End, right?* He doubts himself now.

He had to ask the kid a couple times if he wanted to get on the bus, he was at the stop for god's sake, and so the kid did. Said he wanted to go west. The driver remembers that clearly.

After passengers got off at the shopping centre, the driver noticed the guy rooted on the pavement. But then he got busy with new passengers.

He should call the cops. They wouldn't blame him, would they? He was only trying to help the kid. Built like a man but not right in the head. The driver didn't know him—it wasn't his usual route.

The driver paces some more. He doesn't want the supervisor on his ass again. He looks at the phone on the wall. Touches the receiver, yanks his hand away like he's been burned. Picks up the receiver.

Lulu

On the second morning of Gerald's disappearance, the girls bring their posters to school in garbage bags. They have cut them small, about the size of a record album, so they're easy to pin up. After school they plan to take them to local businesses: the drugstore (Lulu is nervous about asking Mr. Farrell), Buppy's, the sub shop, the convenience store near the Hydrostone, the Frugal Mart, the gas station. Lulu has a list. The day drags on until they're dismissed at three.

No one turns them down, though Farrell makes Lulu feel embarrassed for asking.

"People already know," he says, scratching his head. "But I guess it won't hurt."

They head for the last place on their list, the Frugal Mart. It's going on five o'clock when they arrive, and the small market is packed with shoppers grabbing last-minute supper items. There's a special on fresh haddock and the three cashiers are going full tilt. Someone has smashed a jar of gherkins and the green liquid oozes across the tile near the check-outs. Vinegar mixes with the fug of body odour and butchered meat.

A stock boy arrives with a mop, and Janet nudges Lulu in the ribs. Janet has been doing most of the asking. Lulu steps closer, sidesteps pickle juice, and clears her throat.

"Excuse me, can we speak with the manager?"

The boy doesn't look up, his filthy mop swishing through the mess, barely making a difference. A shard of glass skates across the floor and disappears under a display of toilet paper. He ignores it.

"Can we talk to the manager?" she says louder.

He motions with his head toward the rear of the store.

"Mr. Connelly's in the back."

They weave through shoppers. A little pigtailed girl in a grocery cart stares, her middle finger buried inside one of her nostrils. At the end of the aisle, along the rear, runs a cooler section of fresh meats and dairy products, cartons of locally made sauerkraut and bags of stiff salt cod for fishcakes. A man in a short-sleeved green shirt and black dress pants is reaching far into the showcase. Lulu clears her throat.

"Um, Mr. Connelly?"

He grunts.

"Mr. Connelly? We're wondering if we can ask you something."

"Gimme a second." He stacks some tubes of bologna, then backs up. He stands, smooths his hair. "What can I do you for?" He smiles.

Lulu holds out the poster. "We're wondering if you could hang this in the store? There's a local guy missing."

Connelly takes it and reads. His face goes slack. "Ah no, we don't post stuff like this."

He thrusts it back at her and disappears through a set of heavy swinging doors. A woman in curlers pushes past them to get at the salt cod.

"That was weird," Janet says. "First person to turn us down."

Lulu feels wounded. She looks at the poster, one of the ones she made. She can't see what's wrong with it.

"Missing: Gerald Green, of the Hydrostone. Medium height, brown hair, brown eyes. Last seen Tuesday at Farrell's Drugs. He waves at cars on the corner. Please call police if you see him." No photo but neat printing.

"Why wouldn't he want to help?" Lulu says. "Everyone knows who Gerald is."

Outside, the air's thick and misty and feels wonderful after the heat of the market. Gerald has been missing for over forty-eight hours. There's nothing more to do today except go home.

———

Across town, a police officer jogs down the hill toward the back parking lot of the mall. He's searching outside while his partner checks inside. He scans the building exterior, peers into parked cars. Then spots, hardly visible in the ditch near the tracks, the peak of some sort of lean-to.

He approaches and it's a heavy piece of cardboard, the kind a fridge might be shipped in, propped up in the shape of a tent. He blinks because his eyes must be playing tricks on him. Could swear he saw movement.

The officer squats at the lean-to. A glimpse of blue. Blue jacket, they said. He pulls back the flap. Brown eyes look up at him, scared.

"You Gerald?"

June

June flips over the tin of tomato soup, watches the wobbly red glob plop into the pot. She adds a tinful of milk and begins stirring, cigarette in her left hand. She hopes Mom will eat it—eat anything—though June herself hasn't eaten a crumb since Gerald vanished. The red and the white swirl in the pot but fight a union.

The phone rings and she jumps. Happens every damn time. She's afraid. Afraid of what the call will bring. If it's Trudy or Barry, checking in, she can handle it. But if it's the police…

"Miss Green?"

She can't breathe.

"This is Sergeant Miles with Halifax police. We've got him. He's okay."

"Oh thank *god*," she says, exhaling. "Where is he?"

"We took him to the VG. They're looking him over."

"I'll be right down," she says. The soup's boiling over.

"Oh, and we found him at the mall," the officer says. "In a ditch 'round back. A bus driver called in, remembered dropping Gerald off there."

"Okay." June hangs up. The last bit barely registered.

She absentmindedly turns off the stove, then dials Barry, misdials, tries again. As it rings she yells to her mother to come downstairs. Barry's on his way. Margie screeches and begins rushing around the house. June finds her purse and goes to the front door.

"Come on, Barry, come on," she mutters. She's shaking.

Margie presents herself: nightgown, heavy coat, rain bonnet and slippers, purse slung over a forearm. June does a double take.

"Mom, you wait here," she says. "It'll be crazy down there."

"But June—"

"I'll call as soon as I lay eyes on him."

Margie gives her a cross look. Then Barry pulls up and beeps, and June runs to the car.

"So what the hell?" he asks, glancing at her as he steers through traffic, speeding south. June presses her palm into the dashboard to brace herself.

"I don't know. He's alive, that's all," she says. She closes her eyes, woozy with the car's movement. *He's okay, he's okay.* She opens her eyes.

"Faster," she says.

The mall, a bus driver. None of it makes sense. Did the cop say *ditch*? Barry brakes to enter the hospital parking lot, narrowly misses a man in a white lab coat, and stops at the hospital's Emergency entrance. June's out before he comes to a full stop.

"I have to park," Barry says. His words recede as she hurries inside. June pushes aside a man speaking to a woman behind the counter. The woman frowns at her.

"My son was brought here. I need to see him immediately," June says.

People ask questions and consult charts, it seems endless and she could explode. Finally a nurse leads her to a curtained-off bed, and he's there, lying in a blue johnny shirt. His eyes are closed and a nasty scratch runs down his left cheek.

Gerald opens his eyes. "Mom," he says, "I got lost."

There's a sound, a stifled mix of weeping and laughter, and June realizes it's coming from her. She moves to hold him and the nurse tells her to be careful; they've x-rayed him for broken bones and don't have the results. The nurse leaves to find a doctor. June wants to ask everything at once but checks herself.

"Gerald," she says, her voice breaking, "what happened?" His face crumples and he looks about to cry.

"Don't be mad. I took a ride," he says. "To find the cowboys," he whispers. "I didn't make it."

"No, no, I'm not mad," she says, "but we've all been worried sick." She wants to lick her finger and run it down the length of the scratch, a mother's healing. Barry peeks his head through the curtain and Gerald smiles weakly.

"Jeesh, you gave us some fright, boy," says Barry, ruffling Gerald's hair.

There are dried leaves in his hair and perhaps mud under his fingernails. June can't fathom him getting on a bus.

"At the shopping centre, what happened?" she asks, perching on the bed.

He covers his face with his hands, shakes his head. "I messed up," he says, shaking his head. "Messed up."

"It's okay, buddy," says Barry. "You're going home now. Nana can't wait to see you."

Two men, a doctor and a police officer, step inside the curtain. It's crowded and June takes a shaky breath. The young doctor says the x-rays were clear, no broken bones or signs of head injury. But Gerald has a sprained ankle, some scratches and bruises. June notices Gerald's right foot sticking out from the sheet, the ankle wrapped in bandages.

The patient can go home but needs to stay off the ankle for a bit, the doctor says. He places a hand on Gerald's leg.

"You take care of yourself, okay? No more taking the bus," he says and smiles. Gerald won't look at him. June thanks the doctor and he exits.

The policeman asks if he can speak to Gerald with his mother present. June tells Barry to phone Mom, and he leaves.

The officer pulls out a small notebook and flips the pages. June pulls her cardigan tighter. He asks Gerald to tell him what happened. Gerald looks away. The officer changes tack and asks a specific question. "Why did you get on the bus?"

June holds her breath. Gerald looks to her and she nods.

"Tell him," she says.

"I don't know," Gerald whispers. The cop cups his own ear. "What's that now?" the officer says.

"He says he doesn't know," June says. She may have shouted.

The officer says he wants Gerald to do the talking, but in the end he doesn't get much out of him. A bus appeared. The driver spoke to him. He got on. He got off. Somehow he hurt his ankle. He hid in the ditch in a teepee made of cardboard.

"For two nights?" asks the officer.

Gerald doesn't answer. He looks about to cry and June asks if they can stop. The cop sighs and closes his notebook.

"Well, I guess we'll never know the whole story," he says.

"What about this bus driver?" says June.

"He doesn't appear to have done anything wrong," the officer says. "We won't be laying charges."

June's shocked. *Shouldn't someone pay for this*, she wants to say. But the officer has left.

Barry returns with a nurse who eases Gerald into a wheelchair, tucks in a blanket, and pushes him to the hospital entrance. June carries his wet and dirty clothes in a plastic bag. Barry helps Gerald into the front seat, and June crawls into the back. Tears trickle down her face, sneaky, salty tears. She closes her eyes.

She's vaguely aware of their drive north, past tall Victorian houses, the grassy Commons where men play softball, car dealerships, diners. June has lived here her whole life, forty-five years, but hardly knows this small city. She rarely leaves the North End. But Gerald did.

Barry pulls into their street. Margie comes out of the house and waves her arm.

"Nana," Gerald says, waving back.

Barry tells him to stay put, that he'll help him inside. The sight of Gerald emerging from the car draws a few neighbours from across the boulevard, and Archina and Dougelda even venture down their walkway.

"Gerald, god love ya!" someone yells.

"Nana, I took the bus," Gerald says, clutching Barry's arm.

"I heard. Wanted to do some shoppin' did ya?" Margie says, hugging him. June watches from the sidewalk.

"Mom, leave him be. Let's get in. He's in a johnny shirt for god's sake."

As June helps Gerald into pyjamas, he tells her a nurse gave him a purple Popsicle and a sandwich, but he's still hungry. Margie fixes him a peanut butter sandwich and glass of milk. Kitty rubs against his leg as he eats with badly scratched hands. Gerald, the mystery man. Spent two nights alone, out behind the mall. Unbelievable.

"So how did you hurt your ankle?" June asks. He gulps the milk and it trickles down his chin.

"I had some chocolate. I ate that," he says. "And a pop."

Barry sits down beside him. "Did anyone do anything to ya?" He tries to catch Gerald's eye but Gerald ducks his head and announces he wants to go to bed.

Barry helps him upstairs and June tucks him in, something she hasn't done in years. She kisses him on the forehead, lightly touches the scratch on his face. He closes his eyes.

Down in the kitchen Margie's making tea. June sits and lights a smoke, watches her hand quiver as she brings it to her lips.

"He'll tell us more tomorrow," Barry says. "The kid's exhausted."

The house feels complete now that he's home. June can breathe again, sleep again. But she wants to know why it happened so it never happens again. That effing bus driver, dropping a boy like that on the other side of town. He should be hung out to dry.

"He said something about going to find cowboys," says June. "What in the hell was he talking about?"

"Cowboys?" Margie says.

"Yeah, I guess because of those damn comics, movies. I don't know," says June. She sips her tea.

"Next he'll be hunting for Superman," Barry says, chuckles and moves his arms in a flying motion.

Margie stands and says she's going up to bed too. She shuffles out.

June and Barry sit for a while. He clicks on the radio and as daylight fades they listen to music, exchanging few words. They spend little time together these days. It's kind of nice.

Truth be told, her brother was a godsend looking for Gerald. Worked as hard as anyone. Trying to make up for the times he let them down, the times they couldn't get hold of him, when Sheila was beside herself, Barry gone all night at some card game, that dark time when he mixed with a bad crowd. June studies him; she should say something.

"What?" he says.

She stubs out her cigarette. "I'm drained. I'm going to look in on him."

"Go ahead," he says. "I'll go sleep in my own bed."

Up on the landing, June hears muffled crying. She checks Gerald and he's quiet. She tiptoes in. Rise, fall, rise, fall goes his chest. Alive. She did this when he was a baby. She goes across to the bedroom she shares with her mother.

"Mom, what's wrong?" She can just make her out, lying in bed in the darkness.

"It was my fault, my damn fault, June. Oh I feel so bad. I never thought he'd go." She cries and rocks herself. June kneels beside the bed to get a better look.

"It's okay that you fell asleep. It's the bus driver I want to strangle."

"No, no, the cowboys. I put that cowboy notion in his head."

June frowns.

"He was always asking questions: 'Who's my daddy? Where's my daddy?' What was I supposed to say? I don't even know, heaven help me. So a long time ago I told him his father was a cowboy, like in his books."

Margie pulls a tattered tissue from her sleeve and dabs her nose. "He seemed to like that," she continues. "I said, 'Your dad's out west roping cows, and he's busy. They need him on the ranch. That's why he can't come see you.' Gerald said he'd love to visit him someday."

June rests her forehead on the bed covers.

"I was afraid to tell you," Margie says, placing her hand on June's head. She rolls onto her back.

"I thank God he's found. Thought the No. 9 bus would get him to Alberta."

Lulu

Every Friday morning the radio station gives away ten dollars to the twelfth caller, but you have to listen carefully for the sound of a telephone ringing. That's the signal to call in. Lulu will lie in bed and, when she hears the ringing, hightail it to the kitchen phone. She has the number memorized. She never gets through.

On this morning she calls, then retreats to her room, deflated. She digs and pulls out a pair of rust-coloured corduroys; they still fit but they're worn on the thighs. She flings them to the floor.

The radio announcer begins the local news. Lulu almost doesn't catch it, with her head in her closet, but she leans back and pauses. Did he say? Yes, North End man found. Alive. The announcer moves on to another story.

Lulu stamps her foot. She wants to know more. Where did they find him? She runs and calls Janet.

"Did you hear?" Lulu says. Janet has not, so Lulu fills her in.

"Do you think our posters had anything to do with it?" Lulu says, laughs.

"Yeah right. See you at school."

Lulu wants to tell Viv, she wants to shout. A case solved. Sure, it would have been great if the girl detectives had found him. But to be honest, she's relieved. No more traipsing around the neighbourhood. No more run-ins with Danny and Mikey.

She raps on her parents' bedroom door and her mother says come in. Viv sits on the edge of the bed in a bra and a skirt, holding a blue blouse.

"Guess what?" Lulu says, smiling. "Gerald was found. You know, the guy who was missing? He's okay."

"Oh good," Viv says in a vague sort of way, the way she sounds when Lulu interrupts her in the middle of a crossword. "Lu," she says, "I need to tell you something."

There's no light behind her green eyes.

"Your father and I are splitting up."

"Again?" That winter Dad slept on his mother's chesterfield, until Viv asked him back.

"I can't do it anymore, honey," says Viv. "We were kids when we married—stupid. Life...things haven't gone the way we'd hoped."

"What does this mean?" says Lulu. "Are we moving?"

Viv stands and slips on the blouse. "Dad and I talked this morning. He's moving out."

June

Weeks pass and spring becomes summer. Gerald's escapade, his disappearance, seems almost like a dream, and when June thinks of it she shudders. It could have gone so wrong. Yet he survived two nights outside in May. She often shakes her head in amazement.

Bit by bit, she gets the story out of him. He was on the corner when a bus drew up and the driver asked if he wanted to get on. June asks why he did and he has no answer.

"You wanted to go out west?" she says. "Because of what Nana told you?" He chews a fingernail.

Over the years she dismissed his questions about his father, not realizing how badly he wondered. Maybe thinking it didn't matter, because Gerald was different.

"He's gone away," she'd say each time he asked.

She thought it would be enough that they all loved him, spoiled him. Safe up in his room. But he got on a bus by himself. Defiant? He'd been mad at her the night before because she wouldn't buy him a hot chicken sandwich.

"Why are you so mean?" he'd yelled.

He grabbed onto a lie her mother had to tell because June had been lying too. She's ashamed. Trudy and Barry say she shouldn't blame herself. *It wasn't your fault*, she repeats throughout her days, hoping it will sink in.

One evening she sits beside Gerald in the front room, ready to utter the sentences she's been preparing in her head. His eyes stay on the TV, where American POWs seem to be having a ball in a Nazi prison camp.

"Gerald," she says. "Gerald, look at me." He turns.

"I never talked about your father because he's not part of our life," she says. "You had me and Nana and Barry and we all…You know you're my number one."

"Is he nice?" asks Gerald.

June startles. "I don't really know him," she says slowly. *Please don't ask how babies are made.* "But," she thinks to add, "he isn't a cowboy."

Gerald looks at her.

She says, "Nana was just having fun."

"He's mean?" he says.

She shakes her head. "No." She retreats to the kitchen.

June suspects the events have worsened the hot flashes that began last winter. She'll be walking to work or bent over the sink, rinsing a woman's hair, and it hits her. A wave of intense warmth that begins in her chest and climbs, setting fire to her neck and head. Sweat gathers above her lip, drips from her hairline. She soaks her top and the smock over it. She can barely catch her breath. Wants to strip naked. Change of life, her mother calls it.

At times it makes work unbearable but she's embarrassed to tell Frank. Besides, he has other things on his mind: his wife isn't well and he's thinking of packing it in. He told June last week and she was shocked. She's never let herself think that far ahead. What will she do if the barbershop closes?

On this Thursday morning, Frank tells her he needs to go out for an hour or two. He pauses and adds, "I'm going to the bank."

June straightens the bottles of shampoo and hairspray on the shelf, small adjustments that don't need doing.

"You know, I'd sell to you if you could swing it," he says. "Customers love you. But I figured…"

"Yeah, no, Frank, there's no way I could buy this place."

"I gotta sell, June. The building and all. This is my retirement."

She drops onto a swivel chair and plucks a hair off her smock.

"When the time comes, I'll lay you off. You'll get unemployment." He gives her a small smile. "I wish I could do more."

He hangs up his navy blue smock and hobbles to his car. Like sixty-five going on eighty-five.

Frank was kind to her when Gerald disappeared. Told her to take more time after Gerald was found, so she stayed home another ten days. The incident threw them all for a loop. Gerald seems like he'll weather it okay—he's back walking to the store—but Mom's rolling downhill. She's become June's number one worry.

She lights a cigarette as her next customer walks through the door. This woman will gossip the entire two hours June's cutting and perming her hair. She'll complain about this and tell June to redo that. Then tip zilch. Maybe June's done with this job. Her legs throb every night. She's more needed at home but feels far away. She stands and places her smoke in the ashtray.

"So my dear," she says, inviting the customer into the chair, "what can I do for you today?"

Frank returns some time later and gets to work; a string of men want haircuts for the weekend. At six o'clock he flips the door sign to "Closed," and June sweeps up hair clippings at her station. She decides to bring her smock home to wash it, gathers her lunch sack and purse.

Frank waits at the door. "I talked to my friend," he says, "you know, the barbershop near the bridge, and he thinks he could use some help."

June remembers him well, a lech with a hairy facial mole who tries to grab her bum every time he drops by.

"Anyway," Frank says, "I thought I'd mention it."

"Thanks. I'll think about it."

Frank only has to drive two blocks and he's home. June begins walking in the opposite direction. She'll have to make supper. The kitchen will be a frigging mess, Mom flustered because she forgot what she was going to cook.

"June."

She turns. A smiling man stands beside a car at the curb, his arms resting on the roof. Lorne.

"Just moved back. My sister told me about Gerald." Shakes his head as if in disbelief.

June is unprepared. Eight years. She shifts the weight on her feet, lets one of her bags slip to the ground.

"Let me drive you home," he says, coming around to the passenger side. He grabs the bag and opens the car door. June slides onto the front seat, dazed.

It's a different car but it smells like him, cigarettes and aftershave. It brings a rush of memories: kissing in his old car, Sunday drives in the country. The night they broke up.

She steals a look as he pulls into traffic. The lines around his mouth have deepened; more grey threads his hair. Jeans and a shirt rolled up to the elbows. Those forearms used to drive her crazy.

"So, how you been? How's Gerald?" he says. "It must've been a shock."

"Yeah," she says, "yes it was. He's doing okay though."

"That's good. Man, what was going through his head? Taking the bus to the shopping centre?"

June looks at him.

"I mean," he says, "he never did stuff like that."

"Hmm."

He tells her he's rented an apartment but plans to buy a house. He made a lot of money in Calgary construction and got the hell out. Missed the smell of the ocean.

They turn onto her street but he's on the wrong side of the boulevard. He'll have to drive to the end, enter the busier street, and turn back onto her side.

"Stop. I can get out here," she says, reaching for her things.

"No, I'll do a U-ey up here, take you to the door."

"I'm fine. Let me out."

He raises his eyebrows but stops the car.

"Thanks for the drive." She shuts the door and makes her way onto the boulevard. The grass feels soft beneath her feet.

"June. Hey, I didn't mean anything."

She keeps going, thinks she hears him curse softly. She hopes she's walking okay because she feels shaky. Makes herself not look back, and hears him drive away.

She enters the house, bracing herself. Gerald's watching TV, says hi without taking his eyes off the show.

Homemade cookies sit on the kitchen table. Evelyn was here again. Margie stands surrounded by pots and pans, potatoes spilled across the floor.

"Oh thank god you're home. I can't find my potato masher."

June sets her bags on a chair. "You're holding it."

And June sets aside thoughts of Lorne, of everything outside their little house.

Lulu

Lulu has been exploring the nowhere places, strips of land on the fringes of the neighbourhood, forgotten or ignored, mostly nameless. She'll find a beer bottle with a faded label, one sock. Unexpected wildflowers. She remembers the spring day, as a kid, she gave her mother a fistful of dandelions—healthy blooms that bled a clear, sticky sap over her hands as she broke their fat stems. The friend's backyard awash in yellow where she'd gathered her bouquet was the most magical place she'd ever seen. Mom laughed.

"They're just weeds, Lu," she said.

Lulu wanders, wonders where the old prison field sat on the hill overlooking the water. She was little when it closed. Viv says in her day, kids used to tease Rockhead prisoners out working the gardens, but the prisoners were nice to them. Lulu scrambles down the gaping former quarry called the Pit, where prisoners once worked too.

She circles the school grounds. Schools are lonely in summer. Maybe it's just her mood: she's been working a lot, hasn't seen much of Janet or anybody.

Today she walks past Danny's house, staying on the opposite side of the street, over the train tracks and down to a dusty spot with a view of the city dump and harbour basin beyond. Africville, an old Black community, sat on the shore somewhere around here until the government moved out the people and tore it down, not so long ago.

Dad says the city put all the nasty stuff—a prison, a dump, an incinerator, an abattoir—in the North End where Black people and poor Catholics lived.

She hasn't seen her father in weeks, since grade nine graduation. It was awkward. Someone offered to take a picture of them, and Mom and Dad had to stand on either side of her, smiling. They barely spoke.

Lulu blames the red Mustang. The year she was in grade five, Dad bought a used Mustang sports car—he called it "a classic, a fixer-upper"—and Viv was livid. She screamed that they'd never get a house at this rate. Dad yelled that she blew too much on clothes and junk for the apartment.

Finally, Dad sold the car. But he started taking longer work trips, stayed late at the tavern many weeknights. As far as Lulu could see, her parents never recovered from it. Now it seems they'll get a divorce.

When her schoolmate's parents divorced a few years ago, the neighbourhood talked. The girl's last name changed—one day in school, it was suddenly different—but the nuns forbade anyone from mentioning it. At least in September, Lulu will start high school with a clean slate.

Jimmy sent her a graduation card from Toronto with ten dollars in it. It had a drawing of a puppy wearing one of those flat graduation hats, a mortarboard. "You're Grrreat!" it said. She smiles at the little Timex Gran gave her and realizes she needs to hurry to work.

Liz is serving a customer when she arrives. She's been growing out her dark, curly hair, and it sits on her shoulders. The pale freckles across her nose have deepened this summer and highlight her gold-flecked eyes. She's wearing a white peasant blouse with short puffed sleeves and dangly gold earrings that brush her neck when she moves.

These days Liz and Lulu are running the show at the store while Miriam recovers from an operation.

"We'll be rolling in it," Liz told her, laughing. She's saving for a plane ticket. She's entering her last year of university and says she'll "blow this Popsicle stand" as soon as she graduates. She was considering Toronto but most likely it will be New

York City. Lulu wonders if Liz's boyfriend, Tom, will go too. Sometimes he visits the store and jokes around with them. They seem so in love.

Later that afternoon, when things quiet down, Liz buys them each a Coke. They sit back by the pharmacy where they can watch the front door, and Liz sets her sandalled feet on a stack of boxes. Farrell is snoring in his office, his chin resting on his chest.

"I'm late," Liz says, and takes a swig of pop. Lulu doesn't understand, Liz started today before she did. Liz gestures with the Coke bottle.

"Late, as in my period is late. Almost two weeks. I'm never late." She takes a sip. "You're the first person I've told."

"But"—Lulu feels herself blushing—"I thought you said you're on the pill." Liz shrugs.

"Sometimes it fails. Sometimes I forget to take one." She saw a doctor yesterday. "Don't tell anyone. Ever," she says and returns to the front shop.

Lulu has two immediate thoughts, both of which make her feel guilty: first, she feels grown up having this conversation, and two, she's grateful this isn't happening to her. That's not fair. Liz has to go to New York and become a writer. She talks about this disco called Studio 54 and a painter, Andy Warhol. Soup cans, Lulu looked him up in the school library. But if Liz has a baby, if she can't make it, what chance does anyone else have?

It distracts her all afternoon. She sneaks a look at Liz's tummy, still flat. Guess the baby would be just a bean now, maybe not even that big. Is it a boy bean or a girl bean?

When Lulu gets home, her mother's tearing through her closet and amassing a pile of clothes on the floor, from swimming trunks to a winter coat.

"Your father didn't take all his stuff," Viv says, holding a plaid scarf in each hand. "Never wore these," she says, throwing them on the bed. "Gifts from me, fifty per cent wool, and never looked at them twice."

Lulu wouldn't wear the scarves either—they're ugly and scratchy—but she won't say a word when Viv's like this. She goes to her room and lies down on the bed. She wants to call Janet but won't break Liz's secret. Or call Jimmy, to hear his silly giggle. But it's long distance.

The girls work together every day that week but Liz doesn't mention the pregnancy. One cloudy morning they stand together at the front counter, Lulu aching to ask if Liz has heard anything, when Mikey and Danny enter.

Danny wanders into the handful of aisles, while Mikey struts toward the counter. Lulu turns, pretending to tidy the merchandise on the shelves.

"Hey, it's Tubby," Mikey says.

"Watch your mouth," Liz says, her voice icy. Lulu freezes behind her. She's never heard Liz like this.

"Whoa, I didn't mean anything," he says, half-laughing. "I'm just here for some smokes."

He names the brand and Lulu hands them to Liz without turning around. Lulu can tell Liz is trying to keep track of Danny too. It's an old trick, thieves splitting up to confuse you. Mikey doesn't seem to move. Cellophane crinkles.

"So Liz," he says, "what you doing later?"

"You've got to be kidding me," she says.

"Ha. Your loss."

The phone on the counter rings.

"Farrell's Drugs," Liz says, then pauses. "Yes, this is Liz." She moves away until the phone cord is taut. Lulu can't help staring, Liz going pale behind the comic book rack.

The bell tinkles and Lulu turns to glimpse Mikey jogging down the sidewalk. Danny's gone too. Liz hangs up and brings her hands to her face, her fingers pressing into her closed eyelids.

"Shit," she says. "Shit, shit, shit."

Lulu waits a few beats. "Was it the doctor?"

"I'm getting rid of it." Liz strikes a match. Her hands tremble and it won't light; she has three goes at it, throwing spent matches onto the counter before a flame pops. She draws on her cigarette and exhales. "I already decided."

Lulu knows the church is dead against abortion and that it's hard to get one. That's about it. The McMullins are big churchgoers and Liz is their only child. Liz calls her mother "that bitch."

Lulu has seen Mrs. McMullin in church and met her once, when the sanctuary girls were asked into the rectory to help prepare for the bishop's visit, a big deal for the priest. The housekeeper and some neighbourhood women cooked in the kitchen while Mrs. McMullin oversaw the girls, pacing behind them like a prison guard.

They sat at a long table in the chilly dining room and polished silver: candlesticks, a coffee service, spoons and forks, trays etched with curlicues that were a nightmare to rid of tarnish. Lulu had never seen real silverware.

"Does your mother know you're wearing that?" Liz's mom hissed in her ear.

Lulu looked down at her fuchsia hot pants and taupe pantyhose, which had a ladder tear running down one leg. Hot pants were in. She'd thought the pantyhose, taken from Viv's drawer, would make her legs look thinner. She tried to hide her tears, head bent over a sugar bowl, swirling the pungent polishing cream round and round. No, Liz won't tell her mother about any abortion.

"Hey!" Liz yells, bringing Lulu back to the store. Danny emerges from the shelves, grinning.

"What're you doing here?" Liz's eyes have a wild look.

"What's goin' on down at college, Liz?" Danny says, resting his hands on the counter.

Liz goes still. "Get out," she says, as serious as Lulu has ever heard her.

"Whatcha gettin' rid of?" He leans in, nods toward Liz's tummy. "Got a bun in the oven?"

"Get the hell out!" she explodes.

Danny snorts and heads for the door. He holds up a bottle of aftershave he hasn't paid for, and runs.

"Didn't you know he was still here?" Liz says, angry.

Lulu shakes her head. He must have been ducking down.

"Jesus." Liz leaves the safety of the counter and steps in one direction, then the other. "He won't do anything, right?"

"He's just a punk, like you said," Lulu says softly.

Liz looks toward the windows. She doesn't answer.

June

Barry is taking them for a Saturday drive and June regrets saying yes. Her mother's making egg salad sandwiches, always egg salad for outings, and the smell perfumes the entire stifling house.

Gerald refuses to wear shorts and June could kill him. She stands in his bedroom holding a pair but he sits on his bed, stubborn.

"Let him wear what he wants," Barry calls from the bottom of the stairs. "I wanna hit the road."

June throws the shorts on the bed. "Suit yourself."

She goes into her bedroom and looks in the mirror. She'll die in the heat today. This old gingham sundress is tight now. Mutton dressed as lamb. Who'd ever want this?

Half an hour later they leave, Barry ticked off, Mom in a tizzy, Gerald sulking, June reluctant. She squints in the sunlight. Summer has finally arrived; it's the long weekend marking the beginning of August. She has a splitter and asks Barry to stop at the drugstore for aspirin. Gerald wants to come in too, for a treat. June says no—he's spoiled—until Barry hands him a two-dollar bill.

"It'll keep him happy," Barry says. June shakes her head and she and Gerald get out. Barry, always wasting money.

In the store a brown-haired girl stands behind the counter, and a red-haired girl in braids sits on a stool next to her. They go silent when June and Gerald enter. Gerald heads for the rack of comics.

June brings a bottle of aspirin to the cash and the brown-haired girl rings it in. She pauses and June looks up, waves her hand, dismissing Gerald.

"He'll pay for his own."

She shoves the aspirin into her purse and leans against the counter. Gerald's checking every damn comic. "Hurry up," she says.

"Um, you're Gerald's mother, aren't you?" says the red-haired girl.

"Yeah?" June says.

"We recognized you. We"—she motions to the brown-haired girl—"made posters when he was missing. We wanted to help."

June raises her eyebrows. Weeks after Gerald was found she was startled to see a notice hanging in a store.

"Oh yeah, I heard about that," June says, figures the girls want more. "Thanks."

Gerald brings over his choice and the brown-haired one rings it in.

The redhead prattles on. "Yeah, all the stores wanted to help, it was so great," she says. "They all took posters, except the Frugal Mart. It was weird but the manager, Mr. Connelly, he said no."

June stops cold. His name still makes the hair on her arms stand on end. That bastard. Not wanting anything *at all* to do with Gerald. But he must know. Over the years they've managed to avoid each other, but everyone knows about June's baby.

Barry beeps his horn. June and Gerald get back in the car, and Barry heads for the highway. Mom sings along with the radio, stopping often to comment on the scenery, but June tunes her out. *He* said no. To helping find his own son, the son he has never acknowledged. How dare he.

Barry drives for close to an hour, then exits onto a seaside road that curls along inlets and bays sprinkled with wooded islands and lined by craggy rock. Sailboats bob offshore. Barry stops at a picnic table with a view of a beach.

None of them care to sit on the sand. Gerald hates the feel of it on his feet. June hasn't swum in years. But she has to admit the ocean's pretty, sparkling in the sun. Swimmers dart in and out of the surf. A child screeches and a dog chases a ball into the water. The others eat. June downs two aspirin with Kool-Aid, sickly sweet.

"So, I hear Lorne's back," Barry says.

"Lorne? Did you hear that, June?" her mother says.

June won't bite. They were disappointed when she broke it off, but they can't understand. Too many people making demands on her. Lorne called her at work last week but she made Frank say she was busy. Frank, who has the place up for sale and will soon put her out of work. And now Connelly, front of mind again. Her skin crawls.

Gerald throws a potato chip to a swooping seagull, which snatches it with ease. Gerald laughs and shoves a handful of chips into his mouth. His social worker's been bugging June since he got lost; she wants June to enroll him in the sheltered workshop she's been pushing for years. It's even within walking distance of home, but June doesn't like the sound of a sheltered workshop. They make something there, some product that they sell. Sounds like forced labour. And Gerald wouldn't like it. But the social worker says she's worried about him, that she doesn't want a repeat of what happened. Implying June's a bad mother. Well screw her. Screw them all.

Lulu

The Danny incident scars Liz. She's snappy at work, makes mistakes. They don't talk about it but Lulu knows Liz is worried he'll spill her secret. Liz stares out at his corner. He doesn't appear.

The days stay hot, summer settled in, and as Lulu walks to the store for early shifts, the air is still, the birds silent, as if the neighbourhood holds its breath.

But nothing seems to come of it. Liz relaxes and offers Lulu a rare Saturday off. The store has been dead on weekends. The night before, Viv tells Lulu her father will pick her up in the morning for a fun day together, an early birthday celebration.

Lulu sighs. She and Dad have never been close. He's on the road a lot and when he was still in the apartment with her and Viv, when he wasn't at the tavern or darts or bowling, he'd just sit on the chesterfield.

"Is this what I signed up for?" Viv would say, hands on her hips. He'd watch TV and drink beer.

Lulu wondered what was going on inside his handsome head. He never missed Jimmy's baseball games all those years, loved to talk sports with his son, but he had no questions for her. As if he didn't know what to do with a daughter.

She has a glossy, black-and-white snapshot of her and Dad, tucked into a dresser drawer. He leans forward in an armchair, his arms resting on his knees and a cigarette in one hand. He looks down at Lulu, who's maybe six years old, sitting at his feet in a hitched-up dress, white tights, and black patent shoes. Pigtails. She looks up at him. Neither smiles.

Now she and Dad are supposed to be friends. Now, separated, they're supposed to "spend time together," Viv says. As if that were normal.

He doesn't show until eleven. The car's stuffy and she shifts, unsticks her thighs from the seat. They drive for a while with no destination.

"How about a chicken burger?" he asks in a cheery voice that sounds alien.

She glances over. He likely feels weird too. She agrees and that gives them a purpose. They'll drive around the basin to the chicken burger takeout, a classic spot with a fifties style that her parents loved as teenagers. Viv told her about the day she and Dad were speeding out there, singing with the radio, and a police car stopped them. Viv sprawled with her long legs extended and bare feet stuck out the front window. "Get those feet in," the officer barked. They'd laugh about it.

"Looking forward to high school?" Dad says, fussing with the radio.

"I think so."

"That's good."

He rarely asks about school, never knows what she's studying. Viv signs her report cards and asks about homework.

"Stay in school," Viv will say. "I quit and regret it to this day."

The takeout is jammed but Dad manages to park. They join the line and Lulu decides on a chicken burger and chocolate milkshake. She feels a jolt of happiness; it's exciting to be in a crowd, doing what others are doing, not wondering what you're missing on a sunny Saturday.

She looks at her father ahead of her and feels she should say something meaningful. Jab him playfully on the shoulder and say, "Good job, Dad." She touches the back of his shirt, damp with sweat.

He wheels around, frowning. "What?" he says.

She shakes her head. "Nothing."

They eat in the car with the windows down, listening to fifties music piped from the restaurant. Eating's a good activity when you don't know what to say. Don't talk with your mouth full, and all that. Their return drive is quieter. He probably just wants to get rid of her, go off and do whatever he does.

After he drops her off she stays outside; the apartment will be a furnace and Viv's likely out. She walks the dead streets. Not one kid at the playground—steamy, cracked pavement and broken glass under the swings. A dog tied by a rope lies in a bit of shade in a weedy front yard. The leaves on the trees look limp.

She begins to descend the hill toward the train tracks. Danny's mother stands in her doorway smoking, an elbow resting in her other hand, again in the quilted housecoat.

Lulu crosses the tracks and turns toward the basin and the city dump. She once went to the dump with Dad and Jimmy to throw away an old washing machine and saw people sifting through the mounds of stuff, seeking treasure.

Today she stays clear; she thinks she can smell it from here. A haze hovers over the indigo water of the basin. Seagulls scavenge in the distance, screech, glide, catch the wind. Maybe they'll head out to sea, flap their wings hard and make it to Ireland. It's green there.

The milkshake gurgles in Lulu's stomach. Some sort of warehouse sits ahead, and beside it a shiny black car. She keeps going; maybe she can circle back to the main road this way.

As she passes the car she looks in and sees her, Liz's mother. She's in the front seat wearing a paisley head scarf. But it's definitely Mrs. McMullin, she looks like Liz. The dark-haired man in the driver's seat is not Mr. McMullin. Liz's father is bald.

Lulu can't move. The couple kiss deeply and he places a hand on her breast. When they pull apart, Mrs. McMullin leans back, then stops smiling. She sees Lulu. Mrs. McMullin speaks and the man looks over his shoulder. The car jumps into gear and they take off, gravel and dust flying.

Lulu is wide awake, the nausea gone. Mrs. McMullin—the lady who arranges altar flowers every week in church, who acts like she runs the place, who made Lulu cry in the manse—a sinner.

June

A few weeks into August, Frank sells the barbershop. The buyer plans to turn the building into a second-hand store specializing in military paraphernalia. June has seen this sort of thing: war medals, dented helmets (maybe a pointy German beauty), musty wool uniforms in a colour called "drab," metal toy soldiers that men, not boys, collect to arrange in formations, plus assorted gewgaws. Someone must like that stuff.

Frank will close at the end of September and lay her off, entitling her to unemployment insurance benefits. But UI won't pay the bills. She's aware of a beauty parlour in the North End, but the owner and June hate each other and June would never beg her for a job.

The feud stretches back to elementary school. Perhaps one of the girls stole the other's pencil or admirer. Maybe one considered the other too high on herself. June forgets. But the dislike has festered all these years, and if they pass each other on the street they do not exchange pleasantries. Well into their forties, the women cannot patch it up now.

June chews on this as she makes her way home from work. She will not work for Frank's disgusting friend. She doesn't have the setup at home to cut hair under the table, like some women do. Mom would drive customers crazy with her patter, Gerald getting in the way. She could try retail, but even the measly tips she gets as a hairdresser make a difference. Besides, she's weary of being on her feet all day. She's been lying awake for weeks and doesn't have the answer.

She turns at the sound of a car, and it's Lorne. He stops and reaches over to open the passenger door. Neither speaks as she gets in. As he drives, he begins a speech she figures he's been rehearsing. He says he regrets losing her, that he thought about her all those years and always considered her "the one." He says he never knew how to act with Gerald but wants to try again.

"He's important to you so he's important to me," Lorne says.

June's scared of what the future holds for her and Gerald. Mom spiralling. She hasn't heard nice words like this in a long time. He smiles and she gets goosebumps. She agrees to start seeing him again.

"Gerald is my priority," she warns. She tells him she's been on edge since Gerald went missing. It feels good to confide in him again.

"I bet you're blaming yourself," he says, pulling up to her door. "But you're the best mother I've ever seen."

They go to the movies and for drives. He picks scary movies but cowers on her shoulder like a child, making her laugh. He tells her about the Rockies and cooks her meatloaf, the one thing he does well. June ignores Mom's teasing as she heads out on her dates. She tries to kiss Gerald goodnight but he pushes her away.

One Sunday, she and Lorne and Gerald drive to the Annapolis Valley. Gerald asks to stop for ice cream, and, as they linger near the fruit stand, June's scoop of strawberry topples into the dirt. She marches over and demands a free refill, and the nervous-looking teenager obeys. Lorne chuckles.

"Spunk," he says. "I noticed it first time I saw you in Frank's. Small but mighty. Wouldn't laugh at my jokes."

"Yeah, well, you were pretty obvious," she says, trying not to smile. "You came in so much, you were practically bald."

When they dated that first time they discussed how neither thought they'd ever settle down. But this seemed right. June needed to feel safe and Lorne was used to protecting people.

When Lorne was thirteen, his father ran out on them. Went out one evening for milk and never came back. The eldest of five kids, Lorne had to step up and help his mother, who brought in sewing and ironing, baked pies to earn a few dollars. Lorne had to get bossy, his sisters teased. This story, of young Lorne being forced into manhood, leaving school after grade nine so he could get a job, always makes June weepy.

Eight years after their breakup, he's the same Lorne. A hard worker. Goes on about how he loves working with wood, the smell and feel of it. His mother's long gone but he keeps tabs on his brothers and sisters. Still a great kisser.

Margie welcomes him back with a hug and Barry shakes his hand. Lorne tells him he's sorry to hear about Sheila, says he knows what it's like to sit in an apartment by yourself. Barry doesn't respond, just sips his rum and Coke.

The reunion of Lorne and Gerald isn't as smooth. Gerald is shy and won't shake his hand. One thing about Gerald, he never forgets.

"You think the Leafs will make a run this season?" Lorne asks as they sit opposite each other in the front room. Gerald shrugs.

June leans against the door jamb and can barely watch. The picnic, sure, Gerald was upset that day. He's crushed when kids yell slurs on the street. But she also has a gut feeling Gerald will not accept any man into their lives, not anyone who could come between him and his mother.

On June's birthday in September, Lorne takes her to a steakhouse downtown. Jazz plays in the background as they're led to a white-clothed table; the waiters wear white shirts, red bow ties, and black, buttoned vests. She studies the heavy, leather-bound menu and whispers that this will cost a fortune. Even mushrooms cost extra. Lorne tells her to order anything she wants. She notes the other women and pulls at her blouse. Underdressed.

They reject the suggestion of Caesar salad made tableside—they've never had one and it seems a big fuss, a grown man stirring things in a wooden bowl as you watch—so they order just steaks, well done. The waiter arches an eyebrow.

Then he asks Lorne about wine, June's sure he's trying to embarrass them, and Lorne stutters. They settle on a carafe of the house red but June's not keen on wine and she knows Lorne would rather have a beer. They skip dessert. On the drive home she doesn't look over, just rests her hand on his thigh.

———

"It's your life," Trudy says.

She and June are at bingo. June hates bingo. Trudy plays every week and has coerced June into coming tonight. A thick canopy of smoke floats above the hopefuls who line flimsy tables stretching the length of the bingo hall, an impressive amount of cards arranged like tiles in front of each player. June doesn't know how they keep up.

"B seven," the caller announces, his mouth always too close to the mic, his voice coming through cotton balls.

June skims her few cards. A hum percolates in the hall as it does after every number called near the end of a game, the anticipation of not knowing when someone will break through with "Bingo!" and a raised arm. There are big jackpots tonight.

"I know. It's just," says June. She takes a slow drag of her cigarette. The two women have had this discussion before, and June figures Trudy's tired of it.

"Be honest with yourself. Do you want a man in your life or not?" says Trudy. "Because that hunk wouldn't have to ask me twice to move in with him. But maybe it's not important to you anymore."

"Bingo!"

They crumple up their paper cards and set out new ones for the next game. Trudy has a way of getting under her skin.

Of course June wants to be with Lorne. Her own little family at last. So what's holding her back? Mom, for one. If she moved in with Lorne, it would be a battle—no, a war—trying to convince Mom and Gerald to go with her. Yet she can't just leave.

June sips her cola, flat now. All these years she's tried to do the right thing but it's never seemed enough. Be a good mother, sacrifice your personal life. Make a living, you're a terrible mother.

The bingo caller gives instructions for the next game, around the world and two lines or something, but June has lost interest.

Lulu

Every first day of school since Lulu was five has felt the same. Butterflies in her stomach, a new outfit too warm for early September, the scent of fresh erasers, sharpened pencils and notebooks in her bookbag.

This year, Lulu asked Viv for a large patchwork cloth purse similar to Liz's, to use as a school bag. She hugs it on her lap as she and Janet settle into seats on the city bus heading south. They fidget; they start high school today at the traditionally Catholic school at the Commons. The rival school sits across the intersection, and whichever one you attend, you must assume an immediate hatred of the other. As far as Lulu and Janet are concerned, the other school is for non-Catholics, South Enders, and other sorts of people they have never met.

Janet stunned this morning by showing up with a new layered hairdo, blue eye shadow, and large hoop earrings. She looks about nineteen. Lulu glances at her own top and pants, wishes she were skinnier. Janet says they should aim to get boyfriends by Halloween. Lulu just hopes she can find her classes today.

They get off the bus with a clump of kids they've grown up with. The chatter dies as they near the school grounds. A woman, maybe a teacher, stands at one of the entrances directing students into the gym.

"Line up inside to receive your locker assignments," the woman says again and again.

Students funnel through the double doors and Lulu loses Janet right away. Rattled, she joins the line, wishes she had broken in these new shoes.

"I like your bag."

Lulu turns around. A blond girl in a brown, brimmed hat smiles at her.

"Grade ten?" the girl says.

"Yeah, you too?" Lulu digests the hat and bell-bottom jeans, the strands of colourful beads falling almost to the girl's waist. An old hippie look. The girl nods and bops her head, as if she hears music.

"I'm Lulu."

"I'm Helen. Sucks, huh? Coming back to school."

Lulu has been looking forward to it—escaping her endless, boring summer in the drugstore, Viv's foul moods, and Liz's dramas—but doesn't say so. When they reach the front of the line Helen asks the man at the table if she and Lulu can have lockers near each other. He agrees and hands them slips of paper and their class schedules.

It turns out they're in the same English class, which starts in fifteen minutes. They decipher their lockers and find the classroom, slip behind desks across from each other. Lulu turns her focus to the teacher.

The teacher hands out books and says they'll study some Canadian poetry before moving on to *Romeo and Juliet*. Lulu has never read Shakespeare and is eager to try. She read everything in the small school library and was a regular at the bookmobile that visited her neighbourhood, tickled she could borrow any of the plastic-covered books.

At lunch, she makes her way to the cafeteria in the basement. She hears it first. The room is low-ceilinged and loud, students lining long tables. Tuna fish and BO. Lulu scans the rows, looking for Janet's red hair, but doesn't see her.

Something bumps her shoulder. She turns and Danny brushes past. He pauses and rounds his hands in front of his belly—everyone knows that means pregnant. Lulu feels the colour drain from her face.

"Hey!" Helen is at her side. "I just saw you. Come sit with me."

Lulu follows, too nauseated for the sandwich and packaged cake she prepared last night. Helen has a spot at the far end of a table. She has bought a paper plate of french fries, which sits next to a tattered copy of *Lady Chatterley's Lover*. She's still wearing the hat.

Helen rambles. She says she lives near one of the universities and she's the youngest of four children; her father's a lawyer and her mother's a librarian. Helen wants to become a famous rock musician and doesn't know how long she'll stay in school.

"I play the drums," she says, dipping a fry into a squirt of ketchup.

"Drums?"

Helen laughs. "I begged for them in grade seven. My parents gave in but I'm only allowed to play in the garage. They hate them. What about you?" she asks, twisting her beads.

Lulu pauses. "I live in the North End. Just me and my parents. My brother moved away."

"Cool," Helen says. "I hate sharing a bathroom with my sisters and brother."

Lulu has never thought about the hardship of sharing a bathroom. They have one. Everyone she knows has one.

"Maybe I can come to your house someday. I've never been that far up," Helen says.

"Sure, maybe." It's a lot, Helen's a lot, and Lulu can't figure out why a cool, pretty girl like Helen has latched onto her.

Helen pulls out a lighter and cigarettes and asks Lulu if she wants a puff before class. Lulu doesn't but Helen suggests they meet up tomorrow. She grabs her book and stands.

"Ciao," she says, and Lulu watches her slip through the tables, light on her feet, her outfit saying look at me but ducking her head and moving like she'd rather you didn't.

That afternoon Lulu tries to enjoy each new class, to forget about Liz and Danny. At the end of the day she recognizes Janet at the bus stop and hurries over. Janet is beaming.

"What an amazing first day," Janet says. "Met a bunch of girls from the West End. I'm trying out for volleyball."

"You don't play volleyball."

Janet shrugs. "We played a few times in gym last year. The girls think I can make it. One of them is five ten." She laughs. "They call her Spike."

Sounds like a dog. Lulu snickers. The bus arrives and seats fill rapidly, like a game of musical chairs. They have to stand, grasping the chrome bars.

Lulu studies Janet, cinnamon freckles across her nose and cheekbones, and a chin that juts out when she wants her way. Crazy, Janet has jumped from a wannabe tough girl to a varsity sports hopeful. Maybe it's just whoever she met first today. Either way, it's a rejection of what they've had together.

I'm not so boring, Lulu wants to say. *Today I met—maybe became friends with—a South End girl. Pretty. Rich, probably. A drummer.*

And I know some serious secrets.

Yet Janet doesn't ask Lulu about her day. Lulu could just spill it and get the satisfaction of surprising her, maybe winning the "best first day" sweepstakes. But she keeps it for herself.

June

Lorne and June hunch in his parked car, squinting through rain on the windshield. He's showing her the house he just bought on a quiet street five minutes from her place. It's a basic Halifax two-storey—three rooms up, three down. In the twilight it appears to be dirty white and have a front sun porch with skinny windows. A bleach bottle sits on a sill. The house is vacant, a toy bulldozer abandoned in the gravel driveway. She wonders who lived here and why they left.

He explains he wants to redo the kitchen, give everything a coat of paint. Maybe add a little deck in the back.

"Outside needs to be painted, and I thought you could pick the colour," he says.

She knows it's a bribe, another carrot to get her to commit. He wants her to move in with him, and that means bringing Gerald and her mother. The Hydrostone house has just two bedrooms, his new one has three.

She has not raised it with Mom or Barry. She's never moved in her life. Most people on her street have lived there for decades; a few were early tenants of the Hydrostone.

Lorne's making up for lost time, she supposes. He's almost fifty. They've discussed marriage in a vague way, and that's not the issue. She's past caring if "living in sin" shocks the neighbours. She hasn't set foot in a church in decades and neither has Mom. Margie washed her hands of it when Gerald was born and the priest of the day wouldn't baptize him.

But it bothered June then, the thought of baby Gerald landing in limbo, and a few months later they had him baptized in a Protestant church. It was foreign and sterile, and afterwards at home, people only picked at the cake Margie had baked.

"What do you think?" Lorne asks. June says the house has potential. He grins and turns the key in the ignition.

"Wanna go tell your mother?"

June opens her mouth but says nothing. The car crawls through darkening, glistening streets; trees heavy with wet leaves reveal themselves in the headlights and recede. What should it matter, moving Gerald and Mom five minutes away? Life's turning upside down as it is—she'll soon be unemployed. Lorne's offering her a new stable life. And they're in love.

"Become a kept woman," Trudy teased her the other night. "Be a lady of leisure, for once."

They pull up to June's place and sprint through the rain, now a true September downpour. They land in the front hall and flick water off their hands, push back their sopping hair. Their clothes are splotchy with wet. Mom and Gerald sit on the chesterfield, arms touching, watching TV.

June leaves to put the kettle on. She's always hated this tiny kitchen. Maybe they need a change. A horrible year with Gerald's disappearance and Mom's mental lapses, dementia, the doctor said. And soon June will lose her job of fifteen years. The new dog across the lane barks constantly—it's driving her crazy.

Yes, a fresh start a few blocks away. She could plant things, maybe one of those shrubs with fat, white flowers. Mom calls it a snowball bush.

A shriek travels from the front room. June runs and Lorne and her mother are in some sort of standoff. Lorne looks shocked, Margie has her hands at her hips.

"You are not kicking me out of my home," Margie says. "I've been here forty years. The only way I'm leaving is feet first."

Lorne raises his arms in a look of exasperation.

"What's going on?" says June. Gerald hugs the cat close to his chest.

"Your boyfriend just said he's moving us out," says Margie.

"Now wait a minute," says Lorne. "I'm not forcing anybody. But my place has three bedrooms. This one has two. We can all go."

Margie and Gerald look at June. Lorne looks at June.

"What do you want me to do?" she says, her voice shrill. "Why is it up to me?"

"Because it is up to you, June," says Lorne.

"No, it is not," says Margie. She plunks on her chair and starts rocking.

"Mom?" Gerald says in a small voice. "I don't want to move." June's insides drop.

"Jesus Christ," says Lorne. He throws up his hands again. "I thought we were set, June." He goes into the front hallway and she follows.

"This is all happening so fast," she says.

"We're not getting any younger," he says. "Call me when you've made up your mind." And he runs to his car in the rain.

Lulu

Lulu wakes to a racket Saturday morning, rises, and trips over a long-handled paint roller lying in the hallway. Viv, hair covered by a kerchief, has pushed the living room furniture away from the walls and draped it in bedsheets. She uses her bare foot to move a drop sheet into place on the floor.

"What do you think, Lu?" she says. "It's going to be Georgia Mist."

Lulu eyes the cream walls and tries to imagine Georgia Mist. Grey-blue, maybe. She enters the kitchen and pours some cereal. She's due at the store at nine.

She tips her cereal bowl and slurps the sweet milk. She'll work with Liz today; she hasn't seen her in a few weeks, since she saw Mrs. McMullin with that man. Lulu's head swirls. The pregnancy, Danny, the kiss in the car. Some man's hand on Mrs. McMullin's boob.

She needs to act normal. As if she doesn't know some deep secret about Liz's mom. And she won't tell her about Danny joking around, Liz would freak again. Lulu's always idolized her but doesn't envy her now, not one bit.

A few times Lulu almost told Viv about Mrs. McMullin, but kids don't badmouth other people's parents. And sometimes she doubts her memory, as if she dreamed on that hot, sickening day that she saw Liz's mother having…an affair? A shimmering illusion in the heat that, poof, disappeared.

And the pregnancy. A scandal that an uninvited third person knows about.

Liz arrives late for her eleven o'clock shift and doesn't look Lulu's way as she heads to the pharmacy. Lulu completes a sale at the till and wanders back. Liz sits, flipping through a magazine. Farrell stands pounding two fingers on the old black Olivetti, typing a prescription label.

"Liz, can you call Mrs. Baker? Her ointment's ready." He yanks out the label.

Liz gets on the phone as the front door chimes. Lulu heads back and serves the customer. It goes like this all day, and Lulu and Liz don't get a chance to talk. Disappointed, Lulu retrieves her purse and sweater as her shift ends at four. Liz beckons her to the front counter.

"I haven't even asked you about school," Liz says.

"It's going okay."

"Great. Listen, I'm going to be away for a few days, in early October," Liz says in a low voice. "I'm going to Montreal, to take care of my problem. A girlfriend and I are driving up." Lulu nods.

Liz says, "You haven't told anybody, right? Not a soul?"

Lulu shakes her head no.

"Good. Tom doesn't even know," Liz says. She smiles but her glistening eyes give her away.

There is one guy who knows.

Liz clears her throat. "I need to go away to do this," she says and wipes her nose with the back of her hand. "Halifax is too small." She grabs a tissue and blows. "Don't mind me— hormones." She exhales. "I probably shouldn't have told you in the first place."

Lulu swallows, fiddles with the zipper on her purse. Seeing her like this doesn't feel so good. And now Liz regrets confiding in her. Lulu shifts her weight from foot to foot.

"Get home," Liz says and Lulu takes a couple of steps toward the door, released. "Lulu?"

She turns.

"Now that you're in high school, don't rush into things. You know?"

Lulu gets it. She holds the door ajar.

"Sexual revolution and all that crap," Liz says, looking down at the smoke she's trying to light. "Women still get screwed, in the end."

Lulu leaves and gulps in some air. She didn't realize she'd been holding her breath. Liz will have the bean flushed down a toilet and solve her problem. But as Lulu walks home she doesn't feel relief. Liz didn't seem relieved either. Sad, actually. And her shameful secret, that's still out there.

June

June knows of a family that split apart over a teacup. It was a delicate china teacup and saucer, turquoise and rimmed in gold, a pink rose painted in the well of the cup that became visible as you drank your tea. It was the nicest thing the family owned, its origin unknown.

And when the widow who owned it, a mother of four, died suddenly, one of her daughters claimed it. She said Ma had always wanted her to have it. The others disagreed. The oldest daughter said the set should rightly go to her. The youngest said Ma had let her drink milk out of it while the others were at school, and had promised it to her.

The only son didn't care about the teacup and thought his sisters were acting childish. Still, when asked his opinion, he would not choose one sister over the other. This infuriated the women, who accused their brother of never growing up. One sister grabbed the cup and another had to settle for the saucer. The siblings barely spoke again.

One of June's customers told her this story years ago and they tutted over it in unison, reflected in the shop mirror. How could a family, flesh and blood, sever like that? *Tragic.* The story has come back to June recently. She's worried about a rift in her family.

It's Barry and Mom versus June, Lorne, and Gerald. If she were honest she'd move Gerald to the other side of the ledger, but Gerald doesn't have a choice; he's coming with her to Lorne's house. Mom put her foot down—she's not going.

So Barry, the peacemaker, announced he'll give up his apartment and buy June out of the Hydrostone house. Now that he's got a steady paycheque, he thinks the credit union will give him a loan.

Lorne's excited about the money, they can use it for renovations. But June's unsettled. Not only is her mother furious with her, she'll be alone all day while Barry's at the dockyard. And Gerald seems down. As June packs up their clothes, she tries to bring him around.

"We can paint your room any colour you want," she says. He doesn't answer.

"It's near the other fish and chips place we like," she says. He turns to the wall. She sits on his bed.

"You can visit Nana every day," she offers. A concession to the other side. Gerald opens a comic book and shields his face.

Margie has been crying for weeks. June feels guilty but she's also annoyed. Doesn't she deserve some happiness? Hasn't she sacrificed all her adult life? No surprise, Trudy approves of her decision and predicts Margie will calm down soon enough.

June starts sorting things in the house, and she and Margie play a frustrating game. June will ask if she can toss the rusted flour sifter or the unused cribbage board in the shape of a lobster, the pullover with a moth hole in it, Gerald's old tricycle missing a wheel. Margie always says no. She will throw away nothing. She's losing her grip on the everyday but knows the story behind every household item, and the stories send her down a melancholy road she clings to. June gives up. Let Barry worry about it.

She plans to move after Thanksgiving. She was going to go sooner but can't resist spending one last holiday in the house. She's laid off work now, "on the pogey," Barry teases her.

He tells her, "Go live your life. Me and Mom will be fine here."

One afternoon, June comes downstairs and finds Mom and Evelyn at the kitchen table. The two women, unlikely friends, have somehow found common ground, and Evelyn has become a regular visitor.

"Hello, dear," Evelyn says. "Your mother was just telling me about your new house."

June can only imagine her mother's version. She hunts for her lighter, realizes she looks a fright, greasy hair pinned back and wearing her sloppiest clothes. Evelyn turns in the chair so she faces her.

"I was also wondering if I could visit Gerald at your new place. I wasn't sure, maybe he won't walk by my house so often."

June hasn't thought of this. Gerald will lose his old route, or at least it will be farther away. She's not sure she wants him walking those extra blocks. And he'll fight the change.

"You know, I'm always happy to help with Gerald." Evelyn glances at Margie. "Help in any way I can."

She's no dummy. She's irritating, a bit high-and-mighty, but not so bad, really.

"Oh Evelyn, aren't you a sweetheart," says Margie. "We'll need extra hands when June moves out. Are you any good at moving furniture?"

Evelyn roars.

Lulu

Sometimes, when she's most lonely, Lulu wishes her parents would get back together. Viv's a poor roommate; she's out a lot now—work, Brenda's, the pub—and when she's home, she keeps to herself. She's not as grumpy but she's in her own head, doing a crossword or reading a paperback, a smoke in one hand. She has barely asked Lulu about school. It turns out Georgia Mist is a shade of peach and it's sickly.

But when Lulu fantasizes about Dad returning to the apartment, the scenes always dissolve into arguments. That's worse than the quiet.

She's lost Janet too. They catch the bus together each morning but don't gab like they used to, their conversations stopping and starting like the bus. At school Janet disappears for the day. She makes the volleyball team as a second-stringer and gets consumed by the new girls, the practices and games. Evenings, weekends, she's never free. Lulu stops asking. She feels numb—a ten-year friendship, dead.

At school she's at sea, jostled in the crowded corridors, recognizing few people. She struggles some days to open her locker so carries her belongings from class to class, dropping pencils and apples that roll down the hallway, sweating in her jacket.

Some grade tens find their people right away. A hulking, quiet guy she grew up with gets identified for the football team and is thrust into a new orbit of popularity, glimpsed in huddles of very large boys, flirting with popular girls in the cafeteria.

Lulu tries not to dwell on the misery of the outcasts from her old school: the obese girl with an odd walk, who

for years favoured two raw wieners for her daily recess snack;
the bucktoothed girl shackled into head gear for her braces;
the pimply science whiz in the periodic-table T-shirt, though
Lulu's happy to see he finds his crowd by Thanksgiving.

The surprise is that Lulu has Helen, or is it that Helen has
her? They eat lunch together most days and Helen lends her
books. Lulu can offer nothing in return. Viv plows through
romance novels, trading with Brenda, but Lulu has never paid
attention to them.

Lulu's surprised Helen appears to be on her own. Maybe
the hat and hippie vibe cast her as a loner in junior high. Or
maybe she's changed in high school like Janet has.

Danny's usually at the unofficial smokers' entrance at a
far end of the school. But one day at lunch he struts by the
cafeteria table she and Helen have claimed, Lulu picking at
a sandwich and Helen, in a Jim Morrison T-shirt, sipping a
Coke.

He approaches in a worn leather jacket, collar flipped up,
nods at Lulu, and keeps walking. Helen watches him go.

"James Dean," she says. "How do you know him?"

Lulu's mother talks about old movie idols, so she gets the
reference. James Dean: dangerous, cool, and tragic.

"Danny, from my neighbourhood. He's in grade twelve."

"Kind of cute. I saw you with him, that first day."

Lulu looks at her. Is this the big attraction? She changes
the subject; today she's finally going to Helen's house after
school, after weeks of making excuses.

At three o'clock the girls meet and head down Quinpool
Road, a wide commercial street lined by restaurants and small
shops Lulu has never been in. After a few minutes Helen
turns onto a residential street and leads them on a zigzag
route south.

The houses are different here, older, it seems. Even the
plainest ones—two-storey with a covered porch and two staring windows above, like the eyes on the cover of *The Great*

Gatsby—would be envied in Lulu's end of town. Other houses have scroll details, windows with criss-cross trim, fat front pillars, or a quirky, second-storey window in the shape of a diamond or circle. Mature trees in spectacular fall reds and golds curtsy at the curbs.

As they continue south, the houses grow grander. Nearing Dalhousie, tall houses seem to have been divided into student flats; young people hang outside, talking and smoking and tossing footballs. Other houses are broad, their sides spill outwards, perhaps expanded again and again or built that way years ago by some well-off family. Helen stops at one of these.

"Here we are," she says.

Lulu imagined Helen in a nice house, but this is the finest on the street. It's white and sprawling with a red door and six flared pillars sitting on stone bases, spanning the covered veranda. Above, two matching bow windows bump out, perhaps upstairs bedrooms, and the house stretches higher into an apparent third floor. The girls climb the slate steps to the front door, Lulu counts twelve, and Helen uses her key.

Lulu catches her breath. The foyer is tiled in black and white, perhaps marble, and is centred by a round shiny table displaying a spiky bouquet of real flowers. She gets an immediate sense of the house, which radiates out in three directions. To the left, through open French doors, a living room dominated by a carved stone fireplace and gold mirror; there are high ceilings and mouldings, clusters of uncomfortable-looking furniture in pink and green prints. Beyond is a corner room full of windows, a sunroom perhaps.

The dining room is on the opposite side of the hall: red walls, a sparkly chandelier, and a long table lined with about a dozen chairs. A wide staircase curves upstairs from the entrance, but her eye is drawn to the soft light spilling down the hallway that leads to the back of the house. Helen walks toward this light, dumping her bookbag along the way.

The kitchen feels old and less decorated. It's white with stained, veined marble on the counters and tall glass cabinets crammed with blue-and-white dishes. The cabinets reflect the trees beyond the paned windows on the opposite side of the room. Dappled light falls on a pale wood table and chairs. Lulu would like to linger at that table in that dappled light.

But Helen grabs a bag of cookies and leads Lulu to the third floor. Her bedroom is an attic with edges that disappear in the dimness of the eaves, a double bed dressed in a colourful quilt, a worn armchair, a record player, a tennis racket hanging on the wall. A guitar leans to one side. There are posters, probably musicians but Lulu can't identify them.

She goes to the windows at one end. She's in the golden treetops, looking down at the street. She feels slightly dizzy.

Helen starts the record player and flops onto her bed. "So, tell me about this Danny," she says and bites into a cookie.

Lulu chooses the chair. Her head is full of chandeliers and treetops and she doesn't want to talk about Danny. Helen looks at her; she has a way of making her eyes plead, like a puppy, which she must use often to get her way. Lulu sketches him out, building steam as she goes: his house near the train tracks, the woman Lulu assumes is his mother, his habit of loitering at the intersection with his buddies, his dominance of the little gang of three. She's not sure why but she skips the nastiest details of Danny's past, doesn't say she suspected him in Gerald's disappearance last spring. Or reveal the threat he poses to Liz.

Footsteps and a rap at the door.

"Helen?" A slim woman with short, blond hair enters. She's in burgundy slacks and a matching turtleneck sweater. Pearl stud earrings. Helen looks like her.

"Oh hello," the woman says with a smile. Helen introduces Lulu to her mother, who asks Lulu to call her Cynthia. She's going for a jog and will be back in an hour. Helen's father will be late tonight.

"Will you stay for dinner, Lulu?" Cynthia says. "It'll be just the three of us. Spaghetti."

Lulu's afraid to. There may be too many forks. In a movie she saw people twirling spaghetti on large spoons; is that appropriate? They may ask lots of questions or expect her to speak about current events. At home it's supper, here it's dinner. She has a hole in the elbow of her sweater.

"Um, no thank you. Thanks but I need to get home," she says.

"Oh stay," says Helen. "Please?"

Lulu pauses—doesn't she want to try new things—and says she'll need to let her mother know. Cynthia seems pleased.

"Okay, Mom, bye," says Helen. Her mother shuts the door.

"Sorry," Helen says. "She tries to make friends with all my friends."

Lulu tells her no sweat, her mom seems nice. Helen cradles her guitar and starts strumming, and then she adds words, singing in a low voice. Lulu's no expert but Helen can't sing. She giggles to herself. Still, Helen can play instruments.

Growing up, some kids learned the ukulele through music class, but Lulu knew only one who could play another instrument, a girl whose parents made her take violin lessons. The girl complained bitterly about it. She'd bring the hard, black violin case to school some days and it was so foreign, she may as well have dragged in a pig.

"You play tennis?" says Lulu.

"I used to. We all took lessons, at the Waeg."

"What's that?"

Helen looks puzzled. "The Waegwoltic Club, on the Arm. It's our tennis club, swimming pools, sailing. Everyone goes." She sets the guitar aside. "But I don't care about that stuff anymore."

"Why?"

"Don't know. Just, tennis is not my scene."

Lulu didn't know kids spent summers at a place like the Waeg. She spent her days at hot playgrounds or squeezed into makeshift blanket tents playing crazy eights and eating Gran's bologna sandwiches. When they got older, she and Janet would bus to the Dingle park, also on the Northwest Arm part of the harbour. Once, swimming in the cold water, Lulu saw a turd float by. The city's sewage pumped into the harbour.

They listen to records and discuss the upcoming English quiz. They make a pact to boycott all school football and hockey games. Students are expected to cheer on their teams, but "it's so barbaric," says Helen. Lulu doesn't care about sports so a boycott is fine with her. Then the smell of cooking wafts up and they're called downstairs.

In the kitchen, Cynthia's enveloped in steam, dumping a pot of spaghetti noodles into a strainer in the sink. She has wet hair and appears to have showered, has changed into jeans with the same turtleneck. Bare feet.

"Just sit there, girls," she says. The table's set for three, with cloth placemats, heavy cutlery, and cloth napkins. Chunky blue water glasses, a pitcher of water, and a leafy salad in a wooden bowl. Helen sits and Lulu takes the chair across from her. She places her hands in her lap. Why didn't Viv teach her proper table manners? Helen pours them both water, plucks a piece of lettuce from the bowl.

Cynthia brings Lulu a shallow bowl of spaghetti. It smells wonderful and looks so much better than the tinned sauce Viv uses. She realizes there are no large spoons for twirling. Helen receives her bowl and Lulu watches. Helen captures noodles with her fork and swirls them on the rim of the bowl, then brings the coil to her mouth with a few strands hanging. She slurps them in, wipes her mouth with her napkin. Lulu copies.

Cynthia sits and pours herself a fat glass of red wine. Helen asks if she and Lulu can have some.

"Helen, you know the answer to that," Cynthia says.

"But you said when you were in Italy, kids drank wine."

"I said young adults may drink weak wine. And we're not in Italy."

Lulu looks down at her plate in embarrassment. She wouldn't want Helen's mother to think her a bad influence. Shoot, she forgot to call Viv. She asks if she may use the phone and Cynthia directs her to the adjoining den, then takes a long swallow of wine. It matches the colour of her sweater.

It's a compact, wood-panelled room with worn, velvety furniture, bookcases, a TV, and a horse lamp lit in the corner. Lulu dials the heavy old black phone and Viv answers right away. She's upset that Lulu didn't call sooner, she came home to an empty apartment. Called Gran, even called Janet's house.

"Sorry, I'm sorry, Mom."

"And how are you getting home? You know your father has the car."

"I'll take the bus."

"Well, be careful."

Lulu returns to the table, hoping they didn't hear. Cynthia smiles, asks what part of the city she's from.

"The North End," says Lulu.

"Oh, anywhere near the Hydrostone? Such incredible history," says Cynthia.

"Yeah, close to it. I know people who live there."

Cynthia smiles again. "Aren't you lucky."

The spaghetti's cold and Lulu has fallen behind in the eating. She pretends she's had enough, and Cynthia clears the bowls. The salad comes last, something she's never heard of. It's delicious. Cynthia refills her wine glass and wants to tell them about a funny thing that happened at work. Helen groans.

"Never mind," Cynthia says, setting her mouth. She stands and snatches dishes, tosses them into the sink.

Lulu rises to help but bumps into her. She freezes, unsure. Something clatters out in the hall, and a tall blond man in a dark suit appears in the doorway. She feels like she's been caught doing something she shouldn't. He kisses Cynthia and touches Helen's shoulder.

"No one told me there was a party," he says, smiling at Lulu. She blushes.

"Graham, this is Lulu, Helen's new friend," Cynthia says.

"Lulu? That's fun," he says. He loosens his tie and sinks onto a chair. Cynthia hands him a glass of wine.

"I should get going," says Lulu. It's all so perfect, so taken for granted.

"You have a way home?" says Helen's dad.

Lulu lies, says her mother's picking her up at the corner. No one argues. She hurries to grab her things. The front door is heavy, the brass doorknob full and cold in her hand. The tall trees on the sloped lawn loom over the walkway. It's pitch black.

Lulu inches down the steps, treacherous now. She stops at the sidewalk and waves, not sure if Helen can see her.

"See you tomorrow," calls Helen. "And it's your place next time."

Lulu isn't sure where she is. She tries to retrace the route they took, walks briskly, aiming for a main road and a bus stop. A frenzy of dry leaves rushes across the street. She buttons her jacket. A man, a darker shadow in the shadows, hurries toward her and passes. Lulu exhales.

She finds a bus stop and is grateful when a young woman with a backpack joins her. They wait in silence until a bus arrives about twenty minutes later. Lulu finds a seat to herself, at home in the glaring light and shabbiness of public transit.

Helen seems sure about who she is—or who she wants to be. She's rejected things Lulu didn't know existed. She'd die for Helen's bedroom. And that house—wait until she tells Viv. It's the kind of house you'd see on the cover of a magazine, a family you'd see in a magazine. Everything Lulu could wish for.

Yet Helen seems to have a crush on Danny, and anybody can see he's not boyfriend material. And she was rude to her mother, pushy in a way Lulu would never dare with Viv. Lulu felt uncomfortable. Cynthia got tipsy and pissed off.

"Lulu? That's fun."

June

They get through Thanksgiving. Margie insists on cooking the turkey but June steps in when her mother begins stuffing it with a tin—an unopened tin—of gravy. She sets Mom up at the table peeling vegetables. June will need to redo them later, that's evident, but she holds her temper all day. She and Gerald will move out within the week and she doesn't want any big rows before then.

Lorne and Barry arrive in the afternoon and the five of them squeeze around the kitchen table, set up nice with an old embroidered tablecloth, just one stain on it. The cloth was hand done by Margie's aunt and gets her reminiscing about her childhood on the Shore. Everyone is polite and Mom's pumpkin pie is excellent. But the gathering feels stiff.

June moves carefully through the rest of the week, doesn't hassle Gerald about packing or scold her mother for forgetting. On moving day Lorne arrives early with a buddy and a pickup. They take Gerald's bed and dresser, some bags of clothes, and a few of June's favourite belongings.

For days, she has walked about with a heavy weight. While the men load the truck she goes up to Gerald's bedroom. As a girl she'd lie under these eaves wondering about life. Who would be her Prince Charming? Then came Connelly. She shivers, grabs Gerald's pillow.

Margie is defiant. "Just go then," she says.

June reminds her they'll be mere blocks away and can walk over anytime. Mom says nothing. Gerald appears in the front hall holding Kitty.

"Come here, gimme a hug," Mom asks Gerald, and tries to wrap her arms around the whole package of grandson and cat. Both shrink from her. June says she'll bring her over later for a look.

"Doesn't matter," Mom says, but June knows she's curious. Barry arrives as they're pulling away.

"Nice timing," Lorne yells out the truck window, and Barry laughs.

During the tour of the new house late that afternoon, Margie sniffs a few times and says little. Lorne lists the improvements he has planned. Gerald sits on his bed in his new room, looking glum. The cat hides underneath.

Over the following weeks June plays housewife. She's not much of a cook but tries new recipes from magazines, and sets the kitchen table for the three of them each night.

Lorne will hug her unexpectedly from behind and plant a kiss on the top of her head. At night he can't get enough of her, and June finds she doesn't mind sharing a bed with a man, a luxury compared to the old days when they necked in his car or stole a quick hour at his apartment.

She plants two dozen tulip bulbs under the front windows, red and yellow and white. Stands back and imagines the flowers smiling at her next spring, looks at the bulb package and worries she planted them upside down. She and Lorne paint the front room and their bedroom over two weekends.

One day he surprises her with a new frost-free refrigerator; on another he brings her carnations, just because. She suggests they have his whole family over one Sunday for corned beef and cabbage. She stands flushed in the kitchen, dishing out chunks of the steamy vegetables and red meat, and he catches her eye. They smile at each other.

But she worries about Gerald, who spends entire days in his room. One day she makes him come with her so he can learn the new route to the drugstore. As they walk she realizes how far it is; no, she's uneasy with him doing it on his own.

He doesn't want to anyway. She suggests the nearby corner store for treats but he says, "Nah."

Another day they walk to Evelyn's house and Evelyn throws up her hands when she sees them. Gerald smiles and they go in for tea and banana bread. The house has the feel of June's Nanny Green's house, a quiet, best-behaviour house that smelled like furniture polish.

June explains that Gerald finds the walk here long and Evelyn nods. These visits will not be regular. Evelyn will visit when she can but Albert has just been diagnosed with cancer and she doesn't like to leave him.

"I'm sorry," says June.

Lorne announces just he and Gerald are going out the next Friday night. Smiling, he pulls out two tickets he bought to a Nova Scotia Voyageurs hockey game. But all week, when June brings it up, Gerald wrinkles his nose and leaves the room.

On game night she practically has to push him into Lorne's car. As they drive away, Gerald slumps, staring out the window. They return less than an hour later: Gerald refused to get out of the car and Lorne didn't want to make a scene. Lorne's wild—tickets wasted.

So, at June's suggestion, Lorne sets up a small black-and-white TV on Gerald's dresser. The TV cackles all day, game shows and talk shows transitioning into sitcoms with laugh tracks when evening falls. When June peeks in on him, Gerald doesn't seem to be paying much attention to any of it.

A few times a week she forces him to come on her daily visits to her mother. Each morning Barry leaves Margie a sandwich wrapped in wax paper, but she often doesn't touch it. If the TV's not on, she's blasting the radio, usually some local phone-in show full of strong opinions. Her hearing's going too.

She begins wearing her nightgown all day and develops the odour of someone who needs a wash. June doesn't point it out, just runs her a bath one afternoon. Mom complains but she's chipper and pink-cheeked in her curlers afterward, humming around the kitchen. They sit at the table and June clips her mother's nails.

"I used to do this for you, Junie," Mom says.

That night June calls Barry, furious he's letting Mom get to this state. He promises to pay more attention, and June agrees to handle the bathing.

One cold afternoon, as June walks alone to Mom's, two firetrucks zoom past with sirens wailing. Every hair on her body prickles, and she walks faster. This doesn't feel right. The emergency is on her old street—smoke shoots above the tall trees of the boulevard and onlookers gather at the corner. She runs.

It's their place. Firemen in heavy gear haul hoses from the trucks filling the narrow street, and in through their front door. Smoke rises from the back of the house. June sprints across the boulevard.

Hidden behind a truck, Mom stands on the sidewalk speaking with a fireman, a blanket over her shoulders. *Thank God.* June rushes to hug her.

Mom is befuddled. She was just frying eggs in a bit of bacon fat, so good that way, and she took the garbage out back and then she spied a beer bottle in the yard, those damn kids, and then she came inside and the phone rang, the doctor's office, and she had to sit because her bones were aching and she flicked on the TV to see if her stories were on and then she started coughing and someone, that nice Mr. Fay across the street, was banging on her door because he'd spied smoke.

The lead fireman tells June they're lucky, that a fat fire can burn down a house—can still cause major damage in the supposedly fireproof Hydrostones. The firemen get it under control and then reverse everything: roll up the hose, pack up gear, cap the fire hydrant. By now Mom's next-door neighbour has her inside for a cup of tea, but June stays outside watching in disbelief.

Barry arrives upset, and eventually a fireman takes them inside. The smoky smell is overwhelming and they cough and cough. In the kitchen, the wall behind the stove is charred. The stove is ruined, its plastic knobs melted. The ceiling darkened by soot, the room soaked. Water runs down the walls and pools in the middle of the linoleum floor. A window pane is cracked. June wants to cry.

Putting things right seems impossible. Barry opens the windows and June calls Trudy to ask her to go sit with Gerald. She doesn't know how to reach Lorne, an independent contractor who moves from one job site to another, often unclear about where he's working each week.

She digs out the mop and some old towels and they sop up as much water as they can. June wipes the walls with a towel. Beside the fridge she finds a couple of empty liquor bottles but doesn't say anything. Barry drags the stove away from the wall, the metal's still warm and he'll need help heaving it into the yard. They need a ladder to scrub the ceiling but don't have one, so they leave it for tomorrow.

Around six o'clock June sits and lights a cigarette, gazes into the flame on her butane lighter before she clicks it closed. Her mother could have been killed, burned up the inside of the house, maybe hurt the neighbours. Barry collapses into a chair and says he'll find a new stove but unplug it when he's at work. It still doesn't sound safe.

It's clear now, leaving Mom to fend for herself all day is like leaving a small child home alone. Cooking eggs. Mom's doctor told June the minds of dementia patients are like scrambled eggs. How about fried eggs. On fire.

Mom comes through the front door with the neighbour. Barry and June stand and watch her walk toward the kitchen. She stops.

"Oh my lord," she says, "what happened here?" She turns to them, mouth open. "Barry, did you make this mess?"

"You did this, Mom," he yells. "You could've burned down the damn house. You could've killed yourself." His voice cracks.

Mom says don't pin this on me. She's angry but crying. Maybe she remembers parts of it and is traumatized. Maybe she remembers nothing and is terrified. Embarrassed. She touches the scorched stovetop.

No one speaks. Water drips from the ceiling. Moving the stove has revealed a mouse skeleton. Mom always took pride in her kitchen, sewed the rooster valance over the window a long time ago. The phone rings and they all jump. It's Lorne, who just got home to find Trudy with Gerald. He's infuriated June didn't call him.

"Where am I on your list, June?" he says.

"Is this what you've got for me right now, that you're hurt I didn't call you?" she says. She tells him she'll be home when she'll be home. She slams the receiver into its cradle.

Barry clears his throat and offers to get them supper. June's happy to stay for a while. She and Mom settle in the front room and Barry returns with cheeseburgers; they eat with greasy fingers, even laugh at the TV.

Around nine o'clock June sighs and says she'd better get going. Barry has the neighbour sit with Mom while he drives June home. He says he'll take some days off work, he'll get it cleaned up and not let Mom use the stove anymore.

"Don't worry. All good," he says in the car.

"How can you say that?" she shoots back. "How is anything solved?"

He won't look at her.

"Barry, face it. Mom's not safe at home."

He pounds his hand on the steering wheel. "What am I supposed to do?" he says. "I have to work."

She slams the car door and stomps to the house, ready for a fight if Lorne wants one. But he's already in bed. She kicks off her shoes and circles through the kitchen, the dining nook, and around to the front room. She's too warm. Not ready for sleep, despite the nightmare day.

Scrubbing up Mom's kitchen and pretending everything's the way it was. June shakes her head. Fact is, this feels like the beginning of something. A new phase for Mom, who's almost like a stranger, someone June doesn't recognize.

Her stomach feels hollow. Like that time on a Ferris wheel or sledding as a kid—in free fall, out of control. That February afternoon when the wood and metal sled she was on, squished with the McDonald twins, kept picking up speed, faster, faster, collecting clumps of sod and stones in its path, they couldn't stop, and that small boy crawling across the snow in front of them. They couldn't stop. A hit, then screams. She shudders. Apparently the boy was okay in the end, but she dreamt about it for years.

Flipping through the newspaper the next morning, she sees their disaster reduced, in the list of city fire calls, to: "Fat fire 1:35 P.M."

Lulu

One sunny Saturday in October, one of those perfect, dazzling days, Liz returns to work after her trip to Montreal. She's the same Liz, beautiful, joking with customers, knowing what Farrell needs before he does. She doesn't look unpregnant, any more than she looked pregnant before.

She tells Lulu the drive was tiring but the visit was successful, and hands her a poppyseed bagel—she brought home three dozen. It's the first time Lulu has ever seen one and she saves it for later.

The story, the one Liz told her parents, is that her friend wanted to explore McGill University because she's considering doing her master's there. This is the line Lulu should use if anyone asks where Liz has been. Farrell was fed the line. Tom, the ex-boyfriend, who still calls Liz from time to time, was told this story. Would he be upset if he knew the truth, or thankful?

The trip was expensive—even the abortion cost money. Liz doesn't say how much but hints it was over a hundred dollars, maybe two. She needs to rebuild her savings so she can move to New York and get a job in publishing. New York sounds like a fantasy. Lulu's picked up things from movies and TV: packed avenues of car horns and yellow taxis, robberies called muggings, smart-aleck people living in stylish apartments, cops with an attitude. You need guts to live there.

Over lunch, Liz asks Lulu what's new.

"My friend Janet has pretty much dumped me," she begins, surprising herself. "She found a new group of girls, volleyball players." She swallows at the lump in her throat.

Liz rolls her eyes. "Yeah, some people try to reinvent themselves in high school."

Lulu pulls a crust off her sandwich.

"Hey, if she did that she wasn't a true friend," Liz says. "It happened to me. Losing a friend, it's worse than losing a boyfriend."

Lulu can't compare. She tells her about Helen, about the outfits and the house. Lulu has visited a few times, had to listen to Helen banging on her drums. Then she pauses.

"She has a crush on Danny." They look at each other.

"Tell her he's bad news," Liz says. "Rich girl likes bad boy."

Danny. When he was in junior high there was a rumour he and a friend had tortured and killed a cat. A priest found the cat on the church steps with gouges out of it and patches of fur shaved. Word was, Danny bragged about it, but he was never charged. That may have been the year he was held back in school. A fighter and a known shoplifter—arrested at least once, Lulu's pretty sure—waving the stolen aftershave under her and Liz's noses.

He calls fat girls "fat" to their face and makes life miserable for anyone with acne, glasses, or a high average in school. Taunts the Black girl in Lulu's grade. Bullies Gerald, and by the way she hasn't seen Gerald in ages. Still in school, somehow. And now, a threat to Liz, able to ruin her reputation if he feels like it.

Lulu doesn't know how to explain it to Helen. Tortured cats, violence, possible kidnappings: it makes the neighbourhood sound pretty rough. Helen's already stuck on Danny anyway. One morning, Lulu walks past the school smoking door and Helen's there with him. Helen smiles and waves.

That day at lunch she presses to go to Lulu's place after school, but Lulu's reluctant. What will Helen think of the apartment? But she supposes it's her turn. She gives in, planning to keep Helen outside the whole time. It eats at her all afternoon.

On the bus ride north Helen talks nonstop. Lulu can't follow the threads. As she applies lip gloss, Helen tells her Danny plays bass in a band and they need a new drummer. Lulu almost laughs. A band seems as far-fetched as living in New York. That crowd couldn't afford instruments. Helen leans her head against the window and sings quietly, her delicate, fair features shaded by the brim of her hat.

Lulu's desperate to use the bathroom, so she has to take Helen home. They'll drop their stuff and head out, wander the streets. She worries the place will be a mess but it's not too bad. A stack of clean, folded laundry on the chesterfield, dishes drying in the dish rack. She tells Helen to wait in the kitchen, but when Lulu returns, Helen's sitting on her bed, flipping through the bird book.

"I like your room," Helen says.

Lulu holds out her hand and Helen hands her the book. She doesn't look right here. Today she's in a fringed, suede jacket from a vintage shop. She rests on Lulu's pillow, on the mauve chenille bedspread Lulu once loved, rubbed bare in spots.

"So you think we can find Danny and his friends?" Helen waits, startling blue eyes and perfect teeth.

"You really want to?" Lulu says.

Helen laughs. "Of course. Danny's my boyfriend, kind of." Pigheaded, like she was with her mother. "C'mon," she says, taking Lulu's hand. "Let's go find the guys."

Lulu leads her to the corner. Across the street, Danny, Banger, and Mikey lean against the outside of Buppy's, and as the girls wait at a red light, Helen waves. They must have planned this.

Lulu has watched this scene many times from the store and now she's in it, part of the circle of bad kids. Over in the store, Miriam's serving a white-haired lady, the widow who makes a daily outing of buying her favourite sweets. For a second Lulu wishes she were over there, in the familiar. She'd even work 'til closing.

Helen pulls out a fresh pack of smokes and they all light up, except Lulu. The two times she tried smoking, she coughed uncontrollably. Danny squints at her through the haze.

"So when can I hear your band?" Helen asks him, edging closer and touching her arm to his.

"Another day," he says and presses his hand on top of her hat, squashing it a bit. She giggles.

"Band?" says Mikey.

Danny kicks Mikey's sneakered foot and Mikey shuts up. Banger punches Mikey's arm, and Mikey swats him away. Danny lifts his chin to blow smoke above their heads. He always seems so confident. It's a brazen lie; how will he ever produce a rock band to impress Helen?

Mikey watches Helen. He asks where she lives and which junior high she went to, and she gives half answers. Helen asks Danny where he lives and he says, "Around here."

In the silences they smoke, twist a foot to rub out a butt on the pavement. Banger suggests they split some fries but no one answers. He asks Danny if he can come to his house for supper, and Danny ignores him.

It's past four and long shadows attach themselves to bodies and buildings, seeming to contain the cold. Helen shivers and Danny slips an arm around her shoulders. Both blond, both beautiful, but the strangest couple. Danny's mother in an old housecoat, screaming up the hill at him. Helen's mother, in pearl earrings, going for a jog before cooking dinner in her marble kitchen.

A city bus rolls by and Lulu looks up. Janet gapes out the window at them. Yesterday, Lulu might have relished this sighting, Janet seeing her move on with her life.

"I'm quitting school by Christmas," Mikey says. "My cousin says he can get me into the liquor warehouse."

"But you'll graduate this year, Dan?" Helen says.

Mikey snorts.

"Yeah, I want to quit too," she says.

Mere talk. Cynthia and Graham would never allow it.

"Don't girls like you go to college?" says Mikey.

She shakes her head. "I want to become a drummer, tour the world."

He hoots and she looks hurt. "Yeah, right. And I'm Mick Jagger," he says.

Danny narrows his eyes at him, seems to consider, then turns his attention to Lulu. "Did Lulu tell you," he says, bending his head toward Helen but watching Lulu, "how she follows me around?"

Mikey coughs on his cigarette.

"It was just a game, me and Janet," Lulu says, blushing. Helen looks at her.

"Hey, Tubs." Mikey waddles in a circle, arms curled out to indicate a big belly. "I'm Liz." Danny laughs.

"Who's Liz?" says Helen.

Banger laughs too. They all know, of course. And who else? Liz is in danger.

"I gotta go," Lulu says, backing away. She turns and begins walking fast.

"Hey," Helen yells, "what about my stuff?"

"Come get it," Lulu calls, not stopping.

Helen runs up to her and falls in step. "What gives?" she says, but Lulu doesn't answer. She wants this visit over.

She retrieves Helen's schoolbag from the flat and thinks she'll leave her on the sidewalk. She's mad at her, mixing them in with those guys, using her. But it's dark and Lulu remembers her fear and confusion leaving Helen's that first time. She walks Helen to the bus stop and they wait in silence. Helen plays with the fringe on her jacket.

"What was that about some girl, Liz?" she says after a while. "It set you off."

"Nothing. But Danny..."

The bus pulls up and Lulu is saved. Helen boards and finds a seat in the bright interior as it pulls away, heading south.

Lulu runs then, free in the dark. After supper she broods in her room, wanting to warn Liz but afraid to call. She'd panic if Mrs. McMullin answered, can't let Viv hear. Or maybe she should tell Viv. News may be spreading fast, and that can't be good for Liz.

"Lulu," her mother calls from the kitchen, "Janet's on the phone."

Janet hasn't called in weeks, and Lulu expects a string of questions about what she was doing on the corner. But Janet doesn't mention it.

"Lu," she says, breathless. "My sister heard some gossip. It's about Liz."

June

When Gerald was four, he fell and split open his chin. The cut was deep and about an inch long, and June thought he might need stitches. The local doctors' office said bring him in. It was a production to get him there—June didn't own a car, couldn't even drive, and Barry was missing again, so she walked, carrying the heavy, sobbing boy while pressing a wad of tissue to his chin.

They entered the waiting room a wailing, bleeding steamroller. Everyone turned and looked. The unwed mother with her handicapped boy. June checked in with the receptionist, patting her hair and smoothing her dress. They sat, Gerald on her lap with his face buried in her neck, and she was glad to hug him and look to the floor. They had to wait forty minutes.

The doctor was new, from Africa he said, a large man with a gentle manner. He sat Gerald on the examining table and dabbed at the cut. He agreed stitches were in order and promised Gerald it would be only "a few very pretty ones."

June squeezed her son's hand while the doctor applied topical freezing, threaded the needle, and began. The child whimpered. The doctor paused.

"Has anyone ever told you," he said with a smile, "that you are perfect?" Gerald stopped sniffling and shook his head no.

The question surprised June. On the walk home, she mouthed at it silently the way Gerald was exploring the sucker they'd given him. It returns to her now and then. *Does she think him perfect? Why hasn't she told him? Does she value him as a mother should value a son?*

Today she looks at him, stretched on his bed in the middle of the afternoon, awake, not doing. And worse, she has to bug him again.

"Gerald," she says, "we have to go to Nana's." He shakes his head no.

This back and forth, from Mom to Gerald to Lorne, is crazy. But it's all she can think to do. She doesn't like leaving Gerald alone, and she needs help today carrying heavy casseroles—tuna and mac and cheese. He complains and she can't blame him. It's a raw November day.

The walk seems endless, Gerald lagging behind in apparent spite, June fighting the wind and longing for a warmer coat. When they get there, Mom sits with the TV tray in front of her, as June left her this morning. Snoring.

June dials down the volume of the TV and sinks into a chair. This can't go on. She lets out a sob, brings her fists to her eyes. An idea has been fighting to come to the surface for weeks and she's been pushing it down: move back here, just for a while. Mom would be safer, Gerald happier, June less harried.

After supper she broaches it with Lorne and he says absolutely not. He thought June cared for him and wanted to live with him in their new house. Who knows how long her mother will live? June could be back there for years.

"You'd just love it if she kicked off tomorrow, wouldn't you?" she says.

"Now don't start."

She can't sleep that night. Mom made June and Barry promise years ago they'd never put her in an old age home. She seems to have a particular fear of it, and anyway how would it look, if they put her away? Barry can't take a leave to be home with her, he's too new at work. Mom would fight moving in with June, and shouldn't she be able to stay in her own home during the last part of her life?

Lorne makes a noise in his sleep and June rolls over. He's on his back and a light outside highlights his profile. A strong nose and full, sensual lips. These days, part of her hates him. It's like he's gripping her by the arm, fingers pressing too hard and leaving a mark. He claims he wants his own family, like she does. But they can't seem to figure it out.

She creeps downstairs. Trudy says marriage is a trade-off, that you learn when to fight and when to shut your mouth. June wants this chance, likely her last chance, at happiness.

Surely she had a happy childhood, summer days visiting cousins on the Eastern Shore, taking out the old dory with splintery oars so long and heavy they could barely manage them, screeching in the freezing ocean.

In town, she lived for movies with Trudy and other girls. They jitterbugged for hours at summer dances, then walked home late, exhilarated, mooning over boys they liked and dismissing those they didn't.

But when Connelly forced her, raped her, her light died. All that was Before. In the After, she was alone, shunned. Holidays, photos of the old days—they all brought sadness, not joy. Because that's what the old June did. It's been a long climb back to a middle ground.

These past weeks living with Lorne have been good. They've had some laughs. She hasn't worried about rushing into another job. She can keep an eye on Gerald. Her own kitchen. She can't throw it away. She'll work it out, she'll keep an eye on Mom and stay here. She'll try to bring Gerald around. Somehow, she'll do it all.

Lulu

The English teacher wheels in a television on a cart and shows them a 1968 movie version of *Romeo and Juliet*. Many girls cry at their desks in the dark. They all knew what was coming but the lovers are so gorgeous and tragic, the music so sentimental, Lulu chokes up too. But as the students step into the harsh fluorescent light of the corridor, she doubts it'd ever happen.

Example one, her parents: teenage sweethearts gone wrong.

"We married too young," Viv has said. "We know each other too well." If they'd lived, would Romeo and Juliet have ended up feeling the same way?

Viv seems content without Dad. Lulu hears from him less and less, and she's trying not to care.

Helen and Danny? Won't last, but if their families feuded Lulu wouldn't bet against Danny's mother. As she boards the bus, Lulu thinks of Liz and her boyfriend. No happy ending there either.

She gets off the bus by the drugstore, which glows in the gloomy day. Liz sits at the front counter. Lulu tried all week to warn her about the rumours; she was brave enough to call a few times, but Mrs. McMullin always answered and Lulu hung up. Once, she and Janet squeezed into a phone booth and Janet put on a deep voice, but Mrs. McMullin claimed Liz wasn't home.

Lulu enters the store and Liz looks up, in pain. She summons Lulu over and whispers that she needs to go, she's been waiting for her to arrive.

"Mom kicked me out," Liz says, slipping into her jacket. "I need to get more of my things before Dad gets home."

"What?"

"She found out. Somehow, she heard. Figured out everything. She's out of her mind."

"I, Liz, I think it might have been Danny. I tried to call you."

Liz pulls on a knit cap. "It's okay. It's not your fault."

She slings a bulky kit bag over her shoulder and opens the door and the wind whooshes in, ruffling the corners of the newspapers stacked nearby.

"Where are you going?"

"With a friend." She looks about twelve years old. She steps into the dusk. Kicked out of her house, because she sinned.

A customer enters and Lulu rouses herself to wait on him. All night she peers into the blackness outside, hoping Liz is warm at her friend's place.

It's all suddenly dead serious, beyond secrets shared at work, more than Liz going off on a daring journey, worse than rotten teenagers spreading rumours. Lulu's chest pounds with anxiety. After closing, she rushes home and tells her mother everything. Viv sets down her paperback and says she had no idea Lulu was carrying this load.

"Mom, that's not the point. What about Liz?"

Viv pauses. She says she expects Liz will be just fine in the end, she's a smart girl and won't be raising a baby she didn't want.

"It's always been, Lu. Now there's safe abortion, but women used to use coat hangers, Lysol douches. Girls had babies in secret and gave them up for adoption, or there were shotgun weddings—lots of them. My little cousin Mary grew up thinking her oldest sister was her sister. Turned out she was her mother."

She pours Lulu a tea and pulls a TV dinner out of the oven.

"Being a mother is hard. The hardest," Viv says. "Jimmy was a handful—always questioning, never satisfied. I wanted to smack him some days. But I could never, ever throw one of my children out on the street."

Lulu takes the lukewarm meal into her bedroom. Mrs. McMullin, making out with a strange man last summer within sight of the dump. Sinning and sneaking around, then rejecting her only child for doing the same thing.

She scrapes out the meagre apple dessert from the corner of the aluminum tray. There must be some way she can help. Liz, sparkling in dangly earrings, full of dreams. The one who always seems to know what to do.

June

It's a bitter Saturday night and June and Lorne are expecting Trudy and Martin for cards and drinks. Lorne sets up a borrowed card table in the front room, and June pours peanuts and pretzels into petite glass dishes in the shapes of the four card suits, castoffs from her mother. She feels like June Cleaver.

"Can they play whist? Bridge for dummies," Lorne says as he sets out a quart of amber rum and some glasses. June says Trudy's terrific at games but she's not sure about Martin's mental ability. He laughs.

June assesses herself in the hall mirror. She's made an effort, set her hair in the afternoon, put on makeup, earrings, and perfume from an old Avon bottle that may be skunky. She wears a loose floral blouse to hide her bad bits and keep her cool. She has looked forward to this all week, a distraction from Mom and Gerald, who's watching hockey in his bedroom. Barry, spending his Saturday night with Mom. A saint.

The guests carry in the smell of cold, Martin blows on his hands and Trudy exaggerates a shiver. Martin says it feels like snow.

"Yes, sir," Trudy says when Lorne offers her a drink.

Johnny Cash plays on the hi-fi as they settle onto folding chairs and agree on whist, couple versus couple. Trudy's never played but understands how trump and tricks work, and is willing to try. June doesn't feel as confident but keeps quiet. Lorne starts reciting rules and Martin waves him off.

"Yeah, yeah, I got it," Martin says. "All we do on the ship is play cards."

The game sputters as the couples struggle to establish a rhythm. Partners let each other down, ruin tricks that were supposed to go their partner's way, play a trump card at the wrong time.

"Jesus," Martin says, throwing down his cards. "What in hell are you doing, Trude?"

"You keep overbidding," she says, sticking her face into his. "Don't be so damn cocky."

Martin scowls and picks up his cards. They begin to play better and pull away from Lorne and June, racking up points. Lorne sets his jaw and pours more potent rum and Cokes.

June's not a big drinker but slurps back the sweet drinks, enjoying the release, the warmth, the slackening of her limbs. She forgets about Mom. She becomes overheated and opens a window; the cold air is shocking and Lorne yells to close it but she ignores him.

Martin deals a new hand and Lorne soon barks at her to pay attention. She widens her eyes to focus.

"Smarten up, woman," he says.

She jiggles the ice in her glass and downs the last of the drink. Trudy turns and asks how her mother's doing.

"Doesn't seem too upset about the fire but I don't know," June says. "I'm there every day."

"That's a lot of hauling back and forth," says Trudy, glancing at Lorne.

"Yeah, well—"

"Margie made her bed." Lorne sweeps the cards into a pile. "I asked her to move in but she turned me down, and June wouldn't make her."

June's head bobbles. She stands, sways with the sudden movement and bangs the lightweight table. Her glass falls to the floor and ice cubes skitter across the hardwood. Trudy reaches for her but she pivots.

"Where you going?" Lorne says.

She grasps the staircase railing and climbs, focusing as she places one foot and then the other on the treads.

"I am going," she says, "to check on my son."

Lorne says, "Just leave her." The hi-fi goes silent.

Hockey announcers drone in Gerald's room. It's close in here, and June's stomach lurches. She bats the cat off the end of the bed and squeezes her bum beside him. She rubs his shin, asks how he is, tries to sound sober.

"Are you happy?" The words pop out. He nibbles his thumbnail.

"I don't think you're happy, Gerald. Sad. You've been sad since we moved."

He looks at her and her eyes swim and he's a boy again, smiling, his cheeks rosy from playing in the snow with other boys.

He shrugs. "I miss Nana," he says.

A tap on the door and Trudy sticks her head in.

"We're going, honey. You okay?"

June nods.

"You never could hold your liquor," Trudy says. "Don't let him get to you. He's drunk too." She says she'll call tomorrow. "'Night, Gerald."

June needs to lie down. She doesn't know what to say to Gerald anyway.

"Turn off that TV," she says and closes his door.

She peels off her things and crawls into bed with the overhead light on; the room spins and she closes her eyes. She opens them and faces the cherry-blossom picture, the only household item she brought with her. In her fog she searches for the usual faces and birds, the baby in the corner.

And then she sees a large face, a monstrous face, smack in the centre. How could she have missed this? His bald head comes to a point at the intersection of two branches, dark eyes and a bulging blossom nose, a slash for a mouth. She closes her eyes, opens, and it's still there. The creamy blossoms around it contort into skulls. Now that she has seen it, she can't not see it.

She wakes, it seems much later, when Lorne turns off the light and crawls into bed. She edges toward her side so that she's barely hanging on. Her sleep is full of nightmares: Gerald on a bus that crashes and bursts into flames; Mom wandering the streets looking for him, confused.

Late the next morning she wakes alone with her head in a vice and a gummed-up mouth. Weak November light slants through the window and hurts her eyes. She remembers Johnny Cash, Lorne barking at her, a glass rolling across the floor.

When she feels she can get up, she confronts the blossom picture. Up close it's just flowers, leaves, branches. Nothing sinister. But when she steps back and moves her head, when she lies down, it changes. If she tried to point it out to someone they'd think her insane.

A sharp wave of nausea and she clamps her hand over her mouth. She rushes down the hall and barely makes it, splattering vomit over the toilet and wall. It comes and it comes and it comes, acid burning her throat; her eyes water and tears run down her cheeks. She retches until there's nothing left to give, kneeling, praying for it to stop.

When, finally, it stops, she pulls herself up and grasps the sink. Splashes cold water on her face and makes herself look in the mirror. Smeared mascara and a puffy red face, hair stiff with hairspray moulded into a whirligig. The efforts of the night before always seem ridiculous the next morning.

Lulu

Viv hears through a coworker who hears through a neighbour that Liz is living with a friend near the university. But her parents refuse to pay the rest of her tuition or help her in any way, and she has dropped out. Lulu feels sick about it.

When she arrives for work the following Saturday, anxious to see Liz, Farrell says she quit. His niece will pick up her shifts. He gives no sign he's aware of Liz's circumstances, but he's so wooden, Lulu can't be sure. Liz needs money but it makes sense to avoid the neighbourhood right now.

Work will be miserable without her. And, it's funny, but Liz may be her best friend. A six-year age gap but she's generous, full of smart advice. If Liz doesn't finish her degree it would be a crime.

Lulu kneels on the gritty tile floor beside a carton of shampoo she's meant to price and shelve. The bottles feel unusually weighty and one slips from her hand. The top pops off and blue shampoo crawls across the tile. Damnit. She grabs a roll of paper towel and wipes, but the more she tries, the worse it seems. She lets out a sob.

The door tinkles and a young woman enters. She smiles at Lulu.

"Oh, you've made a mess," she says.

She comes over, squats, and doesn't say anything about Lulu's tears, for which Lulu's thankful. The woman asks if the druggist's in and Lulu nods. The customer stands and pulls out a prescription by the look of it.

"I hear he gives girls a hard time about the pill," she says. She winks and walks to the back.

Lulu will need the mop. The customer's right. Farrell hates to fill prescriptions for birth control, and sometimes has private chats with customers about it. Women and girls seem to leave those conversations ashamed or furious. Once, Liz confronted him and reminded him the pill is legal. His face flushed with anger, and Lulu wondered if he'd have a heart attack.

She mops, swish, circle, swish. *Blame me for using birth control, blame me for getting pregnant. Only have sex within marriage. Well, look at Liz. Look at Liz's mother.*

Over the course of the day, Lulu can't stop thinking about Mrs. McMullin. Probably the boss of that family and the one who booted Liz out. Now Liz is sleeping on someone's couch, a dropout.

As Lulu serves customers and eats lunch alone, she turns an idea over and around in her head. By the end of her shift she has a plan. She's terrified at the thought of it but if she doesn't do it right away, she'll chicken out.

That night she sets her alarm clock so she'll wake in time for nine o'clock Mass. She hasn't been in months; Mom never goes and is sprawled in bed when Lulu leaves, likely hungover.

As she enters church, Lulu spots the McMullins seated in front, Liz's mother in a pink hat shaped like a pencil eraser. She's crazy nervous but as she settles into a back pew, she calms. Sunlight filters through stained glass windows and deposits pools of blue, red, and gold that transform the interior into summer, despite the dampness that requires coats stay on.

She used to take such comfort in church. On cold evenings she'd walk to Mass alone to sing with the girls' choir, thrilling at the rise of their soft voices in the vaulted nave, a mere sprinkling of the devout there to hear.

Mrs. McMullin throws back her head to sing and hurries to the front of the line to receive communion. Lulu remains on the kneeler during communion, where sinners are supposed to stay, scrunches her eyes shut over posed hands, and wonders if she dare pray for strength to do what she's about to do.

When Mass ends she slips out and waits at the corner of the church. The McMullins begin walking the few blocks home. Liz's father keeps well ahead, a thin, long-legged walker who bends forward, his baggy grey suit a fraction behind him. Mrs. McMullin's a stroller. Lulu follows carefully, stopping to hide behind trees and cars. They enter their house, a modest two-storey.

A few houses down Lulu huddles under a tree clinging to its last shrivelled gold leaves. She's going to knock on that door and she's going to confront Mrs. McMullin. He can't answer; she needs Liz's mother alone.

Her nose tickles again and she pulls a bloody tissue from her pocket. A nosebleed like graduation day, when she'd been asked to speak in front of all the parents, and Mom said it was nerves. The bleeding stops and she takes a deep breath.

She approaches the house, up four steps and knock, knock on the door with a shaky hand. Mrs. McMullin answers.

She has removed her coat and shoes but still wears the pink hat. Up close, her face is lined and powdered, her eyes underscored by bags, lipstick poorly applied. She gives off a strong floral scent. She frowns, then gets a look of startled recognition, and Lulu needs to blurt it out before the door's slammed in her face. She swallows.

"I'm going to tell on you. I'm going to tell everybody what I saw, tell your husband, if you don't let Liz move back home."

"What..." Mrs. McMullin says, pulling the door closer. Her toes encased in pantyhose grip the threshold.

Lulu raises her voice. "I saw you kiss that man. I'm going to tell if you don't let Liz move home. Pay for her school."

"Who's there?" her husband calls.

Mrs. McMullin backs up and closes the door, wide-eyed. For a second, Lulu remains nose to the door, then descends the steps on wobbly legs and walks—does not run—down the street. She's likely watching through the sheers. *Look angry. Look like you mean it.*

She has thought it through. She will tell if the McMullins don't take Liz back. It would only take a phone call to Liz's father, everyone knows he works down at the little bank, a letter dropped through a mail slot, a tidbit thrown at one of the gossips who shop at the store. She can describe the black car and the man who was driving. She has no way of reaching Liz but she can help her nonetheless.

At the end of the block she glances over her shoulder. This beats the hell out of playing girl detectives with Janet. She half-runs the rest of the way home and bursts through the apartment door.

Viv's having toast at the kitchen table. Her kimono gapes to reveal her bare breast, her hair spills out of a bun. She and Brenda have been going regularly to the pub and she looks grey.

"Guess what I just did?" Lulu says, removing her jacket. She speaks in a rush, describes Mrs. McMullin in the car last summer, and knocking on their door just now, threatening her.

Viv's jaw drops. "You didn't."

"Liz is homeless. She needs to finish school. It's all I could think of."

Viv brings her hand to her mouth and laughs. "My god, Lu, you're blackmailing Ann McMullin. That ol' bitch."

Viv gets up, seeming energized, fills the kettle and pulls smokes from her pocket. Lulu sits and worries her hands.

"Ann McMullin having a fling," Viv mumbles. "I wouldn't think she'd be interested."

Lulu asks her not to tell anyone and Viv promises she won't.

"What if it doesn't work, Mom? Will I get in trouble?"

"Who's she going to tell? What's she going to say? 'This kid tried to blackmail me because I'm screwing a man who's not my husband.' She won't tell."

Wouldn't it be perfect, Liz returning to the neighbourhood, to the store, and most of all to school? Normal. Until she can get away from her family. Viv fits the lid into the teapot and brings it to the table. She shakes her head and smiles.

"What else are you hiding? You amaze me every day."

Lulu's grateful she's had Viv to talk to lately. A bit mixed up but a good mother. Never mean. It's been sad in this dinky apartment but Lulu wouldn't trade it for Liz's house or Helen's mansion. Definitely not Liz's mother and not even Helen's sophisticated mother. This, the two of them, is okay.

June

June remembers that she forgot. At some point after she and Lorne broke up eight years ago, she forgot all that had been wrong between them. He'd been controlling. Claimed he cared but often found fault with her. Had little patience with Gerald. So when Gerald scratched Lorne's eye at the picnic, and Lorne yelled those words, maybe she shouldn't have been surprised.

She broke with him one day in the car, without planning to, and in the following weeks second-guessed herself. His touch, his laugh, the way he looked at peace in the outdoors. The picnic had just been an off day.

She regretted pushing him away, and the fact of Gerald— his existence—became the reason. If not for him, she'd dare to imagine, she and Lorne would be together. Then she'd shake her head, *No, don't think that. How can you even think that?*

Now, she has to admit it's bad again. The honeymoon is over and Lorne's back to bossing her around.

"You forget I'm not one of your little sisters, needing her shoes tied," June shoots at him one day.

Sure, lots of women put up with crap. Martin's an ass, Trudy cheated, but somehow they make it work. Together since age fifteen and no sign of splitting.

But June is done tolerating. She doesn't want to settle down if it means settling. Gerald's unhappy and her mother needs her. June has a constant headache.

One Saturday evening, she tells Lorne she's walking over to visit Barry and Mom. He's unscrewing hinges and removing doors from the kitchen cupboards; building new cabinets has been downgraded to painting the old ones. The radio moans with country music.

"Gerald's just up watching TV," she says, buttoning her coat.

"K." He doesn't turn around.

She pulls a scarf around her chin and picks her way down the wooden steps. On the sidewalk she takes in the sharp, cold air. The corner street light sparkles the snow-frosted brown grass. It's good to be out alone; she begins walking with a bit of pep.

Some houses have curtains open and lights on. An old man sits by a window, head bent over a book. A woman washes dishes. A couple moves in each other's arms, slow dancing. Children in pyjamas.

When she arrives, Mom and Barry are watching hockey. They've turned off the lamps and the two of them appear, then fade, in the flickering TV light. On the chesterfield side-by-side like zombies. Her mother looks at her, looks back to the game.

"This house is chilly," June says. She sits, still in her coat. She asks and Barry says they had tinned soup for supper, looks at her as if to say, "Don't say a word."

She goes to make warming tea. Red soup is splattered in the sink and pasta alphabet letters lie stranded in the drain. Two sopping tea bags have been tossed in. A fry pan with frilly egg remnants, another rum bottle. She resists the urge to scrub it all away, and returns to the front room with three mugs.

Barry's gaining weight and the bags under his eyes sit atop bloated cheeks. Turned fifty this year. Sitting with his mother night in, night out. He should be with a girlfriend or with friends down at the tavern.

"Mom, how are you tonight?" says June.

Margie's in a nightgown and cardigan. Her grey hair's thinning; June has noticed patches of pink scalp. She always found her clients' bare scalps too intimate. One elderly woman even had an odd growth at the crown of her balding head, an inch-long spike June had to work around until a doctor lanced it. If she touched it by mistake, she couldn't help but shiver.

"Where's Gerald?" Margie says.

"Left him with Lorne. How about I run you a hot bath?"

"Not this time of night. Too cold."

June gets up. She really wants to give her mother a bath, it's been three days. The taps sputter and she finds some bubble bath. As it fills, she looks in on Barry's room. A pile of dirty clothes on the floor, a paperback mystery on the bed. When he moved out to marry Sheila, he likely never dreamed he'd be back one day sleeping in the same room. In Mom's bedroom, June lays out clean nightclothes and the rose talcum powder Mom loves.

Barry brings Margie upstairs. She's annoyed and June has to pull the clothes off her.

"Jesus, Mary, and Joseph," Margie says, inching into the water. "It's boiling."

"Stop complaining," says June, but adds cold water.

The two women are past their awkwardness over this ritual, the reversal of roles between the one who used to do the bathing and the one being bathed. June gets the facecloth extra soapy and sets it on one of her mother's shoulders, lets the suds slide down her bony back. Spots and moles scattered across her shoulder blades, shrunken breasts that sag down her ribcage.

"They're not pretty but I fed both you babies with these," Margie says, as if reading June's mind. "A lot of gals were switching to the bottle then, but not me."

Bubble clouds move across the surface of the water and there's her scar. She had a Caesarean giving birth to June, almost died, she likes to remind her; the baby was lodged and the doctor had to cut her open. She lost buckets of blood and her incision became infected, a terrible time. And caring for a toddler to boot.

It's her war story. Every woman who has given birth has one, traded around kitchen tables where other women nod, commiserate, then take their turn. Margie's scar is pale but will never leave her.

June lifts one of her mother's hands. Blue veins bulge under paper-thin, spotted skin. Skin that's still amazingly soft. She scrubs Mom's nails with a stiff brush, drawing another complaint.

Then she asks her to lean back and she wets her hair with the facecloth, bracing Mom with her other arm so she doesn't slip under. Lathers her hair and rinses. Mom closes her eyes and relaxes in her arms. She always fretted about being plump but weighs nothing now. June holds her a few extra seconds, inhales the citrus shampoo and listens to her breath. The water's cooling fast.

"Okay, let's get you out of here," June says, sitting her up.

She fumbles for a good grip, almost calls Barry, but is able to pull Mom up to standing, shivering. Margie puts a hand on each of June's shoulders, June clasps her mother's waist and gets her out of the tub. June wraps her in towels, gently rubs her hair dry. She brings in the fresh nightgown and talcum powder. Margie douses herself, they both cough and laugh, and June helps her slip on the flannel nightgown spread with blue flowerbuds. Her cheeks glow, pink against her silvery hair.

"You look pretty, Mom."

"Yeah, don't fool with me."

In the bedroom June digs around on the cluttered dresser, finds the Oil of Olay and slathers the cream onto her mother's face. She examines her mother's feet, clips a few toenails, yellow and thickened.

"I'm getting the special treatment tonight, no?" says Mom.

June wishes she had changed the sheets but Mom doesn't care. She sinks under the covers, a thick layer of thin, cheap blankets. Her head hits the pillow, pillowcase mismatched from the bedsheet, and closes her eyes.

"'Night, dear," she mumbles. "Your father will be back tomorrow."

June looks down at this woman who stood by her, through the scandal and the exhausting days of figuring out an infant, then a stubborn toddler. Even when Dad hated her. Even after Dad died of the shame. Always, the one who loved her best. She switches off the light.

She goes downstairs and tells Barry she wants to move back in. He stops mid-drink. She apologizes—it will be a squeeze but they'll figure something out. He says no problem.

"It's for the best," she says.

"What about Lorne?"

She pauses. "It's for the best."

Barry drives her home and tells her to take tomorrow off, he can handle things on Sunday. She lies awake that night searching for the right words, imagining Lorne's reaction. She needs to be firm. But then who knows, maybe he's sick of her? They've barely spoken in days.

The next morning she trails around in her housecoat as Lorne works on the cupboards. She brings Gerald up cereal and a glass of juice. At noon she makes Lorne a sandwich and tells him to come eat. He delays, wants to finish one more thing, and then sits. She waits until he takes a big bite.

"I'm moving back to Mom's."

"What're you talking about?" he says, mouth full of white bread and pink ham and yellow mustard.

"I'm needed there. Gerald and I are moving back, just for a while."

"This is your home. You're needed here."

"Lorne, I've thought about it and it's the right thing. Mom needs help. Barry has to work."

He pauses, drops the sandwich, and stands. She shrinks. He's never hit her—she can give him that—but his words can pummel.

"I want you here," he says. "You check on her every day. Bring her supper. She's okay."

June looks down at her hands. Why does she have to beg? Why can't he just say, "You're right. Your mother needs you"?

"She's not okay," June says, her voice rising. "She's...she's dying, Lorne."

He laughs. "That woman will outlive us all."

He's never liked Mom, because she counters him. She stood up to Dad too. June wishes she were as tough, but under her hard shell, she's pudding.

"Lorne, please."

He turns around, has built up a fury. "No, just no," he says, pointing at her. "You're staying here. We're getting married."

June sits back. Is this a command? They've never discussed marriage with any seriousness.

"She'll be fine," he says. "Grow up, June. Get off momma's teat."

He grabs his mug and clomps down to the basement. June's eyes leak in frustration. Unable to cry for years and lately, she can't stop.

Lulu

Monday morning and the bus swishes through slush heading south along busy Robie Street. Inattentive walkers get showered in the backwash. An early, surprise snowfall, a few inches that won't last. The passengers look cranky; unprepared for snow, they're sentenced to wet sneakers and dress shoes, prune toes, sopping socks and stained nylons that will pinch their feet as they dry and contract throughout the day.

Lulu looks out at the apparent arrival of winter and marvels over her actions yesterday. Wouldn't it be amazing to ride home on the three fifteen and see Liz back in the neighbourhood? Maybe even back at the store. The main thing is that she finishes her degree, that Danny doesn't win, that Mrs. McMullin doesn't ruin her daughter's life.

She taps her forehead against the window glass. The threat was stupid. The high she felt leaving that house has disappeared. She's embarrassed to tell Janet.

At school, Helen and Danny are entwined at the smoking door, hoods up and backs to her but clearly them. Helen must've discovered there's no rock band but hasn't said a word.

During lunch Lulu sits at the usual table, hoping to talk to Helen about their assignment. The caf smells of wet wool. Helen strolls over, Danny clinging and nuzzling her ear. Helen dips her head and giggles at his touch and Lulu feels like slapping her. They sit across the table but pay her no attention.

"Helen, we need to get together to write that assignment," Lulu says. Helen turns to her slowly, reluctant, it seems, to tear her eyes from her Romeo.

"Not today. Dan's coming to my place." *Wonder if Cynthia will ask him to dinner.*

"But it's due soon. We haven't even started," Lulu says.

Helen's smile disappears. "Be cool," she says. "We'll get it done."

"But you keep delaying," Lulu says. She hears herself whine.

"Calm down, little girl," says Danny, laughing.

"Oh, he's awake," Lulu says. "He speaks."

He stills. "What the hell does that mean?"

"Okay, guys?" says Helen. "No sweat. It'll get done."

Lulu lays her sandwich on top of the aluminum foil wrapper. Dumped a second time this year, it seems, by a friend who's found something better. She hates eating lunch with Danny, being with Danny. She wants to shout, "You're ruining Liz's life." Helen is clueless.

"I'm gonna split," he says and stands. "See ya later, babe." He bends and kisses Helen, holds it long and deep. Pulls away and looks at Lulu, then leaves, snatching fries from someone's plate along the way.

"Is he even going to classes?" Lulu says.

"What do you mean? He's a senior."

Lulu crumples the aluminum foil into a ball and rolls it down the table. It falls off the edge.

"You don't like him," says Helen.

If you only knew. Lulu's stress about the assignment, about threatening Mrs. McMullin, bubbles inside.

"You know, last spring I thought he kidnapped somebody," she says. Helen's mouth forms a perfect O. Lulu leans in, elbows on the table.

"Yeah, it was this slow guy who went missing. Danny and Mikey were always mean to him, beating him around. So Janet and I followed them, staked them out."

Helen stares.

"Remember Danny said I followed him? It was because of

the kidnapping. Turned out it wasn't them. But I wouldn't put it past them. They've had run-ins with the police."

Helen's eyes are huge. "You suspected Danny? That's terrible."

Lulu shrugs.

"I don't understand you, Lulu. He's sweet."

"Hmm." Lulu doesn't know what to say next. Did she expect Helen would be scandalized and dump him?

Helen crosses her arms in front of her chest. "Maybe we shouldn't do the assignment together," she says. "Our schedules aren't working anyway."

Lulu pauses. "If you want."

"I'll tell the teacher." Helen gets up and leaves her too.

The laughter and voices of the cafeteria ring around her. At a nearby table a boy has a plastic straw stuck up each nostril. A girl paints her fingernails purple. Science nerds hunch over a textbook in the middle of their table. No one seemed to notice Helen walking out on her.

The cat, she should have told her about the tortured cat. But it wouldn't have mattered. Lulu would just be jealous that her friend has a boyfriend, that she was being ignored.

On the bus home that day, Lulu realizes she can't help herself, she needs to go by the McMullins' to see if there's any sign of Liz. She passes down their sidewalk a couple of times. No one about, but perhaps the sheers rippled. Good, let Mrs. McMullin know she's serious.

After supper she tells Viv she walked by the house, not sure if she wanted to be seen or not.

"What am I doing?" Lulu says. "Why am I threatening some church lady?"

Viv touches Lulu's cheek. "You stuck up for your friend," she says. "Not everyone does that."

The next day in English class, Helen bypasses her old desk and goes to the back corner. Forget Danny's sins, Lulu's sin was being a bitch, wanting to turn Helen off her boyfriend. At the end of class the teacher asks Lulu and Helen to remain. She reads out a note from Helen requesting a new partner for the assignment.

"Do you girls really want to be separated?" the teacher says.

"Yes," Helen says quickly. They stand beside each other, eyes forward.

"Yes," Lulu says.

"Okay," says the teacher, but she doesn't sound convinced. She assigns Helen to work with a girl whose partner had an emergency appendectomy last night. That student will be out for a while.

"There's a transfer student arriving tomorrow," she tells Lulu. "You can work with him. I'll give both groups an extension; too many students leaving and entering class right now."

Lulu takes her time zipping her bag as Helen disappears down the corridor. Friends for just a few months. Will Cynthia ask after her?

A new student. A guy. This should be a disaster. The assignment is to write a five-page scene, something that could change the course of Romeo and Juliet. They can use modern language. The partners are required to perform it, at least read it, in front of the class. The obvious choice is to let one or both lovers survive. But Lulu craves something unexpected, maybe a new character, a girl Romeo falls for or a boy for Juliet. Liz would probably approve. She hopes her new partner will go along with it.

When she arrives home that afternoon, she's surprised to hear life in the apartment. Her mother and father sit in the kitchen and look up as she enters. Already, her parents look strange together, Dad's absence now normal. A visitor in this place that he found and helped pay for, hung pictures in, and lived in for three years. He smiles.

"What's going on?" Lulu says.

"We were just talking," Viv says.

Dad rises and puts an arm around Lulu. "I'm thinking of coming back. If your mother will have me." He seems thinner.

"Jack," says Viv, "nothing's settled." But she smiles too.

They'd be an official family again, though she and Viv are doing okay, in fact are closer than ever. Dad smiles down at Lulu and gives her a squeeze. Their last outing was that drive in the summer. The gap in his front teeth looks kind of grotesque today. She's not even sure she missed him.

June

The new house is drafty. Lorne says it's on the list, to plug some holes and add insulation, but he's been tinkering with other problems since they moved in. This morning, as the November wind whistles through the cracks, it feels like an affront, a personal eff you to June, who's been asking for some warmth since day one.

She makes extra noise with the breakfast dishes, still in her pyjamas. Lorne digs in the front closet for more layers, in a rush to get to the work site. He grumbles the traffic will be brutal in this freak snowfall. The rummaging stops, then a pause.

"Did you make me a lunch?" he calls.

"No bread."

"All right." The front door opens and closes, though does not slam. Let him make his own lunch.

She heads upstairs to wake Gerald; she needs his help carrying more food she made Mom and Barry last night. Getting out the door takes an hour. He's dopey and she can't find him clean socks. Their winter boots appear lost in the move so they settle for sneakers.

It's one of those Monday mornings that make you want to crawl back into bed. Grim-looking people slog to work and school. Her arms ache from the heavy dishes. That's it—she's getting her driver's license. Barry can probably find her a used car for cheap. Lorne would never get it done. She'll pay Barry back bit by bit, maybe start cutting hair in the kitchen. Her own car, what freedom that would be.

"Gerald, I'm going to buy a car. What kind should I get?"

"A convertible."

"Yeah, that'd be perfect this morning."

Margie's slim row house appears across the boulevard. The thinner limbs of the maples sag under heavy snow; all is transformed overnight. She'll kill Barry if he didn't put some heat on for Mom. She opens the sticky door with a jerk and they enter the house, remove their soaked shoes and lay the casseroles on the counter. It's quiet.

"Mom?"

Gerald enters the front room and turns on the TV. A mug and toast remnants sit on the kitchen table. June goes upstairs. Not there. She returns downstairs, a tightness building in her chest. Upstairs, downstairs, like the day Gerald disappeared. She has the same feeling of alarm now.

She stands at a loss, the snowy back lane framed in the rear porch windows, not a footprint in the fresh snow on the stoop. She turns and the door to the cellar's open, a dark void against the pale walls. Her breath catches. Mom wouldn't chance those steep steps.

She makes the landing in two quick movements and before she can call out, she sees the figure lying at the bottom, barely illuminated by the kitchen light. June flies down and halfway her brain registers that Mom's twisted funny. She's on her right side, her right leg bent behind and her left leg thrust forward. Her torso curls inward and her cheek rests on the concrete, arms splayed. June reaches her and notes dried blood streaked down Mom's face from hairline to chin. Her nightgown's bunched around her waist, one fluffy slipper missing.

June crouches and puts her hands to her mother's face. Slightly warm but already not human, rubbery with a vacant air, like her old dolls. Eyes that will never open. She places her head on Mom's chest. No rise or fall. She touches her hands and simple wedding band, which Dad saved up to buy years after they were married.

As the ambulance attendants check Margie over, June closes her eyes, prays, punishes herself for not phoning them immediately. She panicked, froze on the basement floor for half a minute? Ten seconds?

But Margie Green was dead when June got there, gone about an hour, says the emergency room doctor. Clunked her head and likely suffered a brain bleed. Why she fell is unclear. Perhaps she had a dizzy spell. Perhaps it was as mundane as her foot getting caught in her nightgown. The doctor seems content with the uncertainty. June is not.

When she and Barry and Gerald leave the hospital, the bustle and fresh air are a shock. When they were inside, discussing Margie's fall and death, machines beeping and people rushing and that antiseptic smell, life reduced to a pastel universe, June forgot the outside world. Nothing else mattered. She stumbles off the curb, adjusts her gait as they cross the parking lot. The wind plays with her unbuttoned coat.

Gerald weeps quietly in the back seat. June glances at him but can't help. There's a film over her eyes, and she regards the world through a blurry lens. Cars move, people walk—impossible. They drive a few minutes before Barry speaks.

"We need to call Aunt Pansy," he says.

June stiffens. Where was Mom's younger sister these past months when Mom was failing? Insistent that driving an hour from the Shore was too much to ask. That her son, June and Barry's dimwit cousin Ronnie, was too busy to drive her. And how about Dad's family? Never hear from them. Let them read about it in the paper. Her obituary.

"I can't believe this," she says.

"It's unreal," Barry says.

He steers the car into their back lane, and June loses it. Mom won't peek out the porch windows anymore, gossip with Mrs. Parsons across the way, unclip clothes pins and collect her laundry. Sobs convulse her body. The force scares her, but it's a relief too, a letting go. The three of them sit as June's grief fills the car. Howling noises she didn't know she could make.

Gerald leans forward and pats her head. "Don't cry, Mom."

She takes a breath. Barry hands her a balled-up tissue and she blows her nose, then pulls herself out of the car. Mrs. Parsons stands at her window, probably heard the ambulance earlier. *Don't look at us.*

June goes through the unlocked back door and the kitchen's unchanged: Mom's last meal, a sweater tossed over a chair, the upper cupboard still scorched from the fire. The wall phone.

Lorne was hurt she didn't call him after the fire, but she can never get him during the day. She can't concentrate on that problem now. Barry goes to the phone instead while Gerald stalls in the doorway. He adored his Nana. And he's always hated that cellar.

"Come on, I'll make you lunch." June guides him toward the front room.

Aunt Pansy is devastated by the news, Barry reports. She cried into the phone. He expects there'll be a parade of people and cakes, baked hams and scalloped potato casseroles rolling into the city in no time. Next he examines the brittle pieces of paper taped to the wall, clear tape yellowed and ink faded, and finds phone numbers for Dad's two brothers.

June makes Gerald toast and sits at the table. The cellar door remains open. A piece of blue plastic on the floor, likely dropped by the ambulance men. Why, why did Mom go down there? Maybe no reason. Her mind led her astray for months. She shouldn't have been left alone. She, June, should have been here. *Damn you, Lorne. I should've been here.* But she's too numb to sustain even anger for long.

On the phone, Barry relays the story again, the heartbreaking matter of his mother's death already shortened into

153

a version easier to tell. "Steps...June...doctor." He hangs up and says the uncles are saddened. They will attend the funeral and want to know where to send flowers.

"We need to get that sorted," he says.

June comes to. "The church won't do her funeral," she says, wandering into the back porch.

Barry wants to call the priest anyway. Even after all this time, she'd want a Catholic service.

The brown leaves of a potted geranium, which Mom must have been trying to keep alive inside, crumble between June's fingers. She wants to lay her head on Lorne's chest and cry. She wants to blast him for talking her out of moving back. For talking her into leaving in the first place.

The priest will allow a service but not a full Mass with communion. Over the next few days, Barry and June arrange periods of visitation to take place in the funeral home; they discuss flowers—Mom loved pink and yellow roses—choose hymns and approve the church basement reception of crust-less sandwiches, sweets, strong tea, and weak coffee.

June must choose an outfit for her mother to wear in the open casket, morbid but Mom would want it. She pulls a dress from the closet, remembers Mom made her swear never to lay her out in that one.

"You know my brown polka-dot dress?" Margie said about five years ago, back from a funeral home visit. "Do not lay me out in it. Mrs. Bayer had on the same one."

Barry writes an obituary to run in the newspaper. He struggles over it, pen poised above a lined scribbler. He and June argue over certain points of the family tree, and June realizes further loss. She doesn't know this history, and the answers have likely died with her mother, an eldest child. She should have asked more questions.

Marguerite Iris Elizabeth Saunders was born in a fishing village to a fisherman and an occasional midwife who died young, in an exhausting, bloody labour that took both mother and baby. He would have been a brother for Margie and Pansy. Margie was schooled until age fourteen, engaged at eighteen to Westminster Green but forbidden from marrying for years because her father couldn't spare her.

After marrying, Margie and Wes moved to the city. "He couldn't stomach boats, and that killed him," Mom once told June. "So we moved to town for a new start."

Margie clerked in a department store while she waited for babies to come, but she had a handful of miscarriages until finally, a good pregnancy. She had Barry just before her thirtieth birthday. Then June Rose, latest in a line of girls named after flowers. Her doctor told her to stop after that.

The Greens had little even before the Second World War erupted, weeks before June's seventh birthday. Putting a good supper on the table got harder, store shelves often left bare as provisions went to the hordes of Allied troops who found themselves in Halifax.

Margie got them through it. She was an adequate cook and an excellent baker, producing war cakes without eggs or milk, suppers of blueberry grunt when necessary, the best pies. After the war and as her children grew, she seemed to take pleasure in simple things: throwing crusts to the birds, feeding scraps to stray cats, bingo and TV soaps. Laid out her husband's breakfast setting each evening, a bowl for porridge, his favourite chipped mug, a banana or an orange if they had one.

Stubborn. Generous. Widowed young, saddened over the rift between husband and daughter that would never be healed, she aged rapidly. She loved her grandson, illegitimate and different, in every way she knew how.

The obituary mentions little of this, only the basics that sum up a life. Its publication produces a new wave of phone calls and drop-ins, including Evelyn, who appears at the door with yet more food. She's tearful and regrets not visiting Margie in recent weeks, but Albert's gravely ill and in his last stretch, she says.

"We're losing all of the good ones," she says, clasping June's hands.

June closes the door. She supposes her mother *was* one of the good ones. She didn't judge. When she met people, she wanted to like them. She believed people were good, and was always shocked when proven wrong. More Christian than most. The neighbourhood gossip over June's pregnancy pained her, and though Margie was angry enough at the priest to leave the church, June knew her mother missed it. Margie's childhood rosary beads always hung over her bedroom mirror.

Now she's getting a goodbye in church. June stands beside Lorne, Gerald, and Barry in the front pew, Aunt Pansy and Ronnie at the end. She smooths the snug black dress borrowed from Trudy, shy in church though she's thumbed her nose at it for years.

The priest's robe stretches like batwings as he spreads his arms and flexes his hands in a blessing. Before the service she found him cold. They're lesser-thans to him, she imagines. Not churchgoers. Unwed mother. Handicapped son in a new, ill-fitting shirt. Barry like an aging rock star with his shaggy hair and fringed, Western-style shirt, which he insisted is the best thing he owns. Lorne in a brown, checked sport coat and black trousers. She takes a deep breath and identifies the lilies at the altar, sent by Dad's brothers, but not the roses she and Barry ordered. Roses don't smell the same these days.

The organist launches into the final hymn and the soloist, a neighbourhood woman with a thrilling soprano voice, likely pausing her housework to do the funeral, sings them out.

"I once was lost, but now I'm found/Was blind but now I see."

Everyone stares as they file out. It's a good show when relatives cry. In the church basement, June accepts a foam cup of tea and Lorne walks over to talk to Ronnie. She's flanked by Gerald, sniffling the whole day, and stoic Barry.

The mourners arrive and voices rise under the low ceiling, an occasional crack of laughter, people seeking relief after the solemnity upstairs. There are a few neighbours, including Mrs. Parsons, a distant cousin who drove an hour and a half to be here, Evelyn, Trudy and Martin, a coworker from fifty years ago who remembers Margie fondly.

All told it's a measly turnout, the last public accounting of a life. People tell June her mother was a good woman, that she had a good life, that she's finally relieved of her suffering. That she "looked so natural" in the casket the other night. June says little but feels about to burst.

"Maureen wishes she was here," says Aunt Pansy.

I doubt it. Maureen is Pansy's daughter, June's cousin and former best friend. Forbidden from telephoning each other, the girls used to write between June's visits to the Shore— rambling letters in immature cursive that lingered over crushes and slights.

When June got pregnant, it took Mom months to tell Pansy. June didn't expect to hear from Maureen after that, and she didn't. The few times Maureen met Gerald over the years, she smiled and didn't speak.

"Oh cripes," Barry says and elbows June to warn her—the priest is approaching.

The priest takes one of June's hands and looks into her eyes for two uncomfortable, silent seconds. Pale eyes in an ashen face, someone who spends too much time inside. He might be sixty. Likely lonely up at the manse. She can't remember his name.

"From what I hear, your mother was a fine woman," he says. "I wish I'd known her." He shakes Barry's hand, touches Gerald's shoulder, and walks toward the sweets table.

Lulu

Lulu smells flowers. Flowers in the rain.

"Lulu, Lulu," someone calls.

She fights waking.

"Wake up."

She rolls over and it's her mother, in a towel and wet hair dripping onto the covers. She smells of soap and shampoo. Lulu squeezes her eyes shut.

"Guess what?" Viv says. "Sharon just called. Cathy saw Liz."

"Who's Sharon? Who's Cathy?" *God*.

"Sharon works with me. She's friends with Cathy, who lives on the McMullins' street." Viv pauses. "Liz is back home, get it? Your blackmail, or whatever you did, worked."

Lulu sits up. "Really? Liz is home?"

Viv repeats what she was told.

"Do you think it actually worked?" Lulu says.

"Sounds like it."

Lulu flings off the blankets and begins digging through her clothes, then stops and turns. "I want to see for myself. But I don't know."

"What're you going to do, knock on their door?" says Viv. "Go to school. Go spy this afternoon if you want."

All morning, Lulu feels like dancing. She has won something, in a way. But the elation dwindles at lunchtime when she realizes she doesn't have anyone to eat with. She hides in the library, then heads to English class, where Helen sits in her new spot again. Lulu tries to catch her eye but Helen turns her head.

Tapping at the classroom door. A guy enters, apologizes to the teacher, he got lost in the building. She hands him a book and directs him to Helen's old desk.

"Class, this is Matthew," she says. "Or is it Matt?"

"Matt," he says, not looking up, trying to shove his backpack under the desk. His pen rolls under Lulu's desk and she hands it to him.

The teacher seems to take pity on him and ignores him the rest of class. Lulu sneaks a peek: he's tall and skinny, knees touching the underside of the desk; curly brown hair and ruddy cheeks; khaki pants and a baggy, navy blue sweater. Kind of private school. When class ends the teacher calls Lulu and Matt to the front. She introduces them and explains the project to him.

"I'm sorry you're being thrown into this, but it's a major assignment this term," the teacher says. "Have you ever read *Romeo and Juliet?*"

"Yeah, last year, at my old school," he says. His voice is deep and croaky, like he hasn't used it all day.

"In grade nine? Where was that?" the teacher asks.

"Toronto," he says. "It was a different sort of school." He adjusts his backpack.

"That's super. You two and Helen's group can go last, after the other groups have presented. That gives you a couple of weeks."

The teacher presses the clasps shut on her briefcase and hurries out. Lulu looks up at Matt and gulps. She supposes she should take the lead.

"I guess we should start," she says.

He nods. They arrange to meet outside after school and find somewhere to study. They can't talk in the library, and she'd never take him to her place.

At three, he waits for her on the sidewalk in a red windbreaker, and she suggests the diner down the street. She thinks she has enough money to buy something that would justify sitting inside. They walk in silence, Lulu wishing for something clever to say.

It's an odd time of day, between meals, but there are customers. A woman battles to keep two small children in their seats, their food and ketchup migrating from table to floor. In the corner, a man with tobacco-stained fingers reads a newspaper while nursing a coffee.

They choose a table at the front window and order drinks and fries. She's never been out in public with a boy, and wishes suddenly that people would pass by and see her—Helen or Janet, even Danny.

Matt pulls off his windbreaker. He smells like the outdoors, sort of like that sandalwood incense Mom bought. Something exotic. She pushes herself to speak.

"So why'd you move here?"

"My dad got a job at Dalhousie. He's a prof." He shoves a few fries into his mouth. He has long fingers and full, wide lips. Everything about him is bigger and slightly sophisticated, how she imagines Toronto to be.

"He's been out here awhile but Mom and I just arrived. And my little sister."

"It must be hard, moving in high school."

Matt nods. "Yeah, I wasn't thrilled about it. I was on two teams, ran track. But I didn't have a choice."

He doesn't want to be here. An athlete who probably thinks he's landed in a hellhole. And likely pining for an old girlfriend. She's jealous of this imaginary girl, athletic and lean like him.

"What was your school like? You said it was different."

He looks at her. She's being nosy. He seems to make a decision before answering. "It was private, small. I'd been there since kindergarten." He rakes a hand through his curls. "I don't know, maybe I was there too long. It could be incestuous." He pulls out his Shakespeare volume. The word surprises her, not something she'd expect from a jock.

Lulu reveals her idea for a new character, and he likes it. They decide on an older teenage boy who tries to lure Juliet away from Romeo, and name him Antonio. He will be bad news.

"She could meet him on a morning walk," says Lulu.

"No, let's make it nighttime," Matt says. "That will symbolize he's evil. And it fits in with the theme of light and dark in the play."

Lulu looks up from her notes, and he blushes.

"I did a paper on it last year."

She'll begin writing tonight, and Matt will take a turn tomorrow night, alternating until they finish. She's no longer worried about making the deadline. He's much smarter than she is.

"Toronto!"

They turn and three lanky guys in school jackets have come in. One raises an arm above his head in a greeting. Lulu recognizes them as school athletes.

"Hey," one guy yells over, and the young mother, zipping the jacket of one of her preschoolers, looks up. Lulu hates making a scene.

"I hear you're a wicked ball player," the guy calls over. "Come to practice tomorrow."

Matt gives a thumbs up. She can't tell if he's pleased. They decide to stop for the day, and part out on the sidewalk. He walks in the same direction Helen took her, the street crowded with rush hour traffic, headlights blinding in the darkness that arrives so early these days, lights reflecting on wet pavement.

She boards her bus, sick to her stomach. It's the feeling of wanting something desperately but knowing you can never have it. As the bus nears home she wonders if Dad will show up again tonight. Last time he brought Mom a silver charm bracelet. Lulu skips her usual stop and gets off farther up the hill, nearer Liz's.

She walks the sleepy street that has become so familiar, two facing rows of boxy houses. Front windows lit in the darkness. There's a smell of wood smoke. What Mom wouldn't give for this, though Helen's house makes these look terribly plain. She's pretty sure Mom has never been in a house like Helen's. Just as well.

She stops outside the McMullin house. The sheers are drawn but she can tell a ceiling light is on at the back, in the dining room. Lulu knows how these houses are laid out, the living and dining rooms forming an L.

A figure appears under the light and she holds her breath. A taller figure enters the room and sinks, sits. Then a third shadow crosses behind the sheers and goes toward the light. Three people, sitting in the dining room. Home, sweet home. She must hate it, hate them. *Just don't hate me, Liz.*

June

June's instinct the day after the funeral is to call Mom to discuss who came, who's aging poorly, who spent big money on flowers, who didn't show. It's a quick knife jab to the heart when she remembers she can't.

The stabs keep coming, an onslaught of moments over the following days and weeks, felt deep within, when she's reminded her mother's gone, forever. She can be doing the most mindless thing, putting on a sock, drying a plate.

Mom's favourite colour of rose pink, an old song on the radio—music is the worst—the packaged shortbreads she loved with tea: pleasures once but now cruel reminders.

The grief's much worse than when Dad died. Growing up she liked him best, but she knows now you get to be the favourite when you're not the one doing the messy stuff, the nagging to get out of bed, pick up your things, tuck in your blouse, keep up with your studies. Mom made sure Barry stuck it out and finished high school. Dad let Mom handle all that.

He was the funny one, the hugger, the one who could make Mom laugh even on the worst days. He'd return from a long shift on his feet, eat a hot meal, and collapse into his chair for the night. Sometimes he'd hand June a few coins and ask her to run to the store for black licorice cigars. "Keep the change, Junie, for penny candy."

When he turned on her, when she got pregnant, it devastated her. She became a tramp and an embarrassment. Those were his words.

"I'm ashamed to show my face at the brewery," he shouted more than once.

June would run to her room, hating herself. Mom would follow eventually, sit on the bed and stroke June's hair.

Over the years, June wondered if her mother had sensed the pregnancy during those early months. They never discussed it. But that spring, sick with nausea and terror, unable to get out of bed, June was grateful when Mom allowed her to skip early classes. A few times she scrunched money into June's palm for a taxi to school.

"Don't tell your father," she'd say. They'd look at each other, unable to speak.

After June confirmed the pregnancy that summer, her mother—the nag, the plain housewife—carried the load. She found June the way out, the maternity home out of town where she could give birth and come home to start again. When June returned that snowy day with the surprise bundle in her arms, Margie loved him immediately. She helped June love him, too. She suggested his name, after a favourite uncle. Dad wouldn't look at Gerald for the longest time.

June understands what drove Mom. She'd give her life for Gerald. Mothers hoist cars to rescue their children pinned underneath, skip meals so their little ones can eat. They were not a family that used the word "love." Her mother was far from perfect, and they battled regularly. But Mom was her champion, her first and firmest. There's a hole in the world where her mother used to stand. June has never been lonelier.

Barry admits to sleeping poorly. It bothers him knowing Mom's clothes, her hairbrush fluffy with silver strands, her clunky black shoes, are in that room. But June can't face it yet. The room smells of her: arthritis ointment, rose talc, and pee.

"You do it," she says. He shakes his head.

Margie's only real asset was the house, but she died without a will, "intestate," the lawyer says, and it'll take time to sort it out. Barry bought out June anyway, so he should own the house free and clear, regardless of what lawyers say. June understands.

But it's bothering her, that she took the ten thousand dollars from Barry and gave it to Lorne for the new house. He's been quiet since Mom's death, likely awaiting the eruption of "I-told-you-so's." Yet June says little.

She pulls away when he touches her. She stays up late, unfocused in front of the TV. For years she'd found her mother frustrating. June could be impatient and, as the years went on, she took Mom for granted.

There was a scar on her foot. All her life June had never noticed it, but that last day, kneeling in the basement awaiting the ambulance, she spied a raised scar, shiny against surrounding skin, on the inside of Mom's left foot, above the arch. June ran her finger along it now. She'd never be able to ask her about it. Had she really known the person who was her mother?

One morning in early December, a few weeks after Mom's death, Barry calls and says he's coming to drop off a birthday present for Gerald. How could she forget? He's twenty-nine today. She'll dress and go buy him a cake. Find something small as a gift.

As she comes downstairs in slacks and a sweater, Barry arrives. The present is a baseball mitt. They haven't tossed a ball in years but Barry wants to get Gerald out moving again, when the weather's better.

"Sorry, I'll get him up," June says. "He's in bed."

"Nah, leave him be. Tell him to call me later."

She asks if he'll drive her to a store so she can buy a cake. She gets into the car, distracted. First special occasion without Mom. When Barry pulls up to the Frugal Mart she shakes her head.

"I can't go in there."

He looks at her. "Why not? What is it with this place?"

Suddenly, she's smothering in her coat. She looks at her brother, who stares expectantly. She should tell him. A family of secrets. She wishes she'd told Mom things, told her she loved her.

"It brings back bad memories," she says.

"What was so bad about being a cashier?"

She swallows. She said the words just once, to Trudy, a long time ago. He waits.

"Well?"

"He, the assistant manager, he forced me." She exhales shakily.

Barry frowns. "What do you mean, forced you?"

"And then nine months later, Gerald."

A look of horror washes over his face. "Are you saying"—his voice rises—"that he *raped* you?"

June nods, turns away. She feels lighter, lightheaded.

"Jesus Christ," Barry barks. "Why didn't you tell people?"

"I don't know. I needed to erase it from my mind."

"How can you put it out of your mind when the result walks this earth? Gerald's father—"

"No one talked about that shit back then," she cuts in.

"So you let Dad think you were a slut instead?"

Her throat constricts and her eyes fill up. "Why get mad at me? What did I do? For years I thought I'd done something wrong, that it was my fault. But now I say to hell with him, Barry."

"Who is it?" he says.

She shakes her head.

"June, who is it?"

Their fight's fogging up the car windows.

"His name's Connelly," she spits out. "He still works in there. Promoted to manager, Trudy said." She needs to lean against the car door.

Barry gets that mean look she hasn't seen in years. When he was young, he'd punch anyone who ticked him off.

"Don't you dare go in there," she says. "Let's just leave."

He looks at the store and she follows his eyes. They've hung Christmas decorations in the windows, plastic wreaths connected by garlands of spray snow, cardboard elves that hold signs advertising the specials. Imported British fruit-cakes and plum puddings.

"Take me down to the other store. You gotta go to work."

He puts the car in gear, jaw set. His mind's working, she can tell. When he pulls up to the other grocery store, she runs in and grabs a day-old cake encircled by blue frosting flowers, a few comic books, and a handful of candy. At the cash she adds one of those plastic army men attached to a flimsy plastic parachute. You unfold the parachute and release the green man into the wind, knowing he'll get caught in a tree but hoping it's not right away.

Barry takes her home. He hasn't spoken since the Frugal Mart. Before getting out, she looks over.

"Just forget it, okay? Come over tonight for cake."

He nods but doesn't look at her.

She worries all day. She should feel relief, releasing her thirty-year secret into the air. Telling her big brother. But what will Barry do? In the end, will she have to tell Gerald the truth about his father?

That afternoon, she stands on the front stoop and watches Gerald toss the green army man into the wind. It stalls, seems unlikely to fly at all, but catches a sudden gust and jerks higher. Gerald claps in excitement. The parachute hovers over their roof, then drops, rolls, and rests on the shingles. Stranded. Gerald complains to her. But there's nothing she can do.

Lulu

The next day in English class, Matt suggests he and Lulu work at his place after school because it's quieter. He wears the same navy sweater, blue eyes, blue sweater. He probably doesn't even know. Her heart jumps. She barely knows him but wants to go.

"Won't you have basketball practice?" she says, buying time.

He shakes his head. "I haven't signed up yet."

They agree to walk to his house after school. Lulu has trouble concentrating all afternoon. Just before dismissal she rushes into the girls' bathroom, combs her frizzy hair with her fingers, and applies strawberry-flavoured lip gloss. Fat face but no pimples. Flushed, she's been sweating all day in too many layers. Mom says other girls would kill for that complexion and those eyelashes. Lulu can't see it.

"Hey," he says when she joins him on the sidewalk. She feels so squat beside him, but maybe he thinks her petite.

They walk down Quinpool Road, and eventually he turns right instead of left, as Helen did. In this neighbourhood, the houses are close together and old-looking, some splashed in bright colours, green with orange trim, or blue and pink.

They make a couple of turns, Lulu taking big strides to keep up. Eventually he stops and pulls out a key. His house is grey and skinny with a bow window. He lets them into a tiny windowed vestibule with patterned floor tile. They hang their jackets on hooks and enter the dim hallway. A steep flight of wooden stairs rises before them, the ghosts of all who used them these past seventy-five or hundred years condensed into pale, shallow foot pools.

"We'll work in the kitchen," he says.

She glances to her left as they pass. The high-ceilinged front room is stuffed with cardboard boxes, but she can see a fireplace and a red chesterfield, a number of framed paintings leaning against the wall.

The kitchen is brighter and newer. Forest green countertops run along pale wood cabinets, and a tall window reveals a small fenced yard. He throws his backpack onto the table and goes to a cupboard. She sits and digs out the two pages she wrote last night, nervous to show them to him.

He pours them glasses of chocolate milk and sits, takes her handwritten pages without speaking. She watches his eyes move. The digital alarm clock on the counter clicks; numbers printed on black cards fall inside the clear plastic face, like a slow blink. She sips her milk.

"We can change it," she says. "We can erase it all, if you think. I just used modern language."

"This is good," he says, looking up. "I like how he seems shady but Juliet can't see that." He smiles. Lulu wasn't aware she'd done that, but she nods.

"I was thinking, maybe, after they meet, he leaves and Juliet spies on him," she says.

"And realizes who he really is," Matt says, finishing her sentence. "But is it too soon? Maybe Antonio needs to lead her along for a while."

"We only have five pages."

His eyes sparkle. "You're right. I forgot."

"So he's horrible. He doesn't care about love," Lulu says, feeling bolder. "Why does he go after her?"

They look at each other. He chuckles.

"What do you think? Sex. The oldest reason, probably." He laughs but it's not mean, he can't be making fun of her. Her face burns. She's a naïve idiot. She was leading them down a road and didn't know it.

"But we can't say that," she says, pretending to study the lines she knows by heart. How are they sitting in his kitchen, three feet apart, talking about sex? Knees practically touching. He looks relaxed. His family probably discusses sex at the dinner table.

"We won't have to." He lifts the papers from her hand, he almost touches her, and scratches out some of her lines. "Let's make him sound really slimy," he says, scribbling. He holds the paper before him. "How's this? 'Juliet, you make me tingle all over.'"

They laugh. "Don't be ridiculous, Matt."

They decide on a scene finale and he says he'll work on it tonight. She's startled to see darkness and light snowflakes beyond the window. They're reflected in the glass, floating, a boy and a girl in a snow globe. She sucks in her tummy.

The front door opens. "Hello," a woman calls.

Matt introduces his mother, Diane, who has a brown bob and large glasses, a wide, lipsticked smile; and his sister, Haley, who looks about twelve and has his curls.

"Nice to meet you, Lulu," Diane says, removing her coat. She wears a black blazer and black pointy boots visible at the hem of her matching slacks.

Diane insists Matt drive Lulu home. She won't accept Lulu's protests, and within a few minutes the two of them are sitting in the family's little red car.

It's cramped and his head almost touches the roof. She's paralyzed. He pulls away from the curb and says she'll need to direct him. But she doesn't know the streets like a driver. She never pays attention when her parents drive her places, and her sixteenth birthday, when she can get a license, isn't until summer.

They take a few wrong turns until eventually she finds Robie Street, the long main road running north–south. She's relieved. This is her bus route and he can follow it home.

"I live far," she says as they make slow progress in the five o'clock traffic.

"Nothing's far compared to Toronto," he says, stopping at a red light.

"Must seem rinky-dink, huh?"

He shrugs. "Mom says Halifax is a perfect-sized city. They thought Toronto was getting too big."

"But you miss your friends? Your...girlfriend?"

He looks over. "I didn't say I had a girlfriend."

"Oh. I just thought."

He doesn't speak the rest of the way. She's annoyed him. They pull up to her building, he idles the car, and her impulse is to say she's moving to a house soon. But she's mute. They'd been a bright planet, floating in the black glass, laughing. She glances over and he's looking at her. He clears his throat.

"Okay, well, see you tomorrow," he says.

"Sure. Catch ya later."

She closes her eyes and grimaces. Climbs out and watches him pull away.

June

June has picked up the habit in recent years, like an old person, of reading the daily obituaries in the newspaper. Since Mom died, though, she can't look at them. On this morning, she's about to skip the section when she recognizes a name: Albert Winthrop. Evelyn's husband.

June should visit her. She was so good to Mom. Even though Evelyn has a high-class air, and Mom didn't have much schooling, they somehow became friends late in life.

Gerald enters the kitchen, hair sticking up and cranky-looking, the new him. She can't touch his grief. Her own squeezes her and she moves carefully through her days. She considers telling him about Albert, but it would upset him.

He smears peanut butter on a slice of bread, always too much. How would he react if he knew how he'd come into the world? She's unsure of his understanding of sex. If something romantic or racy comes on TV he covers his eyes with his hands, making a show of it, making them laugh. They've never discussed it and if he ever had any desires, he never told her.

She didn't know how much he wanted to know his father. She'd thought she, their little family, was enough. But every TV family has a father. The dads can be stern or wise or goofy, but they're at the centre of those make-believe homes.

"Gerald," she says, "what's up today?"

Nothing, of course. The social worker was by again and says she's worried about his state of mind. It would be good to get him out of the house. She checks the obituary; the funeral's in two days, so Evelyn should be home.

"We're going to visit Evelyn."

Gerald looks up. At least they'll accomplish one thing this day. Half an hour later they're walking, in a damp cold that goes through you. She remembers her wish to buy a car and learn to drive. She reaches to pull the knitted cap over Gerald's ears and he ducks.

Evelyn smiles at the door but seems smaller, older. It smells clean inside, not the funeral lily smell of some houses in mourning. She leads them to the kitchen, where platters of sweets cover the table, an iced bundt cake with a slice cut out of it.

"Our church friends," she explains with a wave of her hand, and begins filling the kettle.

"Here, let me do that," June says. "You don't need to wait on us."

"No, dear, I'm fine. You sit. Gerald, help yourself." He's been eyeing the display and grabs a few treats, then wanders into the front room.

Evelyn tells her about Albert's last, painful weeks, how she finally had to take him to hospital though he'd wished to die at home. She sat vigil with him for three days until, mercifully, he passed. That's what she says, "passed." It sounds gentle. Mom died. She died in a heap and probably in pain, on the floor of the dank basement.

Evelyn looks flat. June knows it's an effort to get it out. She never noticed Evelyn's pretty eyes, sort of violet. A beauty when she was young. June yearns to bring up Mom but it's not right given Evelyn's loss. It should be her time.

"Your mother grieved your father terribly," Evelyn says. A gift to June.

"I don't know if I knew that. Not after so many years."

Evelyn smiles. "She told me all about him, how he wooed her, the strapping young man with a big laugh." Her smile drops. "I suppose I'll grieve Albert just as badly. A life partner, you don't get over that."

June's eyes moisten. When you've lost someone, you long to hear their name. But after the funeral, people don't say it. Most don't ask how you are in case you actually tell them.

Evelyn places a hand on top of June's. "I still miss my mother deeply, thirty years later," she says.

June says, "I just. I wish we'd talked more."

Evelyn's eyes are so clear. She seems so open-minded.

"Did she ever," June begins, "talk about Gerald's...birth?"

"She told me all she knew." She looks into June's eyes. "But she never thought ill of you. She was hurt, wished you'd shared what had happened."

"I couldn't, Evelyn," she says and looks down at the table. "I was ashamed. I felt so dirty."

The ticking of the wall clock seems exaggerated. June broke the seal last week with Barry, and the world kept turning. He's kept it to himself. She needs Evelyn, this stand-in mother, right now. She looks up.

"I was raped. By Mr. Connelly, my boss at the Frugal Mart. I couldn't tell anybody. I thought I'd led him on."

Evelyn's face crumples. "Oh my lord," she says. "You poor thing. You must not blame yourself."

June weeps. Evelyn comes and hugs her so June's head is pressed against her bosom. June flashes to her grandmother, who could soothe any baby against her shelf of a bust.

"That man," Evelyn mumbles. "I feel like marching into that store."

"I couldn't tell Mom and Dad. Dad would've killed him. Mom would've died of shock." June sits back and wipes her eyes.

"No, she was a strong woman," says Evelyn, handing her a tissue.

June leaves the house exhausted, eyes sore. Gerald, on the other hand, has cheered up. He takes her hand and she looks over, surprised. Perhaps he senses her sadness. She'll tell him about Albert later. She wants to say something else. It's scary to utter the words, never spoken in their house.

"I love you, Gerald."

"Love you, Mom."

The words were there, on his tongue. She smiles. It's the happiest she's felt in weeks.

"When are we getting our Christmas tree?"

Oh, she's been avoiding every thought of Christmas. Doesn't want to face it this year or ever again. Everything went through her mother: decorations, gifts, turkey and plum pudding, old carols on the record player. Their little family crowded into the front room, laughing at whatever silly wind-up toy Mom had managed to find Gerald this time. Mom would beam. She made it all happen, saving for the extras all year in her "Christmas Tin." June wishes she could sleep through the coming weeks.

"It's a bit early, isn't it?" she says. He kicks a stone onto the road. Her heart throbs, for him, for Mom, for herself.

"We'll get one, kid," she says, "as soon as the tree lots open."

They walk past their old street. Barry hasn't called since Gerald's birthday. Well frig him. She opened up and he's punishing her for it. Ah well, he's hurting, too. She couldn't live in that house alone.

That evening, she calls and asks him to find her a cheap used car. He sounds surprised but says he'll ask around. Lorne enters the kitchen while she's on the phone, and as she hangs up he asks what's going on.

"I'm getting a car," she says, turning toward the sink full of dishes.

"What do you need a car for? You don't even drive."

She turns and pauses for effect, like an actress. "I want some independence."

He snorts. "You're free to do whatever you want, Junie. Independence. You turning into one of those women's libbers?"

"Yeah, maybe I am. Who knows, Lorne? You better watch yourself."

He looks at her odd.

Lulu

D ad says you need money to make money, and that's why they'll never be rich. He's back, and he and Mom are cuddly and giggly. Sickening. Lulu doesn't want to think about her parents getting romantic. She wraps her pillow around her head to drown out the tittering in their bedroom.

Still, Dad's cheerful and Mom's not going to the pub. She told Lulu she and Dad have been together too long to throw it all away.

"Who else would have us now?" she said and laughed.

Mom's promising Christmas will be extra special this year. Only Jimmy will be missing, spending another holiday in Ontario with some distant cousin.

Lulu figures her new value is she's been seen with a handsome guy. Now she's popular. Helen spoke to her in the corridor yesterday when she was with Matt, and suggested they hang out. Lulu said maybe. Two girls she doesn't really know—cheerleaders—said hello in the bathroom. And now Janet's approaching her on the bus.

Janet swings onto the seat next to Lulu. She wears more makeup these days along with that volleyball jacket.

"How're things, Lulu?"

"Good."

"That's amazing about Liz, huh? They just let her come back for some reason." Janet pulls out a banana and peels it. The banana's too brown and Lulu has to look away.

"So," Janet says, "I hear you've got a boyfriend. The new guy from Toronto." She rolls her eyes. "Cute." She takes a bite.

"We're friends," Lulu says. Then adds, "But I've been to his house."

"Really?" Janet leans in.

Damn, she shouldn't have given her that.

"But like how," Janet says, "how did you, I don't want to be insulting, but how did you become his first friend? How come you?" She tilts her head.

Lulu feels an intense heat. "Why, Janet? Why, because I'm overweight? Because I don't play sports? Because I'm not in a popular group? What exactly do you mean, Janet?"

Janet shrinks back. "I didn't mean," she says. "It's just…"

"What *did* you mean?"

The girl across the aisle stares and Lulu realizes she's almost shouting. Whatever. After all those years together—playing Barbies, wearing matching training bras, lingering outside on fragrant summer nights, not wanting the days to end—Janet can't think of any reason Lulu might land a friend.

Janet hasn't even asked why Lulu was hanging on the corner with Helen and Danny, but it must be driving her crazy.

"You dumped me," says Lulu. "And now you're crawling back because you think I have a cute jock boyfriend." She motions Janet to move. "Get up. I'll stand the rest of the way."

"I didn't dump you," Janet says, but Lulu motions again and Janet has to swing her legs to the side. She looks confused.

Lulu grasps the metal pole and lets her body move, closes her eyes and feels dizzy. But it's good. Dizzy is good. Shaking things up. Things are changing, she can feel it.

She floats through the day and when she sees Matt in English after lunch, she's feeling good about herself. He leans over and hands her the final version of their scene.

"Let me know what you think," he says, grinning.

As the teacher begins the lesson Lulu sneaks a peek. He's changed it. She looks over and he winks. When class ends she wants to talk but he slips away, teasing her. "Meet me at three," he says from halfway down the hall.

He waits in his usual spot, wearing a basketball jacket. On the team already, lured by the coach, no doubt. He's slipping away and soon he'll be swept up, busy with games and cheerleaders. After this assignment she'll have no excuse to talk to him. He holds up his hands in mock defence.

"Now, don't get mad. Hear me out," he says, walking briskly. Lulu follows in a rush.

"I figured Juliet should stand up for herself," he says over his shoulder. "Come on. I'm cold."

"But Matt, she kills Antonio."

"Hilarious, right?"

"But Matt, this is a romance. Juliet is, what, twelve, thirteen? She can't go around killing people."

"Why not? Antonio's a jerk."

They stop and face each other. Students walk around them. Lulu's on the verge of tears. It's been an emotional day, her high on the bus this morning spiralling into this.

"You've ruined it," she says, her voice breaking.

He frowns. "I thought you'd appreciate it. You know, one strong woman to another."

"You just rewrote it without asking."

He shakes his head. "So change it back then."

She holds out the pages and they snap in the wind. He turns and walks away. The deadline will be here in a flash. They're supposed to act it out together in class; they should practice, maybe rewrite. He disappears down a side street. She'll never go to his house again.

She boards the bus for home, where Helen and Danny cuddle in the back. Lulu chooses a spot farther up and slumps in the seat; she's ruined everything. Matt was just trying to have fun, she supposes. What should she care about a couple of fictional characters? But he went off on his own without asking. She thought they had a plan, that they were a team.

"Hey." Lulu turns and Danny's sitting behind her.

"What the fuck you doing, spreading stories about me?" He juts his face toward her and she pulls back. "What is it with you, girl? What you got against me? Kidnapping?" He lets out a sarcastic laugh.

"I—"

"You think I give a shit about Gerald Green?" he growls. "That I'd try to snatch him?"

He bends and spits into the middle of the aisle. It lands as a quivering glob. Two boys across the way screw up their faces in disgust. Danny stands.

"If you know what's good for ya, stay away from me—and my girlfriend." He returns to Helen, who gives Lulu a shrug and an apologetic smile.

Lulu faces front, willing herself not to cry. She's done it now. Danny, a bear poked awake. An actual enemy, and a nasty one. He probably didn't know who she was before she and Janet followed him that day, and now he's threatening her. She should tell Mom and Dad. No, don't breathe another word about him. To anyone.

At the stop by the drugstore, Helen and Danny get off without looking at her. Lulu stays put. Liz is in the store, coat on, talking to Farrell. Lulu stuck her nose in there too, though she meant well.

But when she told Helen about Danny, it was out of spite. Admit it. Maybe she wanted to hurt Helen or get her back in some strange way. And now it's a mess.

In her bedroom she tries to put Danny out of her mind. She pulls out the crumpled pages she and Matt have laboured over, erasing, rewriting, trading off. Two styles of handwriting, hers round and curlicued, his small and tight. They look weird together.

June

Damnit. *Damn him. Damn this car.*

June jams the stick shift, trying to reverse. But her size-five foot lifts off the clutch by mistake, and the Bug stalls. Yeah, a goddamn ten-year-old VW Beetle, painted blue. Like being inside a tin can. Thanks, Barry.

She inhales, tries again, and gets the timing right. The car coughs. She backs out of the driveway and makes a series of jerky stops and starts, hands overworking the steering wheel as if she were piloting a ship in the harbour, until she's in the road facing forward. Wrong direction for Trudy's but she'll circle round.

June squints into the bright morning sunshine. *Keep going, Little Putt Putt.* That's what Gerald calls it. The streets could be slick this morning, with the frost overnight, but she wanted to drive. Made herself.

Lorne shook his head in disgust when she said she was taking the car out Christmas shopping on a Saturday. He's been pissy since she got her beginner's license last week, all done in record time; she and Barry yelling at each other in a parking lot as he gave her a crash course in driving. That's what Lorne called it, "a crash course."

"Get it?" he said, laughing.

June's not supposed to drive by herself. She's supposed to have a licensed driver with her until she gets her full license. But screw it, no harm in sneaking the six blocks to Trudy's.

Trudy waits at the curb, jaunty in a tam, her breath visible in the brisk, silvery air. June stops, feet hovering, balancing. *Don't stall, Putt Putt.* The passenger door squeaks and Trudy climbs in.

"It's freezing," she says. Fiddles with the heating knob and turns to June. "Look at you," she says, "all grown up, driving."

"Don't distract me," June says, squinting. She worries she'll need glasses soon, another expense.

They head for the largest shopping centre in Halifax. June needs to take some busy roads, and the women don't speak until they reach the parking lot. June parks at a bad angle, exhales, and gets out. She peers across the wide road at the other shopping centre, where Gerald ended up that day. Lies. They get people in trouble.

The mall is packed and the two friends stick close together. June would love to buy Gerald a jacket for Christmas, but she doesn't like the prices. Trudy leads them into a department store, and they soon get lost in the business of sampling perfume on their wrists. Trudy spritzes one on, under the eye of a saleswoman in a black dress and pearl beads. Trudy raises her chin and exposes her neck.

"Smell," she says. June obliges, shrugs.

"They all smell the same now," she says.

Trudy runs her hand down the display of tester bottles, uncapping some and sniffing. The saleswoman turns to another customer.

"I want something sexy," Trudy says. "For New Year's."

June groans. Everyone's supposed to have fun on New Year's Eve. So forced, so many bad blind dates. Looking back at a blah year and having no hopes for the coming year. Though she can't wait to say goodbye to this shitty year. Guess it will be a new decade, the 1980s.

"So," June whispers, "I've told a few people."

"Told them what?" says Trudy, sniffing a glass bottle in the shape of a high-heel shoe.

"You know." June wants Trudy to look at her. Trudy turns her head.

June nods once for emphasis. "You know."

Trudy widens her eyes. "You didn't," she says too loudly.

"Who'd you tell?"

June pulls her away from the counter. "Barry. Then Evelyn. She just seems so...motherly."

"Holy shit. What'd they say?"

"Barry was irate I hadn't told Mom and Dad, said I'd let them think I was a slut."

Trudy frowns.

"Maybe he's disgusted," June says. "He helped me with the car but it's like he can't stand being around me."

They ride the escalator to the basement and enter the store café.

"He's your big brother," Trudy says, sliding into a booth. "I bet he's guilty he couldn't protect you or something. He'll get over it."

They order fries and gravy. June feels a moment of contentment, out with a friend and having a big talk. She can't talk to Lorne like this.

"And then Evelyn," she continues. "It just came out. She was close to Mom at the end, so it was almost like telling Mom. I always worried my mother would hate me for what happened in that stockroom. But Evelyn said don't be silly."

"Must've made you feel good."

"I guess." June sips her pop.

Trudy pushes away her half-eaten plate and lights a cigarette. That's how she stays slim. She appears to study June through cigarette smoke. That always makes June edgy.

"What?" June says.

"Have you ever wanted revenge?"

June is taken aback. "What do you mean?"

"You know," Trudy says, "get back at him somehow. Just living his life, wifey cooking for him every night and two girls who went through college, I hear."

June looks at the orange Formica table, shakes her head. "You're crazy." Her voice has softened.

Trudy leans in. "I'm serious. Think about it. I could help you." She stubs out her smoke. "We could get that bastard good."

"Right," June says. "Bonnie and Clyde."

She stalls the car twice on the way home. Trudy tells her to take it easy. As she leaves, Trudy suggests June and Lorne come over tonight to play cards. June promises to call later but knows she won't.

She's grateful for the quiet in the house, Lorne likely down at the hardware store. She yells up to Gerald and he mumbles a response. She sits in the kitchen and lights a cigarette. Revenge. Trudy's cracked. All these years June has barely mustered any anger over the assault. But why?

Anger's powerful and hard to control once it gets inside you. Don't they call it the green monster? Or is that jealousy? Anyway, she knows what always tamped down her anger: shame. That's stronger than anything.

But people—Evelyn, Trudy—are saying she shouldn't blame herself. Still, she hasn't told Lorne for fear he'd be disgusted too. It's ridiculous, him being the last to know. Like the day of Mom's fire.

She rises and opens the fridge door. No ideas for supper. She wanders into the front room. A family—a man and woman and two pink-cheeked children in knitted pom-pom hats—leave the house across the street and get into a car. Trudy said Connelly's two kids went to college. What has he ever done for kid number three?

Lulu

That evening Lulu sits on her bed and rereads Matt's version of the scene. Juliet meets Antonio while out for an evening walk, and soon after he's dead. Antonio makes a pass at Juliet—shoves her against a stone wall and gropes her—and, terrified, she feels above her and pulls out a big rock. She clunks him on the head and he falls, bleeding and unconscious. Juliet flees, crying and believing she's killed him. The scene ends with Antonio taking his last breath.

Lulu had pictured Juliet telling off Antonio in fine style. But Matt's Juliet is more interesting. She meets this Antonio and he turns out to be a monster. A bad encounter in the woods, sort of like Red Riding Hood. She has to admit, Matt wrote a strong Juliet who turns violent. It's an exciting scene.

"Be daring," the English teacher had said.

Lulu takes out fresh paper and begins writing out three identical copies of the scene: one for the teacher and one for each of them. It has some of her original dialogue but it's Matt's version. It's better.

She finishes around eleven o'clock and slips the pages into her bag. She hopes Matt will be pleased about her change of heart, but she's unsure he's even speaking to her. She stands, stiff, and goes out to the kitchen. Viv sits at the table with the little lamp on, pencil in one hand and cigarette in the other. Her crossword is almost finished.

"Hi."

Viv looks up. "Hi, hon. What's up?"

Lulu takes a can of pop out of the fridge. "Not much. Where's Dad?"

"The Legion. How's school?"

She's barely asked all year. Lulu swigs her root beer and considers. Part of her wants to talk about Matt. Viv raises an eyebrow.

"Any boys in the picture?" she says.

"Maybe."

Viv smiles. "Give me the scoop."

"No, it's nothing."

"Come on. Maybe I can help."

Lulu leans against the counter. "There's a guy, moved here from Toronto," she says. "We're doing an English project together. He's perfect. But I think he hates me now."

"Why do you say that?"

"We had an argument over the project."

"Well I doubt he'd hate you because of that." Viv stubs out her cigarette.

Lulu's annoyed. Mothers always downplay things. "You didn't see him." She feels like returning to her bedroom.

"What's he like? What's his name?"

"Matt. Tall, a basketball player. And he's smart."

"Ooh, the deadly combination of looks and brains. That's how your father hooked me."

Lulu laughs. "Dad?"

Viv frowns. "Don't be mean. Your father's one of the smartest people I know. He would have loved to become an engineer or something. But there's no way he could afford it. Same as me." She stands and sloshes the remainder of her tea into the sink.

"That's why he's grumpy a lot of the time, I imagine. He can be hard to live with." She turns to face Lulu. "He wanted to build bridges. Instead he drives around the Maritimes selling car parts. It's dirty, lonely work."

Lulu never looked at her father in this way. He's so quiet, unless he's drinking.

"So don't judge people, Lu, without knowing the full story. Why people are sad or cranky." She places a hand on Lulu's shoulder. "Anyway, sorry honey, we didn't really talk about your guy. But I'm beat."

June

On Monday morning, June lets herself into the old house. Barry's at work and doesn't know she's coming over. It still smells smoky, weeks after the fire. An open pizza box sits on the kitchen counter, dried-up crusts tossed inside. The garbage can overflows with greasy paper wrapping for fish and chips, and takeout burger bags.

She sighs and takes off her coat. Curses—why should she have to clean up after another man? But she hates seeing the house this way, so she whisks the smelly food remains into the garbage, fills the sink with hot soapy water that's a balm in the cold house, and washes the dishes. She sweeps the floor, finally tosses a tea bag into a mug, and pours over boiling water. She sits but not in Mom's chair.

That last morning. Finding Mom through that door and down the stairs. She turns her back and sips the tea gingerly, willing the scalding liquid to distract her. Dust motes dance in the soft December sunlight. Mom spent most of her life in this small room, with a view to the back lane and Mrs. Parsons's garbage cans. Was it enough? June's eyes fill with tears. She shakes herself.

She's come to look at Mom's things. She's not promising she'll do much with them, but she will look. Barry claims he can't handle it. He's one of those old-style men who seems baffled by women's clothing and personal items. He'd probably hold up one of Mom's old girdles and scratch his head. So she'll take a look, a peace offering.

Over the years, Mom's bedroom door was always open, perhaps a habit from her days as a young mother. Barry has pulled the door tight and June needs to shove with her shoulder to get in. The floral curtains are drawn. She hesitates, flicks on the ceiling light.

She always liked this bed, a cream wooden headboard with storage above the pillows, little sliding doors concealing a space to stash paperbacks. The worn bedspread is pulled askew. It should go.

June goes down to the kitchen and returns with garbage bags, packs up the bedspread and mismatched sheets. Dad's Zane Greys are still in the headboard, along with Mom's Harlequins. She sets them aside to give away.

On the dresser sits her mother's wooden hairbrush, face cream, a framed wedding photo, and, strangely, a spatula. June picks up the familiar photo: Mom wears a dark, modest dress past her knees and a quirky little hat; Dad's baggy suit was borrowed. They grin shyly at the camera.

Mom once told June that her wedding day, in the little white church down on the Shore, was the first time she'd had her photograph taken. June has glanced at this photo hundreds of times. She never noticed her parents posed while holding hands.

She inhales, then yanks open the top dresser drawer. There's a tangle of large brassieres and ratty underwear, pantyhose interlaced like tentacles. It smells like her. She grasps the mass and jams it into the garbage bag.

Margie has stashed an assortment of papers in here: her marriage license, Dad's obituary snipped from the newspaper, random report cards for June and Barry, a twenty-year-old receipt for a snow shovel. A plastic sleeve holds two yellowed birth announcements: Barry Edward, born March 12, 1929; June Rose, born September 6, 1933. That must have cost them money.

She's about to close the drawer when she feels something at the back, a small black velvet bag embroidered with the name of a jeweller. A customer once showed her such a bag, containing sapphire earrings her husband had given her for their anniversary. "You should wear sapphires," the woman said, holding one up to June's cheek. "They match your eyes."

June tugs on the silky drawstring and spills the bag's contents into her palm. She frowns, then gets it: baby teeth. Five of them, lumpen and darkened over time.

She sinks onto the bare mattress. *Mom, I'm so sorry. I'm sorry I was a bad daughter. I yelled at you, I lied. I'm sorry. You meant the world to me. I loved you. And I never told you.*

She swallows, fighting the tightening in her throat.

"Don't cry, June," says a voice in her head. "Baby June."

She opens her eyes. Of course she imagined something comforting. But it did sound like Mom. It's been tormenting her, that she can't remember the sound of her mother's voice. The only thing she can hear in Mom's voice is "hello."

She said it every morning when June entered the kitchen before work. Always chipper and drawn out, even when they'd quarrelled the night before or the weather was nasty or they were worried about paying for furnace oil. "Hell-o." Happy to see you. An everyday, throwaway word but June's been replaying it again and again.

She drags the bags down the stairs, thump, thump, depositing them out back beside other garbage. She places Mom's papers in her purse, then considers the velvet bag. What in hell will she do with a bunch of old teeth? She tosses it into the kitchen garbage bin, puts on her coat, and goes to the front door. Stops. Goes back and retrieves the velvet bag.

That night, Lorne gets home around six thirty. June watches him, in his undershirt and thick grey work socks, wolf down warmed-up haddock and potatoes. She was thinking of telling her secret tonight but she's losing her nerve. He pushes away his plate.

"How's your insect?" he says, lighting a cigarette. He knows she hates him calling the Bug an insect.

"Drove it all over town today."

He exhales smoke. "You don't want to get in trouble, do you?"

"Maybe I do. Maybe you don't know me, Lorne. Maybe you don't really know me at all."

He gets up from the table. "Maybe I don't. 'Cause you're sure acting cuckoo these days." He pours a mug of tea.

"My mother just died. In the basement. And maybe I have other reasons to be cuckoo."

He leans his backside against the stove, looking almost as tired as she feels. The bags under his eyes are as dark as his irises. "Is there something you wanna say to me? 'Cause if there is, spit it out."

I'm a tramp, a tease.

She grips her tea cup tighter but the warmth's gone out of it. "Did you ever wonder," she says, "about Gerald's father?"

"You said he was an old boyfriend. Left town after."

June shakes her head. "I lied. Lied to you and to Mom and Dad and to everyone."

"Well, who was it then?" he says, softer. "It's all history anyway."

She takes a deep breath. "I was raped," she says. The house has never felt so quiet. "By the assistant manager at the store where I worked." *Shit, can Gerald hear upstairs?*

Lorne stands straighter. "Raped?"

She fights looking away.

"Why didn't you tell me?" he says, louder. "Why didn't you tell me before?

"You wouldn't wanna know," she says. "You never even asked who the boyfriend was."

"*What?*" He bangs down his mug and faces the window, hangs his head.

"You think differently about me now?" she says.

"Jesus, June, I don't know what to think." He turns to her. "Did you report it to the cops?"

She brings her hands to her face. "I couldn't. I was ashamed to tell anybody."

"And so you let this guy, this *animal*, get away with it."

"I knew this would happen. You're mad at me," she says, her voice cracking. "I was just a kid. I did the best I could." She stands and heads for the front hallway.

"I'm not mad at you," he calls. He steps closer. "What else haven't you told me?" His dark eyes bore into hers and she can barely stand there, Lorne looking at her and seeing what's inside.

"We've known each other how long?" he says. "But you're a stranger to me."

She shakes her head no. He's the cold one, not her. "You sleep down here tonight," she says finally, and starts up the stairs.

"For fuck's sake."

She taps on Gerald's door and pokes her head in. He lies on his bed with the transistor radio on his chest.

He smiles. "Christmas music."

"Nice. Now go to sleep."

"But it's only eight o'clock," he says and giggles.

She goes into her bedroom and shuts the door.

Lulu

It's a messy day. Students enter the English room after lunch, hems of their jeans soaked, snowflakes melting in their hair, textbooks water-stained. Lulu waits outside the classroom for Matt. She's dry, having spent lunchtime inside by herself.

He turns the corner and hurries down the corridor, last to arrive. He hesitates before her, stops. She holds out the final version of their assignment.

"I made good copies," she says.

He takes one and glances at it.

"It's your scene," says Lulu. "You were right. It's better."

He looks up. "You sure?"

"Yeah." She smiles. "Dumb to argue over it."

He opens his mouth to say something, but the teacher calls to come in and close the door. Helen is absent. When class ends, Lulu suggests they go through the scene together today.

"I can't. Basketball practice, and then a game Saturday."

"Well when then? We have to present it next week."

"Come to my place Sunday." He holds out a notebook. "Write down your phone number. I'll call that morning." Lulu writes and he hurries off.

She feels sick but elated. Come to think of it, she's felt this way since starting high school. On the way home she decides to visit the drugstore. She's been thinking about Liz. When she enters, Miriam is stocking shelves.

"Well hello, stranger," Miriam says, turning at the sound of the door. "Our paths don't cross too much."

She's wearing a bulky, collared cardigan with a wolf head spread across the back—likely knit by her reclusive mother, Lulu has heard all about her—and blue eyeshadow up to her brows. Miriam makes Lulu feel dirty, criticizing Farrell behind his back, complaining about her job and her husband, gossiping about pretty well every customer who walks in. Lulu avoids her if she can. She chooses some gum at random and places it on the counter. Miriam waves it off.

"Take it," she says. She gestures toward the back of the store. "He won't know."

"No, I want to pay." Lulu digs out the money and Miriam shrugs.

"So," Lulu says, "I saw Liz was here the other day."

"That one," Miriam says, lighting a cigarette. "Something isn't right with her. Why'd she run away all of a sudden? Off to Montreal or something."

She leans on the counter and Lulu steps back from the coffee and cigarette breath. She assumed Miriam would hear the gossip about Liz but guess not.

"Is she going to start working here again?" Lulu says.

"No idea. I hope Farrell tells her to pound sand. Though we're entering our busy season."

This is funny. Farrell has stocked up on boxed gift sets of cheap cologne, aftershave, and talcum powder, arranged in a pyramid in the front window. He's brought in boxes of Christmas chocolates too, but the prices are outrageous compared to the Frugal Mart. Customers complain about it all the time.

The door tinkles. It's Tom, in a leather Dalhousie jacket and his fair hair longer. He buys a pack of cigarettes, looks at Lulu, and motions with his head: *Meet me outside.*

"Well, I'm going," she says, trying to sound casual.

"Okay, hon," says Miriam. "You're in tomorrow I suppose."

Lulu and Tom exit and walk a few paces past the store windows.

He turns. "I'm looking for Liz. Have you seen her?" He's scanning the street, not even looking at her.

"No, not in a long time."

He sighs.

"Though she came to the store the other day," Lulu offers.

"I need to talk to her. I can't find her on campus."

"Have you tried her house? She's living there again."

He looks at her. "Of course I tried her house. I'm sure her witch of a mother isn't relaying my messages. I just drove by and the place was dark." He seems to study her. "She used to talk to you. She liked you." She tries to look neutral. He dips his chin.

"I know why she went to Montreal," he says in a low voice. "Why didn't she tell me?"

Lulu shakes her head no. As if she knew what Liz was thinking.

"I'm all for women's rights, you know?" he says. "But still."

She hunches her shoulders. "I don't know."

He steps to the curb. "If you see her, tell her I really want to talk."

He darts across the street, through the slush, and into a little Toyota. He didn't even offer her a drive home.

She starts up the hill. She feels bad for him; he seems genuinely wounded. She admired Liz, deciding for herself and going away for a scary operation, paying for it herself. But it was Tom's baby too.

Her sneakers are soaked and she shivers in the dusk. A car horn beeps and Dad pulls up to the curb. She climbs in, the warm air blasting from the vents and the upbeat music the most welcoming hug she's received in a long time.

"Guess what?" he says, grinning. "Don't tell your mother, it's a surprise, but Jimmy's coming home for Christmas. I sent him the train fare."

Lulu smiles. In fact, she cheers.

June

June lies sleepless that night and she's sure Lorne's awake too, his bare back to her. The words seem to hover in the darkness: *rape, lie.* "What else haven't you told me?"

He rises in the weak light of dawn, dresses, and slips out the front door. She rolls over. The rape—she has to keep calling it that, no glossing it over—has shadowed her entire life. She's sick of it. Gerald, she's eternally thankful for. A pearl created in the muck. But her shame, her lies, have held her back.

Lorne said he doesn't know her, even after all these years. Maybe she is a tough nut. But how can they talk when he's so damn cranky all the time? Grumpy after a long day, snappy when she reminds him about the renovations. Still awkward around Gerald. Making fun of her wish to drive.

That afternoon she discovers she's out of potatoes. Mom would be horrified; a Nova Scotia house never runs out of the staple. June considers driving but she's been pushing her luck driving illegally. She pulls on boots and a coat and leans on the newel post at the bottom of the stairs.

"Gerald," she calls, "get your coat on. We need some air."

They head out and the sun feels good on her face. The world is melting and the street gutters run with sparkling water. On Isleville Street she hesitates. They could turn right and go to the nearby convenience store, but she feels a pull, Trudy's words in her head, and finds herself moving north.

"Why we going this way?" says Gerald.

"They have better potatoes up here."

It's slippery, meltwater slicking the sidewalk. It takes a long twenty-five minutes to reach the Frugal Mart. Gerald continues toward the entrance but June says stop. He turns, looking puzzled.

They need potatoes for supper. People come and go from the store. It's a public place; nothing more can happen to her in there. She can walk out anytime. She grasps Gerald's hand and they push through the glass doors.

It's an assault: harsh lights, music, bodies. Cash registers ring. Someone shouts for a delivery boy. It smells like raw meat. Connelly must be in here somewhere. She doesn't want to see him; part of her does want to see him.

"Excuse me," a woman says. They're blocking the entrance. They step farther inside and Gerald slips from her grip and goes toward the produce section on the far wall. June follows as if in a dream. She hasn't been here in almost thirty years, yet it could be 1950 again.

God, that's Sandy at the till, still slaving away. Living with her sister, June has heard, and still favouring pin curls at her temples. Sandy looks up.

Gerald hoists a twenty-pound paper bag of potatoes for June to see. She nods. She had other items on her mental shopping list but it doesn't matter. *Let's make it quick.* She gestures that he follow her to a cash register. Sandy's line is shorter and Gerald is drawn to it, but June shakes her head and grabs his sleeve.

"Over here," she hisses, dragging him into another lineup.

The wait is endless. Beside them, Sandy rings through baking ingredients and wrapping paper. Her face is too lined for a woman her age. When they were teenagers, Sandy confided her dream of becoming a stewardess and travelling the world. She showed June a picture in a magazine of an airplane with a spiral staircase that led to an upstairs cocktail lounge for passengers.

"But I don't have the legs for it," Sandy told her. "Or the face."

June's dreams were simpler. She'd planned to enroll in secretarial school after high school and get an office job, answer phones, type and make tea, be efficient and needed, in her own way. Not slave on her feet all day. Dad worked on his feet at the brewery, Mom too when she clerked in shops. Sitting, a weird symbol of success.

Finally it's their turn and Gerald thumps the potatoes onto the moving belt.

"Just a sec," says the young cashier, "I need to change my tape."

"I don't need a receipt," June says.

The girl fumbles with the used tape in the cash register. "I need a new tape, to record sales," she says, not looking up. June closes her eyes, trying to remain calm. This was a bad idea.

"Here, let me help with that."

His voice. It always had a bit of a joke in it but no one else knew what was funny. June opens her eyes and it's him, squeezed next to the cashier, looking into the bowels of the register. His hair's streaked with grey and he's heavier, but it's Connelly. He inserts the new register tape, slaps closed the lid, and pushes a few buttons.

"There," he says, smiling, "good to go." He steps back so the cashier can take her post, and looks at the customers.

Gerald stands before him, serious and expectant. June holds her wallet, holds her breath. Connelly stops smiling. They haven't seen each other since that day, years ago, when they found themselves on opposite sides of the street. Both hurried off.

Connelly looks at Gerald and back at June. She inhales and tries to harden her eyes. He turns on his heel and hurries away.

The cashier tells June the amount owing, again. June pays and they get out of there, and when she steps onto the pavement outside, she thinks she might crumple. But she doesn't. Gerald leads the way and she follows, she puts one foot in front of the other, and they cross the street on a green light.

She faced him in there. Where he took her innocence, in a back room smelling of rotting produce. Where he got away with it. She avoided this for thirty years. But she did it. And she's still here, still walking.

Lulu

If she ignores the few times Dad dragged her to Jimmy's Little League games, Lulu has never attended a sports event. She's never been to a concert or a play, had never heard live music until a few years ago when the navy band played in the school gym and she got goosebumps, thrilled that the musicians in their crisp uniforms could make those exotic brass instruments sound exactly like the theme from the TV hockey broadcasts that formed the backdrop to childhood Saturday nights.

Now she finds herself, on a cold Saturday evening, dressing for a basketball game. She wishes she owned something green; fans wear green, she's heard. All of Friday kids talked about the game, in class, in the hallways, in the cafeteria—an important home match against the rival school across the intersection.

"This new kid from Toronto is supposed to be good. Real good," a boy said at lunch.

Her insides jumped. She wanted to watch him but had no one to go with. This morning she weighed calling Janet but didn't. Sports teams go out to support the other teams, Janet has told her, so she'll be there but with her volleyball gang.

Lulu can't bear the thought of another Saturday night at home. Once she's in the crowd, people won't guess she came by herself. She sifts through her dresser, abandons the idea of green. Never looked good on her anyway. Viv and Dad are off to an early movie with Aunt Brenda and her husband, and Lulu has told them she's staying home to study.

"I wish, though, that you'd get out, enjoy yourself," Viv says, poking her head into Lulu's room, in her coat, smelling of perfume.

"I'm fine here."

"What about your guy?"

"He's not mine. Goodnight."

When they close the apartment door, she grabs her jacket. It means taking the bus alone, but when she boards, her uneasiness fades. A few students in green are already on the bus, and more pile on as they ride south. The riders are boisterous; two girls share a pint of lemon gin, keeping an eye on the driver as they pass it back and forth.

At school a bottleneck of students struggles to get into the gym, and Lulu finds herself carried in the swarm. For a moment, it's scary.

"Let's go, Irish!" a guy slurs, he seems very drunk, and a boy in rival colours gives him the finger. "Eff you, Carter!" he calls, and the two guys stop and stare. A third boy steps between them.

"Hey," says the man working the door, sounding annoyed but bored. "Knock it off or you're not getting in."

The gym's bright and deafening; a student plays a drum that echoes off the high ceiling. The bleachers are full and Lulu stands at the bottom, unsure. People push past. Then a miracle, a curly-haired girl waves at her, a girl from Math class whose name is Natalie, she thinks. Lulu makes her way to her, up and up and over.

"Can I squeeze in?" she shouts above the noise, and Natalie nods and smiles. Lulu sits, grateful, jostled on both sides, happy that she came. She laughs: so much for Helen's sports boycott.

The teams are warming up, players circle and take turns shooting baskets. She spots Matt right away, skinny shoulders underneath the sleeveless jersey, strong legs. Mostly, she notices his eyes. They look darker; he's focused and serious. He never misses a shot. I know him, she wants to tell Natalie.

Lulu knows little about basketball but she's mesmerized as soon as the opening whistle blows. She can't take her eyes off him and, when she looks around, everyone else is glued to him too. He rushes down the court, pivots, passes smoothly to teammates, finishes off baskets, and starts back the other way with no fanfare.

The game's tense but they win, 71-69. Matt makes a basket at the buzzer to seal it. Lulu and Natalie hug each other and jump up and down, yell with everyone else. They were all in it together. The players slap each other's backs and jog off the court. He didn't see her and that's okay. He'd know why she came.

The bus ride home is loud and the driver warns them to pipe down. Some students seem to be going off to a party. Lulu's on such a high, she doesn't even feel left out. She slips in just before her parents, and when they arrive she lies in the dark and hears their voices, likely raised by drinking. But they're happy voices. She goes over the night again and again.

She has a dream close to morning in which she keeps rubbing her swollen belly—she must be pregnant. People appear before her: Liz, holding a bagel; Matt, smiling in his team jersey. She senses he's the father. A grim nun in a black habit swings rosary beads like a lasso.

"Everyone, stop it," Lulu says and jolts awake. Lies there, heart pounding. Matt, making her pregnant.

All morning she stays close to the kitchen so she can grab the phone when he calls. If he calls. Even though Viv would be excited, she doesn't tell her. Maybe he won't call. But he said he would.

Midmorning the phone rings and she snatches the receiver. Says hello all nonchalant. His voice is deeper, slower, on the phone. She almost says something about the game but checks herself. He says he'll pick her up at two.

She showers, fiddles too much with her outfit, her hair, her makeup. She tugs at her checked shirt, worries it gapes and exposes her bra. She goes to the curb early and waits and, when he pulls up a few minutes later, she feels sick.

"Hey," he says.

She looks at him and giggles, nervous. Her dream comes to her.

"What's so funny?" he says, smiling and pulling away from the curb.

"Nothing. What religion are you?"

He frowns. "No one has ever asked me that. Is it a big deal here?"

Lulu remembers hearing Halifax used to alternate between Catholic and Protestant mayors.

"Yeah, I suppose it is," she says. "I went to a Catholic school, but I don't go to church much."

"I'm Jewish."

Lulu wasn't expecting that. She has never met a Jewish person; she knows there are Jews in Halifax, but none around here. He glances at her. She blushes.

"Oh, cool," she says.

"You look shocked." He laughs, braking at a red light.

"No, no big deal. But I guess, yeah, I wasn't thinking that."

He shrugs. "We're not very religious either."

She wants to ask: Do you avoid pork? Do you light candles at Friday supper? Things she's seen on TV. But she'd sound like a country bumpkin.

Matt's parents wait in their front hall with their coats on. His father, tall with a beard, looks annoyed. Diane wears a black coat and a colourful silky scarf.

"Where were you?" his father asks, his voice sharp. "You know we're going to the symphony."

"Sorry," Matt says. "I forgot."

He turns and introduces Lulu, and his father leans to shake her hand. She offers hers uncertainly, a weak, fingers-only handshake. Matt's dad reclaims his keys and goes through the door.

"Nice to see you, Lulu," Diane says, smiling. "We're grabbing a bite after so we won't be back for hours. Haley's at her friend's." She winks.

They settle at the kitchen table again and Matt pulls out his copy of the scene. They begin reading, the house quiet; a dog barks outside. She glances at him, pictures him zigzagging through defenders, his shots graceful.

"Okay, should we try this?" he says after a few minutes. "You need to start."

She says a few words, clears her throat, then restarts.

"We should stand," he says.

On Friday they watched two sets of partners stand at the front of the class and read their scenes. In one, Juliet arrived just in time to save Romeo from poisoning himself. Predictable. In the other, a space alien touched down and sucked Juliet up into his flying saucer. The alien wore a tinfoil hat. Their teacher looked baffled.

Lulu reads the line to herself, looks up at Matt. "'Who are you, stranger?'"

"'My name's Antonio. And what is your name, lovely lady?'"

"'I am Juliet, of the house of Capulet. What brings you here?'"

"'I heard there are good opportunities. But I didn't expect the girls to be so beautiful.'"

Matt wiggles his eyebrows and Lulu laughs, relieved that he seems back to normal.

"Don't," she says, and tries to compose herself.

"Juliet, you make me tingle all over."

"We cut that line," Lulu says, laughing harder. "Don't you think he sounds like a creep?"

"He is a creep. Keep going."

"'Oh, don't try to flatter me, Antonio. I don't know you. And I must go. My father awaits.'"

"'No, wait.'" Matt grabs her arm. "'Please stay.' I thought he could get aggressive right away?"

Lulu nods.

"'Let go of me,'" she says. "'You're hurting my arm.'"

Matt pushes her slightly and she steps back so she's up against the wall. Though she knows the scene, Lulu's uncomfortable. He towers over her and she gets a sense of how men can overpower women if they feel like it.

"'But Juliet, I'd like to read you some of my poetry.'" He steps back. "Too corny? Should we change that line?"

"Too late. Okay, 'I'm afraid, sir, I really must go. And I have a boyfriend.'"

Matt pauses, looks at the papers in his hand. He steps closer. He's supposed to try to kiss her. She reaches over her head—Juliet's looking for something to hit him with. Her hand knocks a framed print off the wall. Matt grabs it before it comes down on her head, and they giggle.

"You okay?" he says.

She nods and he places the print on the table. Lulu reaches again. Exposing her chest and underarm feels vulnerable. Maybe there's a sweat stain. She pretends to grab something and bring it onto his head. He falls, overplaying it, and bangs into one of the kitchen chairs, knocking it over. He lies on the floor and chuckles. Sits up.

"We've written quite a violent scene," she says.

"It makes you realize, he's trying to…assault her," he says. A word from a police show.

Neither speaks for a bit. He gets up and sits at the table. "Well, the teacher can't say we didn't take chances."

"Do you think we'll get in trouble?"

"Nah, we don't get too graphic or anything."

"I suppose it's realistic," says Lulu, joining him at the table.

"Should we dress up?" she says, thoughtful. "I have nothing to wear."

"Good idea. I'll see what we have."

It's getting dark and she thinks she should go. Matt apologizes that he doesn't have the car, and she says no problem, she'll catch a bus. He offers to walk her to the bus stop.

"No, I'm fine," Lulu says at the door, though his street is especially dark. She steps into the cold, still partially in the Italian garden. Why do girls have to worry about their safety, just walking a few blocks? Guys don't even think about it.

Footsteps beat behind her; she shivers and turns. It's him, running, with no jacket.

"I thought I'd come along," he says, slowing to her pace.

Gallant is the word that pops into her mind. They walk in silence. Her first real crush. Her first Jewish friend.

They reach Robie Street; the northbound bus stop is on the other side, and a few people cluster there. She says she's good by herself now.

"Okay," he says, shivering, hands in his front jeans pockets.

She searches for something clever to say. "No antics in class. Stick to the script," she says, smiling.

"You bet." He salutes and jogs into the dark.

That night she asks Viv if she has something she can wear as Juliet. They look through Viv's closet, Lulu expecting disappointment because none of her mother's clothes will fit her. Viv pulls out a flowy peasant dress in a pink and red print.

"Here it is," she says. "I was worried I threw it away."

It fits Lulu well. The bodice emphasizes her curves, and Viv says the colours bring out her eyes. She uses safety pins to raise the dress to Lulu's ankles. Lulu stands before her mother's full-length mirror and regards herself, swaying so the fabric billows.

"It looks beautiful on you," says Viv. "Here."

She digs in a drawer and pulls out a length of ivory lace

about an inch wide, places it across Lulu's forehead, and pins it at the back of her head so it's secure.

"I think this would be appropriate, don't you?"

Lulu nods. Her long hair's parted in the middle and flows over her shoulders. Maybe people will think she's pretty. Will he? Viv rests her cheek against Lulu's hair and smiles in the mirror. Lulu smiles back.

"See?" says Viv. "You're just big-boned, that's all." Lulu pulls away.

It takes her hours to fall asleep, and when her alarm clock buzzes at seven, she groans. Then she remembers what's before her today.

She dresses and tucks a bit of makeup into her book bag along with Viv's dress. She looks at her feet, digs out last summer's beaten-up buffalo sandals. She had to soak them in water to soften the cheap leather before wearing them, but they still stained her soles brown.

Before English class that afternoon she goes into the girls' bathroom to change. She's all nerves, can't get the lace pinned around her forehead. But a girl emerges from one of the stalls and offers to help.

"You look amazing," the girl says.

Lulu applies rouge and Viv's lipstick and heads for class. Will he think she's overdone it? When she reaches the classroom door, she panics. She's way over the top, people will laugh at her attempt to become the heartthrob Juliet. Her heart pounds. She cannot remember one thing she's supposed to say, though they're allowed to read from their scripts. As she takes a few deep breaths, Matt turns the corner, last-minute as usual. He walks toward her, smiling.

He's gone for it too. He wears a baggy white shirt, a black vest unbuttoned, and a floppy velvet hat, kind of like the ones men wore in the movie. He has even tucked his pants into long white socks to resemble the stockings and shorter pants men wore back then.

"Where did you get that hat?" she says.

"Whoa," he says at the same time. They grin at each other. The teacher comes to the door.

"You two look fantastic. Well done," she says. "Are you ready?"

They follow her in. Someone whoops. Helen mouths "wow" from the back. Lulu's armpits are wet and the lace at her neck itches. What if her nose bleeds again?

"Class, Lulu and Matt are going to start us off," says the teacher. "Don't they look great?" She sits and gestures to begin. Lulu must speak first. She gulps and looks up at Matt. He smiles.

"'Who are you, stranger?'" she says.

She gains confidence as they go on, and raises her volume. Matt, with his eyes, seems to encourage her.

"'Juliet, I'd like to read you some of my poetry,'" Matt/ Antonio says.

"'I'm afraid, sir, I really must go,'" she says, her voice high and odd to her ear. "'And, I have a boyfriend.'" They should have changed that to "sweetheart."

She inches backwards so she can be shoved against the blackboard. Matt follows her cue and pushes her against the wall, gripping her arm like he did in the kitchen. But harder this time. He looks into her eyes. "Juliet."

She gulps. He's supposed to try to steal a kiss. He bends down, blocking out the fluorescent lights. Smells like Irish Spring soap. He brings his mouth close to hers and his lips touch, soft, tentative. She doesn't move.

He leans in and the kiss deepens. Lulu's stunned, they didn't practice this, people are watching and she's mortified, but then something ignites and she can't help it, she's kissing him back. The classroom, the audience, fade away.

Wolf whistles. They break apart and she wobbles, as if drugged. She tries to read his expression but he turns his head.

She's supposed to hit him with a rock. She grabs a chalk-board eraser and clunks him on the head, powdering his hair. Silly, it wouldn't hurt a cat, but he falls to the ground, trem-ors, rests, closes his eyes.

People laugh. She scans the ocean of faces. The teacher wears a tight smile. Lulu rushes from the room, which, she realizes as she goes, fits the scene. Clapping.

She enters the girls' washroom and stops at the sinks, breathing jagged. He kissed her. She kissed him back. Her first kiss. Does he like her? She watches herself in the mirror touching her burning lips, lipstick smudged. The door bangs open and Helen enters with Lulu's things.

"Wow," Helen says, laughing, "that was intense."

Lulu peels off the lace headband, which leaves an elabor-ate pattern on her forehead. She's not in the mood for Helen's teasing.

"He was all over you," says Helen. "Was that planned?"

"Not really." She enters a stall to change and pulls at the dress. It gets stuck at her shoulders and she wants to scream.

"Well you two looked pretty lovey-dovey up there. I think the teacher was impressed with the performance." Helen gig-gles. "You must be going out, huh?"

Lulu zips up her corduroys.

"I gotta run to class," Helen calls. "But let's get together this week." The door slams shut.

Lulu goes out into the corridor, not wanting to run into anyone she knows. Not even him. The kiss. It was so good. But they hadn't discussed it. In fact, he took her by surprise. In front of everyone.

June

The cashier at the Frugal Mart was named Tina, June noticed it on her name tag. She looked about sixteen. June goes over the episode in her head. Did Connelly get too cozy with Tina? Did he rub against her as he squeezed in to fix the register?

June keeps thinking about the girl as she goes about her Saturday morning. She had a wash of cute freckles across her nose, hair cut into a flattering shag. But what did her eyes say? Was she uncomfortable, or excited because Connelly's been showering her with attention?

Lorne enters the kitchen and opens the fridge door. Looking for lunch but too stubborn to ask. She retrieves a can of tuna from the open cupboard, door removed for painting, and hands it to him.

"Thanks," he mumbles, and begins making a sandwich.

She sits and lights up a smoke. She doesn't know where they stand these days. When she told him about Connelly he got upset, what man wouldn't? But why was he mad at her? Why was she mad at him?

He takes his sandwich to the basement, where he's still painting cupboard doors. The house will be a mess for Christmas, but who cares. She doesn't want to celebrate, have company in, or cook a dinner. Not one gift bought. Last night Gerald pestered again about a tree. She doesn't have the strength.

She looks over at the basement door and flashes to Mom on the cellar floor. She dials the phone number she grew up with.

"Hello?" Barry says.

"Gerald wants a Christmas tree."

"Who's this?"

"Very funny."

"Well get the kid a tree, June. You can't skip Christmas."

She takes a drag of her cigarette.

"Look, I know it's tough," he says. "I miss her bad. I'm alone in this house for Christ's sake."

"Did you even notice I threw out some of her things?"

"Well it was either you or a ghost who stripped the room. I saw the bags out in the garbage. How about, I pick you and Gerald up in twenty minutes. We'll go get a tree—two, 'cause I need one too."

She hangs up, feeling better. Gerald gets ready quickly after she tells him.

"I want a fat one," he says, smiling, standing in the front hall in his jacket and hat. He stretches his arms wide to show how big.

June goes to the basement stairs. "Lorne, Barry's taking us to get a tree," she calls down.

He appears at the bottom with a paintbrush in hand. "I thought we were getting one together."

"You never said anything."

"It's our first Christmas in this house, of course I want a tree," he says, his voice surprising her, not angry but hurt. "I know a place, we coulda taken Gerald there to cut one down. Made a day of it."

She hesitates. A car horn beeps out front. She feels bad now.

"Well," she says, "you never said a word and Barry offered. And Gerald won't stop yapping about it."

Lorne walks away. Something smashes down there.

Gerald's in the front passenger seat of Barry's car, the window rolled down, music blasting. "I get shotgun." He laughs. He loves being around Barry.

June slides into the back. Barry takes them a bit south, then west, and parks at the Halifax Forum, a looming, red-brick hockey arena. Someone's selling trees in a corner of the parking lot, multicoloured lights strung up like beads, a hand-drawn sign advertising "Fur Trees." Carols chirp from a radio and the man tending the tree lot hovers near customers twirling evergreens, their conversations appearing as white puffs in the cold afternoon.

The overwhelming smell of balsam fir and pine hits June like a shot of smelling salts. Her Christmases rush back, the early ones with Dad holding her up to gasp at the tinsel-trimmed tree, and her eyes fill.

Barry and Gerald consider one tree and then another. "No, no, no," Gerald keeps saying to Barry's suggestions. Gerald shoves his arm into the heart of a fir and grasps its trunk, holds it steady for June to judge.

"How 'bout this one, Mom?"

"Too big."

He moves on to another. "This one?"

"Too short." Her feet are cold. "You guys pick." She climbs back into the car.

Barry buys two trees and he and Gerald grunt as they secure them onto the broad roof of the car. Branches dangle down the side windows, and June feels shielded. The car crawls back to the neighbourhood, Barry taking it slow. She wishes he would just drive and drive.

"O'er the fields we go/Laughing all the way. Ho, ho, ho," Gerald sings along with the radio.

Barry asks June if he should drop them off at Lorne's. He keeps calling it that. Gerald pleads to help decorate Barry's tree, so they head there. As daylight fades, the guys lug a fir into the house, needles sprinkling along the walkway and into the hall. Mom would get so worked up about needles, sweeping angrily even before the tree was in place. Silently they move it to the correct corner. More fumbling and finally it's in the stand.

Barry has set out two boxes of decorations, and Gerald begins picking through, jacket still on, growing in excitement as he unwraps one familiar bauble after another.

"Remember this?" he says, holding up the tree topper. "Nana's angel."

June escapes into the kitchen. She wishes she were a drinker. Rum and eggnog, Dad always liked that for the tree trimming. She decides to call Lorne.

"Hey," she says, "we're at Barry's. Gerald wanted to help decorate. Why don't you come over?"

"Did you get us a tree?"

"Yeah, we'll do it tomorrow. Come over, we'll buy fish and chips." She pauses. "I need cheering up."

Lorne arrives in paint-splattered clothes, and their eyes meet. Another spat settled, hopefully. Barry hands Lorne a beer as Gerald fights with the tangle of fat, coloured lights.

Barry digs in the other box. "Where are the reflectors?" he says. "We need reflectors."

They've had them forever, maybe since the sixties, scalloped metal collars that slip around the base of each bulb and are supposed to make the tree prettier. Barry's searching becomes frenzied; he throws a wad of tinsel behind him without looking and the strands flutter.

"Where the hell?" he says.

He drops to his knees on the floor and lets out a sob. Bends his head over the box, as if praying over the shiny shards, the decapitated Rudolph, the glitter that can never, ever be cleared away. He weeps, his body shaking, his cries jagged.

June hasn't seen him shed a tear since Mom died. Lorne looks at the floor between his feet. Gerald goes to Barry and hugs him, resting his cheek on his uncle's heaving back.

"It's only Christmas, Uncle Barry."

Of course he's in pain. Even into his middle age, Mom always called him "my boy."

Lulu

That evening, after the kiss, Lulu and Viv wash the supper dishes together and Viv asks how the performance went. "Fine." Lulu doesn't want the kiss cheered or dissected. "I bet you looked sweet though." Lulu doesn't respond. When they finish up, she says she's going for a walk. She needs to move.

"It's freezing out there," her mother says. "And maybe you shouldn't be out in the dark." But she seems to forget as she curls up next to Dad and begins chuckling at the TV.

Lulu bundles up and slips out. It's actually nice, there are a zillion stars, not cold if you're wearing a hat. She avoids the ball field; Danny and Mikey could be anywhere.

She decides to visit Gran. She hasn't seen her in so long, she's ashamed. As she climbs the front steps, the blue TV light flickers through the window. The door's locked and the TV shouts; she can almost make out the dialogue. She has to pound at the door before Gran opens it, one eye peeking through the gap allowed by the chain.

"Oh, it's you."

It smells like cabbage. Gran kisses her cheek and the dog gives a sniff, then curls up beside Gran's chair. Lulu sinks into one of the upholstered rockers, the one Papa used, as Gran goes into the kitchen.

A spindly fake Christmas tree, about two feet tall, leans on top of the hi-fi cabinet. Gran and Papa used to host big, noisy Christmas Eves, two dozen bodies steaming up the windows, grown-ups in the kitchen, clutching drinks and cigarettes, laughing and slapping each other's backs; children, cousins—Lulu in white leotards and a new velvet dress Viv had bought on credit, Jimmy with white shirttails flapping—dancing in the front room by the massive tree, gripping sticky barley candies they could never finish. But after Papa died, fewer relatives came, others died, and Gran's heart wasn't in it.

Gran returns with two glasses of orange juice and a bowl of chips, and sets them on the phone table between the chairs. She eases back into sitting with a grunt.

"You must be busy down at the high school."

"Kind of. I feel bad, I haven't been over."

Gran waves the comment away. "You're young. Enjoy yourself."

They sip juice and rock in the chairs and eat chips. The show ends and another begins. Gran's eyes twinkle. "Any fellas on your dance card?"

"Has Mom been talking to you?"

"No. But I've seen a thing or two."

"There's a guy. But."

Gran feeds a chip to the dog.

"We kissed today. In front of the class."

"Hoo. That's a bit daring."

Lulu feels a flash of impatience. "It was a play. We were acting." She pauses. "But the kiss wasn't planned, he just did it."

Gran watches her, wire glasses slipping down her nose. Lulu never imagined asking her grandmother for advice on boys.

"So, does this mean he likes me?"

"Sounds like it. Sweetie, if you like this boy, let him know." Gran smiles. "Why wouldn't he like my pretty Lulu?"

If Lulu continued it would spill out as a whine: that Matt is handsome and sophisticated and a star athlete, and that she, Lulu, couldn't possibly be his choice. Yet she loves being with him. They're comfortable with each other. And he did kiss her. Still, Gran's suggestion that Matt most certainly likes her makes her cranky. Gran doesn't understand.

Lulu mumbles she should leave but doesn't move. It's so cozy. The two of them could just rock in these chairs and watch game shows all day. Skip school, skip everything. When she was little, Gran would let her polish the coffee table and two-tier end tables with lemon oil. Lulu drank in the smell but couldn't get the oil to sink it. It left a film. When she grew older she realized the shiny wood tops were fake.

The TV news starts up. Lulu puts on her coat and hugs Gran at the door. The lavender cologne and talcum powder set from the drugstore, that's what she'll get her for Christmas.

Plastic, rippled sheeting nailed around the neighbour's veranda snaps in the wind. Wispy snow swirls on the sidewalk, never-ending circles like a Spirograph. Lulu runs, past the little houses and the church and the church park, where the Virgin Mary glitters with snow.

Lulu would emerge into cold nights like this after singing with the girls' choir at weeknight masses, lyrics swimming in her head, perhaps carrying the scent of incense, certain she'd done all she could that day to be a good person. The sense of peace usually ended when she got home.

She enters the apartment and her thighs begin to tingle from the warmth. The TV's turned low and sounds like sports, Viv likely gone to bed. Lulu gets into bed and pulls the covers up to her nose. Of course Gran would think Matt could like her, Gran always takes her side. Around midnight, she clicks on the lamp and opens a textbook. She'll just act normal tomorrow, that's all.

June

The days are bitterly cold and short, and June keeps the lamps lit all day. She envisions the old house while Barry's at work, Mom's ornaments on the dark tree in the dark front room. Mom would have been baking mincemeat tarts and gumdrop cakes around this time. She wanders the new house, smoking, fretting because she has much to do but can't concentrate.

Lorne goes quiet. He leaves for work in the dark and returns in the dark, downs his hot meal, and goes to bed. June stands in the kitchen unsatisfied, in a strange way missing the yelling and slamming of doors. She crawls back into bed many mornings, and when Gerald taps on her door she tells him to find something to eat.

Trudy calls, wondering if June will do her hair Friday; she and Martin are going to a dance. June says she doesn't do hair anymore.

"I'll bring all my stuff. Please, Junie?"

"All right. Come over in the afternoon."

On Friday, June places a kitchen chair near the sink and gathers a few worn towels. She digs out her electric clippers and her best shears, which she'd bought herself and made sure to take when she left Frank's. She coerces Gerald to sit and uses the clippers to give him the trim he desperately needs.

"Ow, ow," he says above the buzz.

"Oh stop. It doesn't hurt and you know it."

When she's done he stands and quivers. She brushes hair off him as best she can, and it rains onto the linoleum.

"There," she says. "Handsome." He makes a face.

Trudy comes in the back door lugging a tote of hairsprays, curlers and a curling iron, brushes and clips and bobby pins.

"I don't know what you expect," says June. She puts the kettle on and Trudy sits, wrapping a towel around her shoulders.

Trudy tells her Martin's mother's kicking up a stink about Christmas, and Martin's sister refuses to come to Trudy's for the dinner, and can June manage an updo?, and Martin thinks he'll be deployed most of next year, and—no word of a lie— she's pretty sure her neighbour's screwing the milkman, and Trudy despises her boss and wishes she could just quit. And what does June think about Trudy going red?

"Like the sexy one on *Gilligan's Island*," Trudy says.

June works her way over Trudy's thick mane, teasing and shaping, grateful she doesn't have to talk. She works almost without thought, the movements and decisions she makes ingrained after so many years at Frank's, and it dawns on her that she has missed this feeling, of being good at something.

Trudy lights a smoke. "So how are things here?"

June inserts a final bobby pin into the updo, which, fingers crossed, should hold during Trudy's jiving. She coats the whole thing in a prolonged mist of hairspray and Trudy covers her teacup with her hand and coughs and says, "Jesus." June finishes with Trudy's sparkly butterfly barrette, then lights up and assesses. The look's out of date but it's what Trudy likes.

"You didn't answer," says Trudy. June licks her finger and tries to tame a curl on Trudy's forehead.

June sits. "How are things? Lorne has clammed up. I told you that I told him, and I don't know, things have changed." She pushes her cold tea away from her.

Trudy leans forward and grasps June's hands. "This has eaten you up for thirty years. Connelly has ruined your life."

June looks up quickly.

"I don't mean—your life isn't ruined. Gerald's a doll. But… for Christ's sake, June, it's affecting your thing with Lorne."

June pulls away and begins wiping her shears with a soft cloth.

Trudy carries on. "He's never had to pay for this. I mean actually pay. You've raised that boy on your own with no support."

June rolls the shears in the cloth and returns them to their quilted bag.

"Maybe you should sue him or something," Trudy says. June snorts.

Trudy kisses her at the door, no longer the concerned friend but excited about the night ahead, June can tell. She'll wear a slinky dress and dance with every handsome man there while Martin steams on the sidelines. Trudy, now there's someone who does whatever the hell she wants. June could never be her, has never wanted to be, but the girl's right: June could stand up for herself once in a while.

Lorne comes in as June sweeps the last of the hair from the floor.

"Where's supper?' he says, stopping at the kitchen entrance. Sawdust is sprinkled through his hair.

"Hello to you too."

"I'm starved. Everyone wants things done before the twenty-fifth. I'm working my ass off and you can't cook me a meal?"

She stops sweeping. "Who do you think you are?"

"Who do you think you are?" He throws his plaid jacket onto a chair and the jacket slips to the floor. "I brought you into my house and you won't even be civil."

"Your house? Did you forget the ten thousand dollars I brought to the table? Everything I ever got from Mom and Dad, I sunk into this house. Into us."

He throws up his hands. "Take it back then. I don't want it." He grabs his jacket and heads for the front door.

"Where you going?" she calls.

He turns. "I can't do this anymore. All we do is fight." He wipes his face from chin to forehead, rests his hand on his hair for a second. "I was gonna wait 'til the new year, but..." Grasps the doorknob. "I'm going to the tavern."

"Lorne," she barks.

He turns to her. "You don't love me," he says. "Gerald, Barry, Trudy even—but not me."

"That's not true." But as she says it she knows he's right. She's been trying but can't muster what she felt the first time.

"Gerald wants nothing to do with me either," he says, shrugs.

"But you begged to get back together." Her voice sounds weak.

He opens the door. "It's never gonna work. You and Gerald, you may as well move out. Might take a while, but I'll pay you back."

"What the hell is going on here?" she yells, a last-ditch stab at standing up for herself. He goes out.

She stands broom in hand, stunned. Yeah, things have been rocky, ages since they've touched. He couldn't handle the news of the rape. She couldn't handle him knowing. But she thought that if it ever ended, she'd be the one to do it. She's shocked because, yes, she realizes, she's been imagining how it might end. And he beat her to it.

Gerald comes in asking about supper.

"I don't know," she snaps. He looks stung.

"Sorry. I just." She looks around the kitchen, which she will never see completed. "I don't know."

"Don't know about supper?"

She sets the broom against the wall. "Let's take the Bug. Let's go to Barry's."

Lulu

Matt doesn't show up to the next English class. As Helen and her partner begin their scene, Lulu watches the classroom door, praying he's merely late. But he doesn't come. She can't take in what Helen's saying; the class's laughter hurts her ears.

All afternoon she fights tears. He made a fool of her and now he's avoiding her. He regrets kissing her. "Why wouldn't he like you?" Gran said. She skips her last class and boards the bus home. Tells herself to get a grip.

But in the empty apartment she falls onto her bed and cries. She feels deeply lonely. Coke commercials lie: being a teenager sucks. She has a rotten sleep that night and wakes with puffy, red eyes. She longs to ditch school but needs to hand in a History assignment. She dresses and catches the bus.

"Lulu," someone calls as she approaches the school doors. She turns and Janet skips toward her.

"Hey girl," Janet says, punching Lulu's arm. "Everyone's talking about you. Necking in English." She grins.

Lulu blushes. "It was just the play."

"Come on. You and Matt? In front of everyone? Bold, Lulu, bold."

Lulu frowns. Who is this person? "I gotta go to class," she says. Janet salutes her, like Matt did that night.

As Lulu enters English class after lunch, the teacher looks at her weird. The teacher knows. No wedding ring, in her cardigans and ugly shoes, another bookish girl who doesn't attract boys. She knows Lulu's fate.

But he's at his desk, grinning in a lopsided way. Lulu sits, her insides bouncing like the Mexican jumping beans Dad once bought her at a gas station. She decides she can handle whatever comes, as long as Matt doesn't avoid her.

He faces front the entire hour and she tries to do the same. But when the bell rings, he asks her to come out to the hall. She follows, feeling helpless. They stop beside a water fountain and he clears his throat.

"About the other day—"

"No," she interrupts, "it's okay."

"No, I, I want to apologize. I shouldn't have done it." She nods.

"We got carried away, right?" he says. "Antonio." He rolls his eyes and laughs awkwardly.

She nods. *Sure, whatever you say. Can I go now?*

"But still," he says, raking his hand through his hair, "you know, I thought, maybe we should go to a movie or something." He pulls at his sleeve.

Lulu can't speak.

"You know, do it properly." He looks at her, his eyes questioning. "If you want to."

"I guess so."

"Okay. How about Thursday, er, tomorrow? I've got basketball all weekend, a tournament."

They agree to a movie and Lulu hurries to her next class. She can't concentrate. Matt asked her out. But acted like he didn't care one way or the other. No, she's reading too much into it; he's just shy. She should be elated. She should tell Viv. But that evening, she doesn't.

He insists on picking her up, so after supper on Thursday Lulu sticks by the kitchen window in her coat. When the red car pulls up she yells that she's going to Janet's, and runs down the stairs in the dark.

"Hey," he says when she climbs in. It's warm and the radio plays softly.

"Hey." They drive in silence for a few blocks.

"So, I'm excited to see this movie. I hear it's good," she says.

"Yeah, me too."

He buys them popcorn and drinks, and they enter the theatre alongside the other couples. When they sit their arms meet on the armrest and they snatch them away. The ads for upcoming movies begin and Lulu munches her popcorn, but not too fast, that would be piggy. The light of the projector outlines his perfect profile.

The movie's silly and she laughs, he laughs, and her shoulders relax. They do not touch and have barely spoken, but it's comfortable again. They leave the theatre discussing how funny so-and-so was, and how another character was sad-funny. The car's as cold as a freezer, and he cranks the heat. She shivers and he rubs his hands and blows on them.

"I, ah, need to get some studying done, so I thought I'd take you home now," he says.

"Yeah. Me too."

The car goes quiet and Lulu wishes she could fix it. *Dear Abby*, a girl might write, *how can I tell if he likes me or just feels sorry for me?* They pass Christmas lights framing windows, plug-in candles with fake orange flames, and she realizes Jimmy will be home soon. He and Matt would have nothing in common. When they pull up to her building, she's relieved.

"Well, thanks a lot. That was fun," she says.

"Yeah, it was."

She grasps the door handle; make a quick exit to avoid embarrassment. Will he kiss her, he's not going to kiss her. She opens the door.

"Hey," he whispers. She turns and he's leaning toward her. He touches his lips to hers, gentle and a bit off the mark.

"See you tomorrow," she says and tries to climb out gracefully. But the car is low to the ground, and she cringes to think what her rear end must look like. He beeps the horn and drives off. She exhales. Her first date, over with.

Inside, Viv asks Lulu where she's been.

"Studying," Lulu says, hanging up her jacket.

"Without books?"

"All right, I was at the movies. With Matt."

Viv throws up her hands. "Hallelujah! It's about time." She smiles and pulls Lulu into her, rests her cheek against Lulu's hair.

"I had my very first date when I was thirteen, skating at the Forum. Your father claims when he saw me that night he knew I was the one. He was smitten."

Lulu has already heard about her mother's teen years, the beauty boys fought over. She wriggles out of the embrace. "I really do need to study."

"Wait. Tell me about it."

Lulu hesitates.

"Did he kiss you? A first kiss?"

"Mom."

"Oh well. Better that than all handsy."

Lulu shuts her bedroom door. Matt, playing the clown falling down during their skit, kissing her in front of everyone, asking her to his house without really knowing her. The cool athlete making baskets under pressure. Not shy.

June

June and Gerald arrive back at the old house with nothing, though Gerald cradles Kitty in a blanket. Barry's sprawled on the chesterfield, a glass in hand. Friday night. The cat leaps out of Gerald's arms and sprints.

"What's going on?" Barry says.

"We're moving back," says Gerald.

Barry sits up. "Moving back? What were you gone, two months?"

"I don't wanna talk about it," June says, sitting down.

"For god's sake, you're gonna talk about it," says Barry. "Did you and Lorne split?"

Gerald plugs in the tree lights.

"We just need to land here, for now. If that's okay," she says.

"'Course it's okay," says Barry. "This will always be your home."

She looks him in the eye. "He's giving me back the ten thousand."

Barry nods and sips the dark drink.

"Why don't you have a girlfriend?" she says.

"Don't," he says. "Gerald, did you eat?"

"Nope, and I'm starving."

Barry gets up. "Let's see what I have," he says, and heads for the kitchen.

Gerald looks at his mother. "Do I get my old room back?"

"Can you sleep on the chesterfield, 'til we figure things out?"

He gives a thumbs up. "Sure." He grins, hasn't looked this happy in weeks. She gazes blankly around the room.

"I'm going to need a job," she mutters.

"You cut hair good," he says, stretching out, claiming the chesterfield already. No, she's already decided she won't go back to doing hair. Barry returns with three grilled-cheese sandwiches.

"This is the best, Uncle Barry," says Gerald.

Barry watches June but she won't look at him. "I'm sorry, Sis."

She tells Gerald to go find Kitty and he leaves. She lights a cigarette. "It's been horrible," she says. "I told him about... what happened. And he couldn't handle it."

Barry sets down his glass. "Don't know if I blame him."

June glares at him. "What is it with men?" she says. "It's not like it happened to you." She exhales. "Even before I told him, he was weird. Said he wanted a family, but I don't know if he's cut out for one. So pissy around the house."

"And how about you?"

"Me?" June says. "Of course I wanted a family. I've got a family."

He produces a bottle of rum from beside the chesterfield and pours a glug into his glass, tops it up with Coke.

"You're drinking too much. Again," she says. He takes a big mouthful.

"I shouldn't have gone back with him," she says. "My head was so messed up, almost losing Gerald, losing my job. Mom, losing herself."

Barry just looks at her.

"And he killed Mom," she says.

"*What?*"

"If Lorne hadn't talked me into moving out, I would've been here the morning she died." This is the awful truth she's been holding in for weeks.

Barry holds up a hand as if telling her to stop. "You can't go down that road."

"I know it in my gut." She stubs out the cigarette. "I will take that guilt to my grave."

He shakes his head. "Well, I'm glad you're back."

"I need a job."

"Worry about that after Christmas."

Gerald returns, holding the cat. "Kitty's happy to be home," he says, stroking him. "But I told him, 'Don't go into the basement, 'cause that's where Nana was killed.'"

Lulu

Excitement courses through school on the last day of classes before Christmas break. Friends exchange joke gifts at their lockers; a boy gives a girl a heart-shaped pendant in the cafeteria—Lulu watches her hold it up under the fluorescent lights—and is rewarded with a long, sloppy kiss. Helen invites Lulu to skip afternoon classes and go to her place.

But Lulu can't leave school yet. Maybe Matt will come to English, which is last on the rotating schedule today. A sorry band of students shows up, those who would never dare miss a class: the pudgy guy already boasting a full moustache; the keener who immigrated here with his family and tells everyone he'll be the doctor who cures cancer; three girls, not friends, who keep their heads down in the halls, likely praying for invisibility. No Matt.

The teacher has brought treats. She starts up Christmas carols and sits at an empty student desk, ready to chat. The students loosen up. Lulu accepts an intricately iced sugar cookie and wonders if Matt's off preparing for his tournament. He might be celebrating Hanukkah around now, how does that work? She comes to as the teacher finishes a story about her year in Paris, pointing out the vintage earrings she bought by the Seine, and realizes she's missed the best part.

Afterwards she buses to the drugstore for her shift, braced for the busy evening Farrell has predicted. Inside, Liz stands beside Miriam at the till, bagging customers' purchases. Lulu pauses in surprise.

"He brought in reinforcements," Liz says.

Miriam tugs her coat over her sweater—red with silver jingle bells sewn into the shape of a Christmas tree, surely a home project—and retrieves a large bag of merchandise she'd stashed behind the counter. Lulu wonders if she paid for it.

"Hope Santa doesn't leave you girls a lump of coal," Miriam says, jingling out the door.

"When I was little, my Papa said that to me and I didn't know what coal was," Lulu tells Liz.

A middle-aged woman in curlers buys three cartons of cigarettes, gifts for her three sons, she tells them. A white-haired man asks loudly for "lots of safes—a present for the missus," and grins at the nun in a habit standing behind him. She goes deep red. He has stained, crooked teeth, a smoker's yellow moustache, and dandruff speckling the shoulders of his dark coat. Lulu tastes her lunch coming back. The nun buys a few religious Christmas cards. When the store empties, Liz lights a smoke.

"Tom told me he was in to see you," she says.

Lulu gulps. "He was looking for you," she says. "I didn't tell him anything."

Liz takes a deep drag. "It's okay. I know how he found out." Lulu waits but Liz just keeps smoking.

"I haven't seen you in a while," says Lulu.

"Yeah, well, my parents—the king and queen—asked me to move home. I didn't want to. But Jenn's place—her boy-friend and I do not get along."

She squishes the last of her cigarette into the hard plastic ashtray, stamped with the name of some insurance company, and looks out into the dark. Across the street, the steamed-up windows at Buppy's are decorated with silver garland and flashing lights. Buppy stops a customer on his way out and slings an arm around his shoulders. The two men laugh.

"God, I hate this place," says Liz. "The ass end of a small-minded city—if you wanna call it a city."

It stings. It's not so bad here. And she has no idea what Lulu did for her. What Lulu saw. Lulu thinks she was kind of brave at the McMullins' door, threatening Liz's mother. She should tell her.

"I saw your mother," Lulu says. Liz looks over. Would she appreciate what Lulu did? Would Liz really want to know that about her mother? Lulu falters.

"On the street one day, I saw her," she says. Liz raises an eyebrow. Lulu needs to change the subject. "And I have a boyfriend," she says. "He's from Toronto. Really cute and on the basketball team."

Liz points an index finger in Lulu's direction. "Don't get pregnant," she says, and heads toward the bathroom, just a toilet plunked in the stock cupboard that never seems to have toilet paper. Lulu frowns. Why's Liz so bitter? She did what she wanted.

When Lulu gets home that night, her father pulls her into the kitchen and puts a finger to his lips.

"I'm picking up Jimmy from the train station tomorrow," he whispers. "You keep your mother busy while I'm gone."

Dad must be watching spy movies. She reminds him she's working tomorrow; she's disappointed she'll miss the homecoming. By the time she's done work, the surprise will have died, like the fizz in a glass of pop.

"Oh well, you'll see him then," he says.

Liz is working Saturday too. She's in a better mood as they open the store for business, Farrell already filling prescriptions out back, and asks Lulu what her guy's like. Lulu's less keen to talk.

"I don't know. Just normal I guess."

Liz sips a coffee she bought at the diner. "Where does he live?"

"Not far from school. His dad's a professor at Dal."

Liz laughs. "I hope he's not one of my profs. They're all ogres. What's the last name?"

Lulu pauses. Is it Simon? She's in love with the guy and doesn't even know his name. Is she?

Around lunchtime, Farrell says he's ducking out for an hour. Liz buys Lulu a club sandwich from Buppy's, "a Christmas present," and as they're finishing up Helen and Danny walk in. Helen's in a white furry hat, probably her mother's, and a long camel coat.

"Hi, Lulu," she says.

Liz looks up. "You're banned from here," she tells Danny.

"Says who?" he says.

"You stole that aftershave. Get out or I'll call the cops," Liz says.

He laughs. "Yeah, right." He joins Helen, who's browsing the ladies' toiletry section. Liz goes and stands at the end of the aisle, arms crossed.

Danny exaggerates a sweep of his arm. "Can't you see, we're shopping for our mothers here?"

Helen picks up a box set of soap and presses her nose against the plastic cover. "Mom loves lemon," she says.

"You gettin' that for the old hag?" he says. Helen doesn't react.

Lulu rings in the soap, embarrassed just as she is whenever she waits on someone she knows.

"We should get together over Christmas," says Helen. Her cheeks are pink and she looks like a model in a teen magazine.

"Sure," says Lulu, though it doesn't entice her. Helen seems to have forgotten Danny's threat that Lulu stay away. Helen lingers, looks over her shoulder at Danny, then turns and mouths something. Lulu shakes her head; she didn't catch it.

"I'm going to break it off," Helen whispers.

"Do it then," Lulu whispers back.

"I'll call later," says Helen.

In the aisles, Danny makes a show of fondling deodorant and iodine, wart remover and baby oil, reading the labels, sniffing, placing each one back. Liz watches and rolls her eyes.

A startling bang bang on the window. Lulu jumps. Mikey's plastered against the glass like a starfish, splaying his hands in fingerless gloves. He licks the window in a slow circle, his tongue thick and pink. The tongues of his scruffy Adidas loll out too, laces dragging on the pavement.

"Mikey, my man," Danny says and hurries out the door, letting it bang into Helen as she follows. Danny punches Mikey in the shoulder. Danny turns to the window, where Lulu and Liz watch, and pulls a tin of English talcum powder, the good stuff, from his pocket. He shakes it and he and Mikey take off, laughing. Helen strolls behind.

"That little Christer." Liz hurries out onto the sidewalk. "Hey," she yells in their direction, "I'm calling the cops!"

Lulu wedges herself in the open door and strains to see, shivering. How did he take that with Liz watching?

Liz comes back inside, frowning. "He just does it for spite," she says. She places her hand on the phone. "No sense calling the police," she says, then glances at the dispensary. "Though Farrell would insist on it." She seems to weigh what to do.

Lulu goes over to straighten Danny's mess. Flowery talcum powder. Odd thing to take but a nice gift for a mother. That wasn't spite; that was Danny, doing his Christmas shopping. Even his mother, cursing him up the hill, will get something.

She's worried about Helen—maybe she's scared of Danny. Mind-boggling that she's stayed with him this long. She glances out the window. There's something she hasn't seen in ages.

"Look," she says to Liz, who has not called the police, "there's Gerald Green. He's back at his corner."

June

June lies on a cot in Gerald's old room, her eyes tracing a jagged crack in the plaster ceiling, and is suffocated by awful memories: unwanted pregnancy, Gerald's disappearance, Mom's dementia. She can't come back here. She and Lorne have made a mistake. This break is just growing pains.

Barry's bedroom door creaks and she hears him thump down the steps, slow movements. Stiff, or hungover. She'll call Lorne now before he leaves for work. He was planning to work all weekend to catch up.

"June," Barry calls up to her a minute later. "You better come down."

She grabs her sweater and goes downstairs, where Gerald snores rolled in a blanket on the chesterfield. She joins Barry at the front window. Lorne's pulling stuff out of his car trunk. June's stuff. She squeals and runs to the door, flinging it open.

"What in the hell are you doing?" she yells.

Lorne comes up the walkway with a green garbage bag, June's spring coat, and something else that she can't register.

"We gotta cut the ties. Now that we've made up our minds." He looks down at the bag. "I packed up for ya."

"Jesus Christ, my toothbrush is still probably wet over there," she says, choking on her words. She moves to grab the bag and slides on the slick wooden stair. Lorne hands it to her, folds the coat over the railing.

She's so furious she can't speak. She's shocked to realize she wants to spit on him. Dumping her, like a piece of garbage, after upsetting her life forever. *After begging her.* He sets another item against the steps, June's cherry-blossom picture.

She looks at the cheap print. Weeks ago she identified evil in the blossoms, menacing faces. She ignored it. Now this picture that she once loved, the only piece of decoration she has ever bought herself, that she thought was classy, that she carted to Lorne's to start a new life, seems to mock her. She tosses it toward the bushes under the window. It sails, the plastic frame light, teeters atop the bare branches, and slips between shrubs and house.

"Jesus."

"Don't Jesus me."

He fetches more bags, Gerald's radio, and deposits everything they own at the bottom of the steps. Says he'll bring back Gerald's bedroom furniture. She senses Barry and Gerald behind her in the entryway. A neighbour alights from a house across the boulevard, that one who goes to work in skirts and heels and thinks she's better than everybody else. The neighbour looks over at the commotion, in a fox fur coat on a Saturday morning. June isn't even wearing a bra. She looks at Lorne.

"You hate Gerald. Because he hurt your eye," she says.

"You're crazy." He wheels around and goes to his car. "Bye, June," he calls before getting in. "Merry Christmas."

The engine's harsh in the frosty morning. She doesn't move. He always was matter-of-fact. The grass on the boulevard sparkles under the strengthening sun. She feels a hand on her shoulder.

"C'mon inside," Barry says. "We'll grab these bags."

He leads her into the house, and he and Gerald bring in the belongings. June goes to the kitchen and, with quivering hands, tries to light a cigarette. She's never been so humiliated. Rage boils within and she swipes at a couple of dirty drinking glasses on the counter. They crash into the sink, which brings Barry and Gerald rushing into the room.

"You and Lorne fight, Mom?"

"Not now, Gerald," she says. Oh, she's been short with him lately.

Barry places a hand on her shoulder and she closes her eyes.

"Have you ever seen a bigger loser than me?" she says.

"He's the loser, not you."

That day she picks through the things Lorne brought over. She calls Trudy twice but can't get hold of her. Remembers the ten thousand dollars and gets furious again. If he tries to rip her off, she'll call the Mounties. She'll call him tonight to blast him.

But she can't get hold of Lorne either. His phone rings and rings, she can almost hear it echoing in the small house that never felt full, even with the three of them in it. She tells Barry she's worried about the money.

"He won't stoop that low. Lorne's an honest fella," he says. "Though I didn't see this coming."

In bed that night she weeps fat, hot tears. She goes over their conversations, looks for her missteps, his too. Last on her list, he said. Did he expect to take Gerald's place at the top?

"What else haven't you told me?"

He can't understand her thirty years of shame, guilt, regret. Because she should have done something, back then. She should've made Connelly pay. And because she didn't, people are disgusted with her now.

She rolls over and looks at the perfect half-moon through the window. Her only foray out of this house, her only stab at independence, her only chance at love, a failure.

Lulu

Jimmy has filled out. That's good, in guys. It's the first thing Lulu's father says when she walks in the door.

"Will you look at him, Lu?" he asks. Lulu looks. Mom paces the apartment, smiling.

Jimmy hugs Lulu, his new grown-up thing or maybe it's a Toronto thing. It's awkward—they're not a hugging family. But Lulu's happy to rest against his body, which she knew so well, bony and boyish, sharing a canvas navy hammock in Gran's backyard; cuddled under Jimmy's covers, jiggling legs, giggling, impatient for Viv to find them and exclaim in mock surprise.

"You're a lady now," he says to her.

"Modern women don't want to be called 'lady,'" she says and swats him playfully. He's more handsome, more like Dad, the same dark, uncontrollable hair. A cowlick.

Her father's all wound up and suggests they go out to supper to celebrate. But they don't know where to go. Lulu can't remember the four of them ever being in a restaurant together, except maybe a diner on a day trip. In the end, they order fish and chips.

"Good ol' east coast food," says Dad. It's Lulu's second helping of fries today, and she pokes her fingers into her belly through her jeans.

Jimmy has moved up to apprentice drywall finisher. Taping and mudding—now that's an art, he says. He says the money's just okay but the work's steady. He has a new room-mate, Jeff, who's from Saskatchewan. Jeff's six foot four, a gift for an interior painter.

"What do you do for fun?" says Viv.

Jimmy shrugs. "We live above a bar. We shoot a lot of pool."

"You can do that here," Viv says.

"He's living the life, up in the big city," says Dad. Trying to convince them all. Jimmy, living Dad's dream.

"You ever get to any hockey games?" Dad asks.

"Nah, can't afford it." Jimmy slouches in the kitchen chair, flicks a floppy french fry. He looks at Lulu and grins, sort of sheepish. "Remember Pinky?" he says.

She nods. When Jimmy beat down Mom and Dad for a pet. She could tell him her news, about doing well in high school and acting out Shakespeare; meeting new people, South Enders and parents who are professors and go to afternoon classical concerts. About Matt. About unmarried women who go off to live in Paris.

"Danny McMichael stole something from the store today," she says.

Everyone looks at her. Viv says Danny's from a long line of crooks, and Dad says Danny's father went to jail years ago for beating someone up, real bad. He might still be in there. Jimmy remembers Danny, two years behind him in school, fighting every day.

"Even when he was small," says Jimmy, "he'd scrap with bigger guys."

"And don't forget that poor cat," Viv says.

This would be a good time for Lulu to tell them Danny has threatened her. But how could she explain it? That it all began with her little-girl search for Gerald, mostly to impress Janet. Making posters, how childish it sounds now. Telling Helen about Danny, to be mean. Spit quivering on the bus floor. That she hasn't been especially nice, through any of it.

"Lulu has a boyfriend," says Viv. Lulu rolls her eyes.

"Who is the bugger? I'd better give him the once-over," Jimmy says and laughs.

"He's just a friend," she says.

Matt may be playing basketball this very moment. She always wanted a boyfriend at Christmas so she could receive a romantic gift, like the heart pendant in the cafeteria.

The next day, they parade Jimmy around the North End, to Gran's and to Aunt Brenda's, then to Dad's side, just his mother left now and a couple of brothers. Dad's mother, Nam, lives in a tiny house with a wide view of the harbour. The whole area flattened after the Explosion, Nam has told Lulu.

"Will you look at him," says Nam, reaching up and squeezing Jimmy's cheeks with her palms. It makes his lips bulge. He hunches his shoulders and she stops.

"Too good for us now, wha?" she says, but pats him on the cheek and hands him and Lulu Christmas cards in red envelopes. Lulu expects they each contain a five-dollar bill, same as last year.

Finally, Jimmy rings up some old friends, and Lulu doesn't see much of him for a day or so. At work she agonizes over his gift, she's been putting it off and never did get to the mall. She settles on an Old Spice gift set—she's grown to like the smell in the store—and two Mars bars, his favourite. It's not much. He could probably find anything he wanted in Toronto.

June

When dawn comes, seemingly reluctant and after seven on this, one of the shortest days of the year, June rises and dresses. She's been awake for hours.

Barry leaves early to do his shopping. June checks on Gerald sleeping in the front room, and gets into her car. She has to gun the Bug a few times before it clears the ice in their parking area out back. The car putters down the back lane toward the street.

Christmas Eve morning and, despite herself, she feels the electricity of the day. A woman, already burdened with shopping bags, hurries down Isleville Street. A man carries a plastic-wrapped turkey on his shoulder, must be twenty-five pounds, maybe a Christmas bonus from work. Boys throw a Frisbee across a boulevard, likely told to get out of someone's hair. Everyone is out.

June rounds the corner, and the tight Frugal Mart parking lot is nuts; vehicles pull in and out, a car honks, a bag boy drops a paper bag and brilliant tangerines roll under a wood-panelled station wagon. She parks across the street.

They couldn't fit another person inside. Shoppers hug hams, potted poinsettias, bottles of those disgusting green and red syrups adults dilute and give to kids as a treat. Registers ding; rusted shopping carts squeak by; a baby wails; and the speaker blares "I'll Be Home for Christmas." All for what, in the end?

Sandy's ringing in an enormous order. It's for that snooty Ann McMullin, who stands waiting in a fur-collared coat. But

June is determined and inserts herself behind Ann, in front of the next shopper in line. She waves at Sandy.

"Excuse me," the other shopper says.

June leans in. "Can you page Connelly?" she says loudly, wanting to be heard above the hubbub.

"Gimme a second, June." Sandy punches in something on the register.

"No," June says, "now." Ann turns and notices her.

Sandy looks up. Surely she's guessed. Connelly was all over June for months; then June quit that summer, obviously pregnant. Her old boyfriend made sure everyone knew it wasn't his.

"She was frigid, wouldn't let me touch her," he reportedly told friends, the sweetness that had attracted her gone. Barry heard the stories but didn't tell her for a long time.

Sandy picks up the pink phone receiver mounted beside her on a post. "Paging Mr. Connelly. Mr. Connelly, please come to the front cash." Her voice tinny.

"Would you mind finishing my order?" says Ann McMullin.

June steps back and lets the next shopper take her rightful place in line, and waits, rocking on her feet. She counts her breaths: one-two, one-two. That was her instinct during childbirth, counting through contractions to get through it, but the nurse kept telling her to shut up and push.

Connelly winds his way through the crowd, she spies his greasy, slicked-back hair as he squeezes to the front. He signals at Sandy with his arm held high.

"Did you want me?" he calls.

"No, I did," June says.

He looks down at her and blanches. June wishes she were taller. She takes a breath. She takes another breath. She can't back out now. She extends her arm and points at him with a shaking hand.

"This man," she says. She gulps.

"This man raped me," she says louder. A petite silver-haired woman beside Connelly recoils and peers up at him.

"Years ago, when…" June fights to strengthen her voice.

He looks horrified. "Hey, hey," he says and grabs her, sort of a tackle, he clamps his hand over her mouth, and a woman, not her, screeches.

June bites hard, the fleshy part below his thumb, and he yelps and pulls away. She wants to spit out the rancid taste of him. She straightens her back.

"Ed Connelly raped me," she yells, "in the stockroom when I was sixteen years old. He was my boss."

There's a ringing in her ears but she thinks the other noises have settled down. Yes, registers are not dinging. People are not talking. Even babies are not crying.

"Stop!" barks Connelly.

June glances at Sandy, who does not appear surprised or stand open-mouthed.

"I got pregnant," June yells. "Had to quit school. And this, this monster got away with it."

"Shame," someone cries.

He moves toward her. She steps back and bumps into something but she needs to get it all out.

"You've seen my boy? He's yours. You're a father of three."

"Stop your lying!" Connelly roars. "Get the hell out of here!"

He lunges at her but two men grab his arms. She wishes she could see Sandy's reaction. But oh god there's Evelyn, clutching a loaf of bread. June pushes through shoppers and bursts through the exit doors, crashing into a woman. She wobbles but the woman grabs her arm and smiles.

"You okay?" asks the woman, who's trailed by three small children. June nods and rights herself.

She sits in her car, gulping air. What did she just do? She did it, that's what she did. Over at the store, customers come and go as before. Word will spread fast. She rolls down the window and tugs at the neckline of her sweater; she's boiling again.

Eventually she drives home, to her real home, feeling windswept as if she'd been walking in a gale, naked of makeup and hair a fright but feeling cleansed. Gerald has turned on the tree lights and sits, admiring. June settles beside him, her heart still pounding.

"What's your favourite ornament, Mom?" He gets up and points to a blue glass ball with a pointed bottom, glitter spilling down it in ribbons and a village scene painted inside a pink hollow. "I like this one."

"I like them all."

He begins touching the ornaments gently. Mom never minded, even when he was small and clumsy. She squints at the lights. She exposed her shame. Everyone looking, Evelyn and Sandy and Ann McMullin. Maybe the hardest thing she's ever done, and maybe nothing will come of it. Just a mad, sad woman ranting on Christmas Eve.

There's a knock at the door. Oh no, the cops are here for her. He called the cops. Gerald looks at her because she knows he doesn't like to answer doors. But she can't move. The knock again. What would they charge her with? Slander? Or maybe it's him, come for her.

The door opens. "Hello?" a soft voice says.

Evelyn enters the hallway and June exhales. Evelyn comes and sits beside her, setting a grocery bag on the floor. She takes June's hand, then smiles at Gerald.

"Dear," she says, "can you put the kettle on so your mother and I can have tea?"

"Why do I always have to leave?" he says.

June gives him the eye.

"Okay, for you, Evelyn," he says, and stomps out.

June turns to Evelyn. "How did you find me?"

"I was on my way to the other house and saw your car."

"When you knocked I thought he'd sent the cops."

Evelyn frowns. "My dear, the last thing he's going to do is go to the police. You just accused him of rape, in front of the entire North End." She squeezes June's hand.

June shakes her head. "I can't believe I did it."

In no particular order she tells Evelyn about the past few months, how she regretted opening up about the assault: Barry disgusted, Lorne furious, Trudy egging her on to get revenge. How her dream of a happily ever after with Lorne fizzled. How Lorne kicked her out. How she blames Lorne—blames herself—for Mom's death. And now she and Gerald are back here, with Gerald sleeping in the front room. She needs her money back and she needs a job. The words pour out, like blood gushing from a wound.

"And I kept thinking about that pig, getting away with it," says June. "Still using stinky pomade like he did in the fifties."

"Ever the hairdresser."

June looks at her. "Did I mess up?"

Evelyn seems to think about it. "That man—no man—should be able to get away with what he did. You were brave, confronting him."

"I don't even care about telling the police; I just want him to admit it, to himself."

"Well the whole neighbourhood knows now. Interesting to see what the court of public opinion has in store for him."

"If people believe me."

"I've always found him smarmy, myself." Evelyn chuckles. "When you bit his hand."

Gerald returns and says, "Kettle's tooting."

The tea soothes, and afterwards June craves a cigarette but stops herself because she knows it bothers Evelyn. She watches the back door, expecting Barry or Trudy to burst in with bad news: the police are looking for her, people are calling her a sick liar, Lorne's already shacked up with someone else. She must stop.

"So, who do you have for Christmas?" she asks Evelyn.

Evelyn looks down at her hands. "Well, my sister was coming from Ontario, but they all have a stomach flu."

June nods. "You will come here."

Evelyn protests but June insists and it's arranged that Evelyn will return this evening for supper, and come tomorrow after she attends church. Evelyn leaves and June digs out the vacuum cleaner. She thought she'd feel healed, confronting him, but she's a ball of nerves again.

Barry returns in the afternoon with half a dozen shopping bags. Immediately, he calls up the stairs. "Gerald, come 'ere. I've got a surprise." He grins at June. "I found a dancing Santa."

"Evelyn's coming for supper and for turkey tomorrow."

"Oh? How come?"

"I ran into her at the grocery store. She has no one."

She watches Santa Claus wiggle his bum and Gerald laugh and Barry slap his thigh, his eyes wet with tears, and she can't tell Barry what she did. Not yet. She produces a supper of sorts and Evelyn arrives with a cake, red and green maraschino cherries forming a wreath on the white icing. She smells nice and has pinned a sparkly snowflake brooch to her emerald sweater. June's glad she invited her.

Everyone except Gerald toasts with glasses of the Baby Duck that Barry bought. The wine is sweet and fizzy and June tries to feel something, the elusive Christmas spirit, but her heart aches for her mother.

Lorne's probably at his oldest sister's. Surely she will ask after June and be shocked that he's ended it. June sips the wine and hopes he's getting a dressing-down.

Around midnight, long after Evelyn has left and they forced Gerald to bed—as excited as a kid about the following morning—June sits and watches Barry stuff candy into a stocking for Gerald. He sets it under the tree along with the gifts he brought home: a football and a warm jacket for Gerald, and something in a wrapped department store box for June. The gloomy black-and-white movie A Christmas Carol plays on TV with the sound turned low.

"You saved me. Getting those things for Gerald," she says.

He goes back to his rum and eggnog. "Well someone's gotta turn into Mom. Look, I'm getting so fat I'm growing boobs." She laughs.

In the movie, a ghost's forcing Ebenezer Scrooge to recognize the mistakes he made throughout his life.

Barry points at the screen. "We can drive ourselves crazy worrying about the past," he says.

"It's hard to let the old ghosts go."

"Mom would have loved tonight." He drains his drink. "I was thinking, me and Gerald can bunk in the big room, and you stay in the little room."

"We're taking away your privacy," she says.

"Privacy? I was going batty by myself."

Lulu

On Christmas morning, Viv makes those cinnamon rolls that come in a tube you bang on the counter to open, then bake and frost. Jimmy's croaking for a coffee; he turned into a coffee drinker up there and tea doesn't do the trick anymore.

"Drink yer tea and be quiet," Dad says and smiles.

Jimmy's gift to Lulu is an angora sweater, cream-coloured with a round neck and long sleeves. It's the most beautiful sweater she has ever seen, and her mind races to wearing it to school, the latest Toronto style. She's embarrassed handing him the wrapped Old Spice, but he acts thrilled, says the boys on the job won't know what to make of him.

"Maybe you'll meet a nice girl who'll appreciate it," Viv says with a wink, and Jimmy sticks out his tongue at her.

They go to Aunt Brenda's for turkey dinner, Viv bringing cooked carrots and turnip. Gran gives Lulu a pair of gold hoop earrings, "not real gold, mind you," and a ten-dollar bill in a card. Gran keeps sniffing the lavender bath set from Lulu, and the tip of her nose ends up powdered from the talc.

Lulu imagines Danny presenting the stolen English talcum powder to his mother: would he biff it at her? Would she bother to get him anything?

Throughout the day, despite the food and laughter and Viv and Brenda waltzing in the kitchen, Lulu has a jumpy feeling in her stomach, like she's missing out on something. She wonders what Matt's family does on Christmas Day. There's no way she can call him but maybe, in the spirit of the holiday, she'll call Janet. She slips into Brenda's bedroom to use the bedside phone. There's a book on the nightstand, *The Joy of Sex*. Lulu dials the number while flipping through the book, gets disturbed by the naked hippies, and shuts it.

"God, I need to get out too," says Janet. "Want to meet up at the school?"

Lulu tells them she's going to Janet's house. She's not dressed warmly because she travelled by car earlier, and as she goes out the door in a thin jacket, Viv points that out. The night's so quiet, Lulu hears her sneakers squeaking on the packed snow. Every window at every house glows; cars line the streets, parked halfway up the snowbanks.

The school's on a rise and the wind bites her face. The sheltered courtyard they've agreed on is poorly lit. She huddles against the wall and tries to pull the jacket collar over her chin.

Janet arrives within a few minutes, panting from running up the hill. She's in a new knitted hat and scarf, and Lulu envies her. With a flourish Janet pulls a pint of amber liquor out of her coat.

"Rum," she says, "to warm us up."

She takes a drink, shudders, and hands it to Lulu. Lulu drinks, coughs. A flame runs through her. They squat against the wall and discover they both got the latest Fleetwood Mac album for Christmas.

"Hey," Janet says suddenly, "remember we met Gerald's mother that time, in the store? Mom says she attacked the manager in the Frugal Mart yesterday, said he raped her or something."

"Gerald's mother?"

"Yeah. Can you imagine?" Janet takes another drink and licks her lips. "I mean, wouldn't you be humiliated, saying that in front of everybody?"

"She must have really wanted to."

"How could it even happen?" Janet whispers. "An old guy like that, when would he ever get the chance? To get her alone?"

The girls go quiet. *Rape* is a terrifying word, something to flee like the bogeyman, a word mothers and aunts use solemnly when recounting the tragedy of a girl they knew in school, or so-and-so's niece; a girl who'd been ruined, who never went anywhere in life, whose father wouldn't talk to her anymore, who wasn't believed, who was trying to trap a man, who dressed slutty and was asking for it, who lost her fiancé over it, who got pregnant, who became a nun, who moved to another town to escape the looks on the sidewalk, or worse, no looks at all.

"I don't feel too good," says Lulu. She struggles to stand.

Janet laughs. "You're drunk."

"So are you," says Lulu, who moves away, afraid—no, certain—she's going to throw up. She bends and places her hands on her thighs. Nothing.

They begin taking baby steps to Lulu's place. The wind swirls. Lulu slips on ice and Janet grabs her by the sleeve.

"We'll never make it," Lulu cries. She has never been so miserable.

"Shut up."

"Hey girls!" A man yells from across the street.

"Keep going," Janet says through clenched teeth.

"Lulu?" She looks up and it's her brother, jogging toward them.

"Jimmy! We thought you were going to rape us," Lulu says.

He shakes his head. "You're pissed." He puts an arm around her to help her along. Janet doesn't leave for home, just walks with them. "Janet, is this your doing?" he says.

"Can you drive me home later?" she says.

Lulu stops. She bends, gags twice, and vomits; the stream steams when it hits the ground and, in the street light, Lulu spies cranberries in it.

"Gross," says Janet.

"That feels better," says Lulu. Jimmy tugs at her again, and they make their way in silence to the apartment.

"What's going on?" Viv calls when they come in the door.

"Nothing. We're home," says Jimmy. He eases Lulu onto her bed and closes the door. Janet starts yanking off Lulu's shoes and jacket. Lulu turns her face into the pillow and moans.

"Fun night, huh?" Janet says.

Lulu lifts her head and looks at her. "Are you my friend?" she says.

"Yes. Now shut up and go to sleep." Janet pulls up the bedspread, and Lulu closes her eyes.

June

After Christmas dinner, Evelyn washes and June puts away while Frank Sinatra croons carols on the record player. Barry simmers the turkey carcass for soup; Mom liked to start it right away. Gerald's off reading the comics Evelyn gave him.

"I never believe Sinatra when he sings Christmas songs," Evelyn says, scrubbing the roaster. "He doesn't seem the sort to care about a sentimental old holiday."

"Too busy with Vegas showgirls," says Barry. Evelyn snickers.

June feels a rush of gratitude. Barry, who pulled off the day for Gerald and went easy on the liquor. Evelyn, who hasn't said a word about June's mother or Lorne or the grocery store but has let June know, through glances and squeezes of the hand, that she thinks everything's going to be okay. It's helped, if only for brief moments. The phone rings and Barry answers, hands it to June.

"Well Merry Christmas," says Trudy, jarring after a day on the sauce, no doubt. "I just heard what you did."

"Shh." June hurries down the hallway as far as the cord allows. "How did you hear?" she whispers.

"My niece was there. Right on, Junie. She said the place was buzzing after you left. I wish to hell I'd been there."

"I don't know. Everybody must be talking."

"Yeah and I say 'good.' The villagers coming at him with pitchforks."

June tries to imagine Ann McMullin and Sandy and Tina the cashier and the stock boys and maybe even the priest jabbing Connelly with pitchforks. Where does someone even get a pitchfork?

"Oh honey, I'm sorry. You're probably having a shitty Christmas," Trudy says. "Missing your mom. Lorne, that asshole."

"It's tough. But Barry's been great. Evelyn's here."

"The old lady who was obsessed with Gerald?"

"Do you think his wife knows?"

"I hope she boots him out and he gets canned and thrown in jail." Someone laughs in the background and Trudy ends the call, promising to visit tomorrow.

In the coming days, June tries to find peace with what she's done. Enjoy the revenge, as Trudy said. She peers out the front window, wondering if the whole street knows. One morning she scurries halfway down the block, chasing a section of their newspaper in the wind, and swears Archina and Dougelda scowl at her from a break in their curtains.

Another day she strikes up the nerve to tell Barry. He looks stunned. She's brought shame on the family—again. But he laughs. He roars in his chair.

"I wanted to kill that bastard after you told me. But you got him good."

"I thought you'd be mad."

Barry gets up. "I'm going to call my buddy who lives on his street. See if he's heard anything."

June follows. "I don't want your friends knowing about this."

"Too late for that." But there's no drama; Barry's friend says all appears quiet over at the Connellys'.

The next morning, Barry leaves the house and returns shortly after. He tells June he went into the Frugal Mart and there was no sign of Connelly.

"I hope they fired him," he says.

"Maybe he's just on Christmas vacation."

"Oh and Sandy said to say hi."

Evelyn hears the news first. Come January, Ed Connelly will take an early retirement. She stands in June's kitchen and describes overhearing the wife of the Mart's head butcher, gossiping in the drugstore.

"The butcher's wife told Miriam it's 'a *forced* retirement.' You know Miriam, the odd one in the wolf sweater," says Evelyn.

June covers her nose and mouth with her hands. "Oh my god."

"Didn't take long, hmm?" says Evelyn. June takes a ragged breath.

"See," Evelyn says, "people believe you."

June walks to the sink and lights a cigarette. "Or the store doesn't want the scandal," she says.

"I worried," June continues. "I worried about that little cashier up there. That he might try something with her."

"Then you've done a good thing."

After Evelyn leaves, June tackles the breakfast dishes. How does Connelly explain to his wife that he's up and leaving the job he's had for decades? She'd hear the story on the street. What's that like, learning the man you've slept beside most of your life raped a young girl in the stockroom? No, she couldn't believe it and lie there, listening to his snoring, absorbing the warmth of his body under the blankets. Cooking him pork chops. Or maybe she does believe it. Maybe there was something about him, all along.

Lulu

Lulu begs to skip the Boxing Day turkey sandwiches at Brenda's. Dad looks at her flaked on the chesterfield, under the brown and orange afghan that Nam crocheted.

"Looks like a hangover to me," he says.

"Jack, just leave her," says Viv, but she places a cool hand on Lulu's forehead.

Jimmy says he'll be over soon, and squeezes beside Lulu's feet. Mom and Dad go out the door.

"You ever drink before?" Jimmy says, picking out a chocolate from the variety box on the coffee table.

"Kind of." Lulu reaches for her glass of water. So thirsty. She threw up twice more this morning, hoping no one would hear.

"You like it up in Toronto, Jim?"

"Yeah, it's decent enough." He picks up the newspaper from the floor. "Just needed a change."

"Were you running away, from us?"

He looks at her. "No, why would ya say that?"

She shrugs. "I just thought, you know, their fights, moving around."

"You remember Candy?" he says. "We went out for a long time. Kept it quiet. When we broke up, I needed to get away."

"Oh, sorry. She was pretty." A blond girl with big earrings and tight T-shirts, and everyone knew they were going out. He flips a page of the Sports section.

"I don't really have a boyfriend," Lulu says. He looks sidelong at her. "I mean, we kissed. We went to a movie. But I think he liked me better as a friend."

"You never know. Guys are weird."

Eventually, Jimmy walks over to Brenda's for a hot turkey sandwich and Lulu dozes. The phone wakes her sometime in the afternoon, and she drags herself up to answer. Janet asks Lulu how she's feeling.

"I've been better."

"Your first hangover." Janet, so sophisticated. "There's talk of people hanging at the school tomorrow night. Maybe a bonfire. My brother's going to the liquor store. Wanna go?"

Lulu moans softly. She froze last night and feels terrible today. She says she's not sure, but Janet persists.

"C'mon," she says. "I'll call tomorrow and you'll feel like it."

Lulu thinks she should eat something, and as she's making toast, the phone rings again. It's Helen. She invites Lulu to her place today, says her family's driving her bonkers. Lulu pictures a towering Christmas tree in that fancy pink and green living room. It would be something to see. But she tells Helen she's hungover.

"Partying hard, huh?" Helen says and laughs.

Lulu bites the dry toast. Tasteless. "What did you mean, in the drugstore?" she says, trying to swallow the toast. "About wanting to leave Danny?"

"I'm tired of him. He's not a very nice person."

"Well just break it off." There's a silence. "Are you afraid, Helen?"

"No," she says quickly. "But I'm all he's got."

Lulu can imagine Danny getting pretty mad at being dumped.

"Want to come to a party tomorrow night?" she says. "Some people are having a bonfire up at the school. My old school."

"That sounds fun. I just need to live through my uncle's stories today."

Lulu turns on the TV and goes back to the chesterfield. Janet won't like Helen coming. She ignores her when she sees her and Lulu together. If Lulu had guts, she'd call Matt and invite him too.

June

Gerald's wandering again. Every day he visits the drugstore to chip away at the Christmas money June gave him. And he's probably waving at cars, though she doesn't like to think about that. It embarrasses her; she had no idea until Barry stopped at that intersection a number of years ago and saw his nephew at the curb. Made her think she didn't know her son, wanting attention like that, needing more than he got at home. Strangers looking. She scolded him but he wouldn't stop.

This time she warns him: stay away from buses. He won't look her in the eye.

"Yup, yup," he says and goes out into the snow.

She and Barry watch him rolling his shoulders in his new jacket, the pompom of his black-and-gold toque bouncing with each step.

"It gives him something to do," Barry says, and shuts the door firmly against the cold.

June returns to the kitchen and picks up the envelope again. Barry found it this morning, wedged in the door. A cheque, from Lorne, for one hundred dollars. On the envelope he'd written, "This is only a start." June brings the envelope closer. It looks like he wrote "sorry" but scratched it out.

"Want me to take you to the bank?" says Barry. "They should be open again."

Someone knocks at the door. June hesitates then goes into the hall, noticing the tree in the front room already looks tired.

Sandy looks up shyly as the door opens. "Hi, June. Thought I'd pay you a visit."

June ushers her in, stunned. Sandy takes off her boots and coat, and they go to the kitchen. June won't look at Barry, just puts on the kettle.

"Hi, Sandy, good to see you," he says, and goes upstairs.

The women sit. June crosses her hands on the table, uncrosses them.

"I guess you—" she says.

Sandy breaks in. "I was wondering how you were," she says. June widens her eyes. "Since the other day, I've been thinking about you. About it all," Sandy says.

"I caused quite the stir, I bet." June gets up to make the tea.

"It came back to me—he was always around you, giving you more 'training,'" says Sandy. "I was jealous. Didn't we all find him just a little bit handsome?"

June blushes as she sets the brown teapot on the table, shakes her head. *No that's not true.*

"And I thought I was too ugly for him to flirt with," Sandy says.

"Sandy," says June, pouring their tea. She brings her the last slice of Evelyn's cake.

"I didn't know. About the stockroom." Sandy presses her lips together. "You were seeing that Murphy fella."

The tea scalds June's mouth and brings tears to her eyes. She clears her throat. "No one knew."

"I felt bad when you quit school. It must have been hell, getting pregnant back then."

June drinks her tea. After she left the Frugal Mart, she never heard from Sandy or any other cashiers; not one friend from school called except Trudy.

"So I wanted to tell you, Connelly's gone. In the new year," says Sandy.

"Yeah, I heard."

"Management got wind of the ruckus," Sandy says, licking icing off her fork. "From what I hear, it wasn't what you said about him. It was because he grabbed a customer."

June nods and says, "Does his wife know?"

Sandy leans in. "Apparently, she's sticking by him," she says quietly. "Won't believe a word of it. My sister's friends with her sister."

"Do people think I'm crazy?"

Sandy shrugs. "Who cares? No, I don't think so." She takes a bite of cake. "Definitely not."

June remembers Tina. "What about the little one, Tina? Do you think he ever tried anything on her?"

Sandy laughs. "No, she's got a mouth on her. She'd tell him where to go."

June looks down at the table.

"Look, you did nothing wrong." Sandy points the fork at June. "You done good."

June nods. She could've done more. But she did something. And he lost his job over it.

"Did you make this?" says Sandy, finishing off the cake. "It's gorgeous."

"It was my friend Evelyn. You'll have to meet her."

Out on the stoop, Sandy pauses. The curls at her temples flutter in the breeze. "It was me," she says.

June frowns.

"I was the one who called head office. Disguised my voice. Thought I'd tell them what Ed Connelly had been accused of. They came in immediately and talked to the staff about it."

June laughs in surprise. Sandy goes down the steps. Her coat's a brown-and-olive-green tweed, picked threads hanging in spots, cut boxy in the old style. But it has quality silk lining, June noticed when she handed it to her, and the tag said "Made in Montreal." Probably cost her a fortune twenty-odd years ago. Sandy stops on the sidewalk.

"That's our secret, okay, June?"

"When are you gonna quit that place, anyway?" June says, smiling.

"Why should I quit now? I'm getting a new boss."

Lulu

In her last grocery order before Christmas, in honour of Jimmy's return, Viv stocked up on all the old junk food, including the breakfast cereals they loved as kids. This one turns the milk chocolatey brown. Lulu and Jimmy sit at the kitchen table slurping big bowls of it.

"You should call 'im," says Jimmy.

"Who?"

"The guy who's not your boyfriend," he says, and tips the bowl to his mouth for the best part.

She'd look so *needy*. "Guys hate that." Even she knows it.

Jimmy sets down the bowl. "If I was more honest with Candy, maybe we'd still be together."

Lulu thinks about it. She showers and dresses, she changes the sheets on her bed—they smell like sick—she even tries to read a book. And she thinks about calling Matt. She could ask him to the bonfire.

Around noon she works up the nerve to call the operator for his phone number. She looks at the numbers she wrote down, just fours and sevens and twos, nothing scary. She makes sure Mom and Dad and Jimmy are in the front room, and dials the kitchen phone. His father answers and she asks for Matt. She wants to throw up again.

"Hello?" he says.

"Matt, it's Lulu. How's Christmas? I mean, you don't get to do Christmas, right?" She cringes and he chuckles.

"I'm good. What's going on? I was going to call."

"You were?"

"Yeah, maybe do something again."

She closes her eyes and the feeling of release is so strong she has to squeeze her legs so she doesn't pee on the floor, like a happy puppy. She asks him to the bonfire. She's been promising everyone a bonfire; there sure better be one.

"Sounds great," he says. "I'll swing by around seven."

Lulu hurries to her room and plugs in her curling iron. She has no patience with this sort of thing but does what she can. From under the tree, she digs out the angora sweater. She'll dress warmer this time but make sure people see it.

Helen arrives first, just before seven, and Matt is close behind. They stand in their coats as Lulu rushes to get her things on. She doesn't want to have to introduce anyone.

"Love your sweater," says Helen.

"Thanks," says Lulu, who's crouched tying her boots.

"Now who's this?" Viv says. Lulu looks up, bits of angora stuck to her lip gloss.

Helen and Matt introduce themselves, and Dad steps forward and shakes Matt's hand. Jimmy leans against the wall watching. They need to get out before Dad says something stupid or Viv embarrasses her. But Viv is asking Helen and Matt where they live and if they want a glass of orange pop.

"Beautiful kimono, Mrs. Dawes," says Helen, and Viv explains that it's real silk, made in Japan, and Helen tells her she loves vintage.

"Okay, we're leaving," says Lulu, squeezing between Matt and Helen to open the door.

"Bye, kids. Don't do anything I wouldn't do," Viv says in a singsong, and Lulu wants to die.

Out on the street, she starts off in a rush but then tells herself to calm down. She exhales and waits for them to catch up.

"Your mom's beautiful," says Helen. "I see the resemblance."

"Yeah, right," says Lulu.

"No, I see it too," Matt says.

A few blocks away, Janet waits at the corner. She ignores Helen but makes a fuss over Matt, asking about the recent tournament. She tells him her brothers are all basketball fanatics—news to Lulu. Helen links her arm through Lulu's and slows their pace behind the others.

"I couldn't do it," Helen says.

"Break up?"

"I talked to him last night but I couldn't do it."

They reach the school and enter the paved courtyard where Lulu and Janet drank two nights before. Someone has dragged an old oil drum onto the grounds and started a fire in it; flames shoot toward the inky sky, there's the wonderful smell of woodsmoke, and about half a dozen guys and girls stand around it, drinking beer. Lulu recognizes most of the faces, older kids from down Janet's way including her older brother, Steve.

Steve's stocky with bushy red hair and long sideburns. Lulu has never felt comfortable around him. Growing up, he was snarly and often absent, always in trouble with his parents. Kicked out of high school for hitting a teacher; maybe a shoplifting charge too. Janet's father came down hard on him and Steve disappeared for a year, hitchhiked all the way across Canada. Came home with a tattoo of a west coast totem pole. He drives a bread truck now, and Janet brags they always have loads of food that "fell off the truck."

Janet goes over and he pulls beers from the two-fours near the wall. She returns, hugging four Schooner stubbies to her chest.

"We can probably get more," she says, and hands them each a bottle. "You owe him for these." Steve whistles and tosses them a Bic lighter, which Matt uses to flip off the bottle caps.

Lulu can't stand the smell of beer, let alone the taste. She sips. Hasn't improved. The fire looks so warming but she knows it's their place, as the younger ones, to keep back. She's flanked by Matt and Helen, who has already attracted one of the older guys to her side. He's tall with shaggy hair and a toque, and wears a couple of layers of plaid jackets.

"Aren't you cold with your coat unzipped?" Matt asks Lulu.

"Nope."

"Have a good Christmas?"

"Yeah," she says. "My brother's home."

"That guy at your place, I figured it must be your brother."

And Lulu knows she should have introduced Jimmy. "He works in drywall. It's an art apparently," she says.

Matt nods and takes a swig. "I wish I knew what I wanted to do," he says. "A lot of lawyers in my family but it sounds dry as dust."

"I want to go to university," Lulu says, and it seems to bounce off the asphalt during a quiet moment. He looks at her. "No one in my family ever went," she adds.

"Then you should," he says. "You're intelligent enough."

After a while Janet wrangles more beer out of Steve, who demands payment so they dig around in their pockets. Lulu turns down a second. The flames dance and light up the school windows, revealing a stack of binders on a desk, backward paper letters taped to the inside of the glass that spell out "Joyeux Noël."

The older guy has stuck by Helen all night and he's making her laugh. She stops abruptly. Lulu follows Helen's eyes toward the opening of the courtyard, where Danny, Mikey, and Banger hover.

"Don't mind if I do," Danny says and bobs over to one of the older guys.

"He's drunk," Helen whispers.

Danny bugs Steve for beer and Steve asks for money first.

"Banger," says Danny, "pay the man."

Danny and his boys weave into the fire circle, and the talk and laughter go up a notch. Lulu's group has settled in a shadowy corner, but the courtyard is not that big and they're trapped there. Within a few minutes, Mikey glances over.

"Look, it's Tubby," he says, and Danny turns. He approaches Helen, holding a beer.

"What you doin' here?" he says. "Slummin' again?" He turns to Lulu. "And I thought I told you, stay away from my girlfriend."

She swallows.

"I'm not your girlfriend anymore," says Helen, setting her jaw. Danny steps toward her, and Lulu senses Matt tense next to her. But it's Helen's new admirer who steps between Danny and Helen.

"Back off, punk," he says, pushing Danny in the chest.

Danny pushes him back hard, and the older guy punches him right in the face. Danny staggers. Lulu and Matt and Helen lunge out of the way, but Janet trips. Her bottle shatters around them as people run over—Steve and Mikey and boys Lulu can't put a name to.

Matt helps Janet up and Lulu pulls Helen to the wall. Steve has Mikey by the collar, practically lifting him off the ground. Curses and grunts. Another guy from Steve's crowd confronts Banger, who holds up his hands as if to say, "I'm no fighter."

Danny recovers from the punch and tries to land one, but Helen's admirer jabs him hard in the stomach, and Danny doubles over. The guy says something into his face and walks away. Danny, half-slumped against the wall, doesn't move.

Steve still has Mikey and the two of them are yammering at each other. Something flashes at Mikey's throat, just a moment caught by firelight. Lulu's not even sure she saw it. Steve releases his grip and Mikey falls into the glass. Steve points toward the snowy sports field.

"Get the fuck outta here," he yells. "Ya jackasses."

He returns to the bonfire, where someone's ripping up an empty beer box and feeding it in. A girl laughs. Mikey rises slowly and Danny straightens up behind him.

"C'mon, Banger," says Danny. He turns and limps toward the darkness. Banger hurries to catch up and Mikey follows, and as he passes the fire it reveals blood dripping from his hand. Helen waves away her admirer, who eventually takes the hint.

"We should go," Matt says, his voice shaky.

Janet calls goodbye to her brother, cheery like nothing happened.

"Don't bring your special friends next time," he tells her, and his pals laugh.

When they leave the shelter of the courtyard, the night feels bitter. Lulu does up her jacket partway and Helen entwines their arms again.

"Did you see the knife?" Helen whispers. "Steve had a knife."

Janet asks them to her house, down the hill toward the harbour. Lulu would rather go home but she stays and they cross the field in silence, boots crunching on snow. God knows what Matt thinks about his night out in the North End.

"Can you believe that? Danny and Mikey?" Janet says after a few minutes.

Lulu doesn't answer because yes, she can believe it, just as Helen likely can. Yet those guys were just whooped by Janet's brother and his buddies, who are much more dangerous. Janet, always with her head in the sand.

Lulu flashes back then to her and Janet on another winter day. Maybe grade three. They were in Janet's overheated kitchen, in the little house so close to the new bridge, you'd swear you could touch it. The girls rolled snickerdoodles as Janet's mother wrestled a hefty ham out of a pot of steaming water. A younger sister, licking cinnamon sugar off her fingers, asked about another brother, Dave or Don or Doug. Lulu had never heard of him.

"When's he coming home?" the little sister said, and the room fell silent. Janet's mother's eyes bore a hole through the loose-tongued child.

Lulu never heard the name again, it was as if it never happened, and it slipped out of her memory until now. Janet always tells people there are five kids in her family, but there must have been six. The sixth someone shameful not to be mentioned. Janet, always smiling, letting on her family is big and fun.

They hurry past the Pit and the lights of Dartmouth across the harbour, then another half dozen blocks. But before they turn onto Janet's street, figures emerge. Danny, Banger, and Mikey.

"You kids still up?" Danny says. A shiner's already forming on his left eye.

"Just leave us alone," says Helen.

He clamps an arm around her shoulders, squishing up her nice coat, and forces her to walk with him awkwardly, where the paved road trickles into a path that runs toward the new bridge.

"I wanna show you all something," he calls out.

"Hey!" Matt says, moving toward them, but Mikey blocks his way and begins poking him in the collarbone with a bleeding finger. In the street light, Mikey looks unfocused, drunk, not right. There may be a cut on his neck. Matt frowns.

"Let her go," yells Janet, running toward the bridge.

"Down here, to look at the pretty lights," calls Danny.

They trail behind, reluctant followers. The path slopes and the snow's deep around them; dead plants with bobble heads poke out of the drifts.

Danny stops and looks up. They're beneath the steel underbelly of the bridge. Cars above make a clackety-clack, like a train. Lulu didn't know someone could get here. She can just make out a wide piece of steel running the length of the span, backed by shorter pieces running the opposite way, like a ribcage. The cars above ending their journey from Dartmouth.

"You ever see it like this, Helen?" Danny says. He lets go of her and she stands staring up. He points toward the basin, past the road taking cars in the opposite direction, past the ribbons of concrete that separate them from the water.

"That's where the coloureds used to live. You got any coloureds down your way?" he says.

"You shouldn't say that. That word," says Matt.

Danny turns. "What's that, faggot?" he says. Everyone stills. Banger giggles. Clackety-clack.

"Don't ya know, little Lulu, that your boyfriend's a fruit?" Danny says. Lulu has a river running through her ears.

"Screw you," Matt says and flies at Danny. They grapple; someone screams. Danny punches and Matt falls. He sits up slowly and touches his mouth.

Legs running through snow, a blur of lights, and Lulu's hitting Danny's chest and face, for all of the horrible things he's done and will continue to do. He grabs her flailing wrists.

Then Helen and Janet are at her side and Matt's trying to pull Lulu and Danny apart. A mass of arms; an elbow jabs Lulu in the face. Janet and Helen pin down Banger, and Matt ends up standing behind Danny, locking Danny's arms behind his back. Matt's a bit taller. Danny breathes hard; he's had a rough night.

"I hate you!" Helen screams at him. "I wanted to save you. But I don't care anymore."

Danny lifts his head and looks at her. It's a dead look, like the caged animals at the wildlife park. "I don't need to be saved."

"Hey, look at me!"

They follow the voice up, where Mikey, a dark silhouette, stands on the outer guardrail of the bridge above.

"Mike!" Danny yells. "Get down!" He struggles and Matt releases him.

Danny starts scrambling up a steep snowy slope, a wedge of land that rises to the surface of the bridge, but it's slippery and he doesn't get anywhere. Mikey somehow fought his way up and teeters atop the guardrail, which is maybe three feet high and has horizontal slats. Lulu can just see the roofs of the cars travelling behind him.

"Get down, Mike!" Danny pleads, half-standing, bracing himself on the ground with one hand.

"Mikey?" Banger says, like a question.

If he falls it's what, maybe thirty, fifty feet down to the path? Lulu's no good at that sort of thing. She looks at Janet.

"Run home and call the police," she says, and Janet takes off.

Lulu watches her and wants to run too. What's she doing, on this freezing night, in the kind of place teenagers gather to drink, with Danny and Mikey? But she turns and Matt has arrived at the top of the slope. Mikey's about twenty feet away from him, wobbling on the rail. Matt offers his hand and seems to call to him, but the cars muffle his words. Mikey turns his head.

When Mikey falls, it's not forward onto the path below the bridge, the thirty or fifty feet down, but backwards, onto the surface of the bridge. Into traffic. Cars can't stop on a dime, in the dark, on wet, slippery pavement. Everybody knows that.

June

June's squashed in the back seat of Martin's car, shivering in a dress Trudy made her wear and a coat too thin, smelling the bad aftershave of the new guy on her left, tensing to avoid touching Trudy's brother Reg, on her right, who's always had a thing for June.

Trudy swivels in the front seat and smiles back at them, her red lipstick catching the light but her eye sockets shadowed. Like a ghoul, June thinks, annoyed Trudy's forcing her to come. Forcing her to show her face in public.

"It's gonna be so much fun tonight, Junie," says Trudy.

June says nothing.

"It's a live band, right, Mart?" Trudy says, pinching the sleeve of his sport coat. He grunts and makes a left turn.

"And the scoff, my god June you won't believe the food," Trudy goes on. "They bring it out at midnight."

As Martin parks the car, Trudy squeezes in one more thing—talking June into New Year's Eve—before they pile out.

"Blois here's a...what is it, Blois?" she says. "Purser?"

"Petty officer," he says.

"I'm an assistant manager," says Reg.

"Yeah, at the Woolco," says Trudy.

June tiptoes across the parking lot, praying Trudy's heels don't bring her down. Underneath the coat, the dress rides up her behind. Reg offers his arm and she ignores it. She longs to be home, though Barry invited the guys over for poker. At least he's enjoying himself. She bought Gerald extra candy to ease her guilt.

She yanks down the dress again and tucks the coat check chit into her sparkly little purse. Trudy called it a disco bag. Follows the others into the dark hall, where the band plays "Mustang Sally." A handful of early dancers twirl in front of the low stage; they jive and make behind-the-back passes, seem to sense where their partners are, move like couples who've danced together forever. Trudy hands her a drink ticket and June figures she may as well use it. Get through this thing.

Blois is already at the bar with a beer. June gives him a close-mouthed smile and waits for the bartender to notice her, unsure what to order when he does. She can feel Blois looking at her.

"You don't wanna be here either," he says.

She tilts her head, getting a better look than she did in the car. Tall and slim, dark hair and olive colouring, thin lips; a grade B Clark Gable. A lot of women would find him attractive. June can't decide.

"Is it that obvious?" she says. The bartender points at her, she has a moment of panic and orders vodka and 7 Up.

"Divorced?" he says.

"What?" she says. "Oh, divorced, no. Just…single."

"I am," he says. "Divorced." He bends so she can hear him, practically touching his mouth to her ear. She's glad she sprayed on perfume.

"Kids?" he says. She tastes the drink and screws up her face.

"One. A son."

"What does he do?" His dark eyes look tired. Sad, maybe.

"Nothing," she says. Blois chuckles.

"They can be lazy buggers, eh?" he says. "My two can't keep a job."

The ice is watering down June's drink. It's better but her feet are killing her.

"Jeez," he says, "did you hear some kid jumped off the bridge the other night?"

"I need to sit," she says, and lurches from the bar. She doesn't care if he follows. His questions are simple enough but they have complicated answers.

She spies an empty table in the far corner. On the splintered, thin wood tabletop sit a beer bottle and a couple of cardboard crowns that say "Happy New Year!" A paper plate of Cheezies. The plastic chairs are made for stacking. June plunks and stretches her feet, scowls at the skinny shoe straps digging into her instep.

The band has switched to fifties music, "Rock Around the Clock." It was one of their favourites; she'd swing Gerald's chubby hands and make him dance, he'd tip his head way back, giggle until he toppled over, and she'd collapse too, laughing, lying on her back and breathing hard. He'd give her a wet kiss on the lips before running off. That was her Friday night. She wasn't even twenty-five.

Blois approaches and she straightens her back and sucks in her stomach. He sets down two fresh drinks and takes the chair next to her. Raises his beer in a toast.

"Here's to a new year," he says. "Gotta be better than the last dozen." He takes a long drink.

June grasps the clear plastic glass he brought but doesn't taste it yet. Last time she got drunk was the card game. A fight and then sick. Lorne, who she thought was her future. But they tried twice and it didn't work, twice. Bet he's not at a dance tonight.

She sips the vodka and eyes Blois. She's not drawn to dark-haired men, despite "tall, dark, and handsome," despite Mom telling her, strangely, "Never trust a fair-haired man." But shit, she was attracted, once. *Admit it.* She squeezes her eyes shut.

"Wanna dance?" he says.

She wants to say, *No, I do not want to dance. These effing shoes are murder and I feel fat in this dress and I'd rather be home, overhearing men argue about cards in another room. I hate New Year's. I hate that Trudy tried to set us up.*

"Sure," she says.

They dance to two or three songs. He's not bad and she loosens up, laughs when he tries something fancy, in a joking way. She hasn't danced in she doesn't know how long. They dance a slow one; he puts his hand on her bum and she's startled: is this how it's done now? Trudy waves from across the packed floor, pleased with herself, no doubt. They return to the table and drink thirstily.

Blois asks if she'd like to go out sometime, a movie or bowling. She's been expecting it. Does he actually like her, June, the person? Even find her attractive? Or does he just need someone, anyone, to hold?

Over egg rolls and fried rice, they'd sketch their stories—she wouldn't tell him much—clutch each other in the car, agree to another date. Then she'd expect a phone call, feel hurt if it came late or not at all.

She's tired. She doesn't want to listen to another sad story and absorb it as part of her own, worry about him, wish she could wash it away. She's out of room.

"I can't," she says, and his smile drops. "Thanks, but I'm just not ready."

"Oh," he says, "I thought. That's all right." He puts the bottle to his lips but it's empty.

"I'm tired."

"You wanna go then?" He jumps at the change in subject. "I can get you a cab."

"No that's okay—sure, why not? Get me a cab."

They get up, as if resigned to something unpleasant, their chairs scraping the floor during a lull in the music. There's a phone near the entrance with a direct line to a cab company—June could do all this herself—but she collects her coat and watches him talk into the receiver, then hang up.

"They say it's gonna take a while. New Year's," he says.

"That's okay. You"—she gestures toward the dance floor, the pulsing music heavy on the bass, the lone flashing strobe, the bodies gyrating in the dim hall—"go back in. I'll wait here."

"If you're sure. Think I'll stay."

She nods. "Yeah, go. Thanks, Blois."

He goes and soon she can't make him out in the crowd.

Outside she breathes in the sharp air, tickled she's getting away with this. Trudy will be mad. The cabbie will spy her here under the light, which is revealing a gentle snowfall. She pulls her coat closer, stamps her feet to try to get feeling back in her toes, pulls the sparkly butterfly clip from her hair. The door creaks and Reg comes out, smiling sheepishly.

"You going, June?"

"Yeah. Waiting for a cab."

"Mind if I share? Cabs hard to come by tonight."

"Sure, why not." He sidles in and zips up his jacket.

"You don't like dances?" he says.

"Oh, dances are all right," she says. "I just don't feel like it."

Lulu

Word spreads: Mikey Frenette killed himself. Jumped off the old bridge. Zigzagged naked down the middle of the new bridge, and *splat*. Out of his mind on dope. Washed up nude beside the oceanography institute, bloated and blue. The scientists thought it was a porpoise—Viv heard that one at work. Marie Frenette could barely identify her son and there were no dental records to help, because none of them had ever seen a dentist. That one sounded likely.

When Lulu returns to school after New Year's, she avoids people. It's all kids are talking about, and she can't say a thing without choking up—over Mikey, who tortured her. Viv says it's because she's in shock. Matt shakes his head no if anyone even looks like they want to ask about it. Some are surprised to hear Helen was there, but she just tells the nosy to piss off.

Janet won't shut up. For two weeks, she holds court in the corridors and girls' locker room, in the cafeteria and on the bus, explaining with flourishes and dramatic pauses what really happened. She neglects to say she wasn't there when Mikey was hit by the snowplough, that she and her father ran up just after. But Lulu's not going to correct her.

Danny disappears. Janet hears he left Halifax, someone saw him entering the bus terminal. She tells Lulu this on the phone; they've taken to talking every night. Viv won't let Lulu out and checks on her every fifteen minutes, but Lulu doesn't want to go anywhere anyway.

She and Matt still sit beside each other in English but have stopped spending time together. There will be no more dates. *Are you?* she wants to ask. *Because it's okay if you are.* They get 90 percent on the Shakespeare assignment and he gives her a stingy smile.

"How are you doing?" she asks one day, it takes so much for her to ask, and he just says, "Good." As if the old Matt were crushed that night, too.

Yet throughout the winter, he continues to star on the basketball court. During morning announcements, the vice principal reports how many points Matt got the night before, top scorer in yet another win. Lulu won't go watch, despite Janet's pestering.

"It's like he's possessed out there," Janet says. The accusation, the one Danny threw at Matt that night, hasn't made it into school, and none of the girls repeat it.

Lulu goes to Helen's a couple of times; Helen has lost interest in the drums, just stays home and listens to James Taylor. Though they discuss the knife, a glimmer at Mikey's throat.

"I wasn't sure what I was seeing," says Lulu.

"I saw Steve pop it open," Helen says. "I think he cut him with it."

Cynthia's frosty. Helen says her parents were livid she was there that night. They clearly blame Lulu for drawing Helen into Danny's world. Cynthia does not ask her to dinner, and Lulu slips out the heavy door into the cold, the smell of something delicious filling the house behind her. She now knows where to catch the bus and has shaken off the willies over walking in the dark. The days are getting longer anyway.

Liz is still doing shifts at the drugstore. One Saturday, as they eat lunch, Lulu decides to tell her about that night. Liz is the only person who hasn't asked. Lulu says Danny seemed drunk when he arrived at the school and then Helen broke it off with him. Lulu was worried he'd explode. To cap it off, Steve and his friends humiliated Danny and Mikey in a fight. She tells her about the knife and Mikey's blood. Liz sucks on her straw, her eyes never leaving Lulu.

"After he fell, things got crazy," Lulu says. "The grown-ups took over. Janet's dad ran up. Sirens. The ambulance had to stop on the bridge and it caused a traffic jam, even late at night. That's what the news said."

The police questioned them, the witnesses, and that's when Lulu noticed Danny and Banger had taken off. Janet's dad led them to the house and they all called their parents. As Lulu and Dad stood on the sidewalk with Janet's parents and Matt's dad, Matt keeping a distance, all of them speaking in half-sentences, Helen's father, Graham, pulled up.

He got out and took in the house dwarfed by a looming metal utility tower, at the bridge shooting across the harbour behind. Janet's father always called it the best view in the city. Helen's dad didn't even speak to the other parents, just ordered Helen into the Volvo.

When Lulu got home that night, exhausted and numb, she peeled off the angora sweater and threw it on the floor. Ruined, by a red blotch near the neckline. Blood.

She doesn't tell Liz the main thing on her mind. She can't figure him out. He kissed her, really kissed her, in class. He seemed to like her. Maybe he can't figure it out either. She'd been beating herself up: she wasn't skinny or interesting enough. But maybe that wasn't it at all.

What did Danny see? Or was it just a slur, one of the nastiest things a guy can hurl at another?

"How annoying, Lu," Janet says one night on the phone. "You finally get this great boyfriend and he turns out to be..."

Lulu rolls her eyes. "Janet, we don't know anything. Yeah, it would've been nice to have a boyfriend." She pictures Matt, silent in English class. "But mostly, I just miss my friend."

June

Nothing has changed at the doctors' office since June was last here: wood panelling, bulky gunmetal desks, orange vinyl chairs. Vivian Dawes is on the phone when June enters. She smiles, motions for June to sit.

"The druggist can give you something for that, Mrs. Smith," Vivian says, nods and adds some uh-huhs and oh-that's-a-shames.

June squeezes between an old woman in a quilted hat like a tea cozy, and a young man with his arm in a sling. One of them reeks; June decides it's the woman. Poor thing probably lives alone and has trouble bathing, like Mom did. The waiting room's packed and the other phone, on the empty desk, keeps ringing. That's why June's here—a job interview. They've just lost a receptionist and need another one fast.

"Vivian said to call right away," Evelyn urged June two days before. "I was just there and it's mayhem."

It took June a day to work up the nerve but now she sits, wishing her short winter boots looked better with a skirt, waiting to speak to one of the three doctors. Jiggling her purse on her lap. After twenty minutes, Vivian directs her to an office door.

"You'll be great," Vivian says.

The doctor has his back to her, writing at his desk, but says to sit down. After a moment he twirls the chair and faces her. It will be no love match, as Trudy teased her: he's about sixty-five with wire glasses down his nose and a pot-belly behind the white coat and tie. Blue ink stain on the chest pocket. Wedding ring.

"Mrs. Green," he says. "You think you can handle it here?" The direct question throws her.

"I'd like to try," she says.

"Do you type? File?"

She's not qualified, she told Evelyn that. She clears her throat. "I type a bit. And I know the alphabet." Dumb.

He wrinkles his brow, then leans back, his chair tilts seemingly too far and he laughs. "Well I suppose, yes, the alphabet's crucial to a filing system," he says and laughs again. He clicks his ballpoint pen in-out, in-out.

"Okay, let's give it a shot," he says. "Mostly, we need someone with maturity, good with people. We're bringing on a nurse too, god willing."

"I've worked with the public all my life," June says and smiles.

"Excellent." He offers his hand to shake hers. "I'm Dr. Dauphinee, by the way. Vivian will get you set up."

June has a stupid grin when she emerges into the slushy January afternoon. Three days a week for now, eight o'clock to five. Beginning tomorrow. If she had a hat she'd toss it in the air, like Mary Tyler Moore. Between this and the money from Lorne, splitting expenses with Barry, they'll be okay.

Yet as she walks farther from the office, she sobers up. There's Gerald, and she wants no more joy rides or disappearances. As soon as she gets in the door she calls Evelyn, who has offered to help. Evelyn will spend tomorrow with him.

"But you know, June," she says, "it's time to look into the sheltered workshop. I go by on my walks, and the young people all look so happy."

June hangs up and fingers a business card taped to the fridge. She calls the number and tells Gerald's social worker they're interested. The social worker sounds relieved, thinks there's a spot available; they could probably take him next week. Gerald enters the kitchen while June's on the phone. She has to tell him. He does not take it well.

"No, no, no, no," he says, and runs up to his room. She grimaces, then marches to the bottom of the stairs.

"Gerald," she calls up, "we have to try. Mommy has to go to work."

She hasn't called herself that in years. Mommy, like speaking to a small child. But this feels like the old days, forcing a kid to go to school. Grade five, when that brat teased him mercilessly.

When Evelyn arrives early the next morning, Gerald's moping in his bedroom. Barry wishes June a good first day. He's walking too, his car on the blink again.

Evelyn coaxes June out the door. "Don't worry, we'll have fun. We're going to make cookies." She holds up a bag of ingredients.

June arrives at the office perspiring, pantyhose wet through her boots, carrying shoes and a ham sandwich in a plastic bag. She goes up the wooden wheelchair ramp that's been added to the old house and worries she's the first one here. Peeks in the bow window and Vivian's at her desk. June taps on the glass.

Viv—"Call me Viv"—shows her the cramped back room for storing her coat and purse, the kettle, boxes of bandages and medical forms, a mop. She leads her to the empty desk and June sits gingerly in the wooden swivel chair.

"This is you," says Viv. "I cleared out the last of Sharon's things. The phones are straightforward but we're getting fancier ones soon."

The phones start ringing before the doctors arrive and then the patients come. A lot of people with white hair, mothers with children, the priest, who seems embarrassed. June realizes she'll need to be discreet. The morning passes in an instant; she doesn't even have time to pee.

She eats her sandwich in the back room, gazing out a tiny window that overlooks the side street. Clumps of children —coats wide open, mittens on strings dragging along the ground, hats stuffed in pockets—return to school, throwing snowballs and hooting. Gerald needs to have an arrangement; he has to try the workshop.

Around four o'clock, a woman holding a toddler enters. She looks down at June's blotter and raises her eyes just enough.

"The lady said come, you'll squeeze us in," the woman says softly. June looks at Viv, who's on the phone. Viv nods.

The woman adjusts the child at her shoulder, a boy two or three in a ripped snowsuit. He has a phlegmy cough. June smiles and asks for her name, pen poised above the hard-covered record book.

"Mrs.?" says June. The woman twitches.

"Just write Patty Parker," she says.

"And your boy?"

"Lawrence."

Patty and Lawrence sit over an hour while the doctors see scheduled patients. At quarter past five they're still waiting, the last ones there, but Viv says she can't stay any longer on this particular day. June offers to remain until they've been called in.

"You sure?" says Viv. "Your first day."

"I'll be okay."

"By the way," Viv says at the door, "my Lulu loves Gerald. I mean, she was worried sick about him last year. He comes into her store."

Then it's just June and Patty and Lawrence. The phones stop. Suppertime traffic passes outside. Baseboard heaters pump out a dry heat. Water drips somewhere.

"Hungry," Lawrence whines to his mother.

That day, when June carried Gerald here with the bleeding chin, to the doctor from Africa who was so kind. June has no food for the child.

"I have a son," she says. Patty looks up.

"He's grown now, twenty-nine." *I raised him without a husband, too.* Patty sort of smiles.

A patient leaves and Dr. Dauphinee sticks his head out and calls Lawrence's name. June stands. *Guess she can go home now. She sat all day but she's exhausted.*

Lulu

Winter drags on, they get snow flurries in April, and it seems spring will never come. Lulu buckles down and concentrates on school, tries to ignore the fact Matt's ignoring her.

One afternoon in May, an actual spring-like day, they wind up leaving English together. It's the final class of the day and they emerge into the sunshine without speaking. Lulu turns toward the bus stop, not planning to say goodbye. He never does. But Matt asks if she wants to walk a bit.

"I found this little park by the water," he says.

They pass the shops and restaurants of Quinpool Road, the Oxford movie theatre, large houses with generous verandas. The road falls and the Arm becomes visible. At the bottom of the hill, where the road curls toward the busy traffic rotary, a sliver of grassy land, like a comma, juts into the water. Lulu has seen it from the back seat of the car.

They go down the slope to the water's edge. It's a day fit for daffodils and dandelions—the shock of yellow. A day that can heal the hurts of winter. Beyond the stone seawall, sailboats are anchored in the shimmering water; big houses line the shore and there's the Dingle Tower opposite, where Lulu used to swim. The Waeg's somewhere here too; Helen says they'll swim in the lido this summer.

"Do you think about it much?" Matt says.

"All the time. You?"

"Yup." He picks up a stone and examines it.

"Do you think he was high?" she says. He shrugs.

She waits for him to bring it up. The other thing. Instead

of skipping the rock, he takes a big wind-up and throws it toward the water. It plops, a disappointment. They need to talk about it. That's why he asked her here.

"I don't care," she says. He looks over. "What Danny said." His face goes still. "I just wanna be friends," she says. "I miss—"

"He was wrong," he cuts in. His voice says *subject closed*.

She blushes.

"I've started seeing Katie Bishop," he blurts.

She inhales sharply. Katie Bishop, a blond ponytail and legs as long as Lulu. Prancing in the hallway in tiny volleyball shorts, always smiling with big, white teeth. She'll look fantastic next to him. Lulu swallows. He looks at her and his eyes soften.

"I wanted to tell you in person," he says.

She wills her eyes not to fill. It's just a surprise, that's all.

"That's great," she says and tries to smile. "She's more your type."

A woman with a beagle on a leash walks in their direction. Lulu pushes past Matt and starts up the hill.

"Lulu," he calls.

"Gotta go. See ya."

He doesn't follow. She takes the sidewalk toward the rotary, traffic streaming by. She can let the tears go; if anyone notices she's just a girl, crying.

She knew it couldn't be the same, so why's she so devastated? Her thoughts, her eyes, all blurry. She concentrates on crossing busy streets without getting killed, on her thirst, on her aching feet. She enters an unfamiliar convenience store in the West End to buy a pop, and the young man behind the counter greets her warmly. He might be from India. The store smells spicy and there's a basket of strange red-green fruit, it must be fruit, beside the cash register.

"Mangoes," he says with a smile. "Taste."

He offers a saucer of glossy, deep yellow cubes. It tastes like peach and banana and pineapple all rolled into one.

"That's amazing," Lulu says. She leaves smiling, promising to return. The pop tastes so fake after.

It takes over an hour to walk home. She sinks onto their chesterfield and it comes: it's not fair. It's not fair her relationship with Matt ended that night at the bridge. That they're awkward around each other. Not fair some girls have long legs and the confidence to play sports. That Matt feels he should date a girl like Katie, should date at all. And Mikey. A bully, a thief, "a bad egg," as Gran might say, but he didn't deserve that.

Lulu's stomach hurts for days. At school she passes Matt and Katie chatting by the lockers. Her chest pinches but she walks erect. His eyes follow her. She can't talk to Viv because it might come out—the accusation, her questions—about Matt. She can't bear Janet's flippant analysis, and Helen's down one of her rabbit holes these days. The whole school will soon know about Matt and Katie anyway.

On Saturday she has a shift at the drugstore with Liz. The day after she graduates, in just a few weeks, Liz is boarding a plane to New York. She has written publishers asking for job interviews; she'll share a studio apartment with a friend's second cousin. Her dream come true. Lulu tells her about Danny's slurs and Matt dating Katie.

"Matt's gotta do what he's gotta do," Liz says. "We all do."

Lulu nestles more packs of cigarettes onto a shelf. It's not the answer she was hoping for, but maybe she expected it. Out the window, Gerald's waving at cars. Viv had his mother in for tea last week, and they laughed a lot.

"My parents fight constantly these days," says Liz. "I can't wait to get out. But I'll miss you. Smart beyond your years."

Lulu will miss Liz too, but she'll be okay without her. Playing top dog over Farrell's niece or whoever works along-side her this summer. Ordering the new girl to fetch lunch at Buppy's. Banking her measly paycheques. And as soon as she turns sixteen this summer, she'll get her driver's license.

They close the store at six, and when she gets home her parents are waiting.

Viv squeezes her palms together at her mouth, as if in prayer. "Lu," she says, "we found a house. We're buying a house."

They drive over, it's not far from Gran's. Small with a pointy roof—Dad calls it a one-and-a-half storey—and an enclosed porch barely wider than the front door. Mint green with dark green trim. Like the simple, make-believe houses Lulu drew as a kid, smoke twisting from the crayon chimney.

"There's a plum tree in the backyard," Viv says. "Can you imagine? Our own fresh fruit."

They'll move this summer, paint her bedroom whatever colour she chooses. From the back seat, Lulu studies the upstairs window they pointed out as hers. She can see it, a luscious mango. No one else has a room that colour. She giggles: Dad will blow his top.

Viv looks back at her. "You'll still live at home for a while, right?" she says. "There's a bus stop handy, for going to university." Lulu never mentioned university to her mother. But she knew.

It all sounds okay. Her parents happy, hopefully for a good stretch. Room for Jimmy when he visits. And when Lulu does move out, whenever and to wherever that may be, she can picture them in this little house near Gran. With a plum tree and a mango bedroom.

June

The one-year anniversary of Gerald's disappearance arrives in May, and though June has told herself she won't dwell on it, does not remind Gerald or Barry of the date, she has an odd day at work. She's sluggish and mopey, and then she remembers again.

She doesn't want to upset Gerald, he's doing so well at the sheltered workshop. Comes home talking about the friends he eats lunch with, Jessie and Kevin and a girl named Sally. She brings him peanut butter cookies from home, and though June's rattled by the idea Gerald might have *a girlfriend*, the workshop director tells her it's fine, don't worry.

"Shouldn't we all feel special?" the director says.

The Saturday after the anniversary falls sunny and warm, and June decides to go for a drive—with her full driver's license. She and Gerald travel over the bridge and he strains to get a glimpse of the navy and coast guard ships below. She's going to take him to the Shore.

The drive's longer than she remembered—she's never driven this far—and as the Bug picks up speed cruising down coastal hills, as she pulls on the steering wheel to make the sharp bends, her heart thumps. At times, she feels out of control. The lines on the road coming at her. *Calm down.*

Lorne visited the other day. Still handsome. He brought another cheque and said he hopes to pay it all back by fall.

"I guess I'm just meant to be alone," he said at the door.

Then why did you chase me after you moved back? Hearts broken all over again. But his words touched her.

"I wasn't perfect either," she said.

She glances to her right. Glittering blue water in cove embraces, little islands of furry evergreens, ochre seaweed blanketing speckled rocks. Must have been hard for Mom and Dad to leave. It's past lunchtime when they turn onto Foggy Loop, and summer visits with her parents come back, the excitement of seeing the road sign, knowing soon she'd be running with cousins through tall grass and down to the water.

Aunt Pansy's front porch lacks a railing but no one uses that door anyway. The house has a flat face, like the plain houses in the North End, and moss coats many of the faded red roof shingles. June hasn't called ahead but there's a pickup truck in the driveway.

"Oh my word," Pansy says when she sees them. She clutches her chest and June kicks herself for not calling.

The sprawling kitchen's the same: ancient linoleum printed with daisies, a round table in the middle, the old enamel cooking range to the side, not used in decades but Pansy won't see it go. A worn settee, perfect for napping. The radio plays hymns.

Didn't matter if it was hot as Hades, Pansy would often be in the throes of baking or canning when they arrived, so many jars of grey-green chow lining the counter. There's no sign of work today. A plaid armchair has been moved to the window and a teacup rests on the sill, amber rings on white paint, and June sees how Pansy spends her days.

Pansy feeds them bologna sandwiches on stale white bread, and the cookies are from a box. She reminds June so much of Mom; it all just makes her sad. Pansy explains cousin Ronnie has walked a few houses down to help a neighbour with a lawnmower.

June asks after Maureen. There will always be a sting but she's trying to rise above these things. She reaches across and rubs Gerald's shoulder.

"Wears a suit every day to the bank," says Aunt Pansy, "and their new house, if I could only find the snap of it." She gets up and digs through the sideboard. From behind June could swear it was Mom, small and sturdy.

Maureen's house is a brick two-storey, on a street far away. A baby tree planted near the curb, no sidewalk. Two cars in the driveway. June doesn't envy it.

"I think we'll scoot," she says. "I want to show Gerald some sights."

Foggy Loop Cemetery sits on a spectacular piece of land. It's a crest with a clear view out to sea, protected on either side by spruces and by a cliffside row of wild rose bushes, fragrant pink flowers that somehow bloom each summer. Today, the bushes still look dead. There's a metal arch meant to be an entrance.

"A waste of a fine piece of property," Dad used to say. "You think corpses care about a view?"

June treads lightly across the small graveyard, sunken and mossy in places. There are perhaps thirty headstones, some weathered black or tipped over, others graced by plastic bouquets. She finds the family markers and turns to Gerald. He's still outside the arch, paralyzed and wide-eyed.

"It's okay, honey, it's only grass and hunks of rock," she says. She extends her arm. "Come here, I want to show you our people."

He shakes his head. "I'm scared of ghosts."

She smiles. "Casper was a friendly ghost," she says.

He shakes his head.

"Bad idea. Look here." She squats in front of a headstone. "This is your great-grandfather, William Henry Green. Born 1870, died 1942." She turns to face him. "Grandad's father."

"What about my dad?" he says. "Where're his people?"

"I told you," she says, her strangely buoyant cemetery mood burst. She walks toward him. "We don't think about him."

Mercifully, Connelly and his wife have moved out of the neighbourhood, "pushed out by gossip," Trudy said.

"Is he a bad man?" Gerald says. Such thoughts could give him nightmares, perhaps make him feel bad about himself.

June wraps her arms around him and squeezes, closes her eyes. "No," she says into the breeze behind him, "just not our friend." It doesn't seem adequate but it'll do for today.

At the edge of the gravel parking area, a black iron bench faces the water and, according to the brass plaque, it's dedicated to someone dearly missed. They sit. The whitecaps have picked up. An aluminum boat with an outboard motor putts by, and the man and woman in it wave. Gerald waves back.

"In the summer," June says, "we'll come back and swim."

"Looks cold."

"Freezing."

When June was a girl, her mother called her a water rat: always in it, tasting, floating on her back, twirling, trying to capture it in her arms. But it always slipped through her fingers.

She'll need a bathing suit. Evelyn and Viv could come. Lulu too, if she wants. Trudy. And Sandy, who never gets out. June stands and reaches her hand to her son.

"It's been years since I had a swim," she tells him. "I don't know why I stopped."

Gerald

Gerald slides the girl the money, the girl Lulu with brown hair who said her mother works with Mom at the doctors'.

"Here you go," she says, handing over his change. She smiles.

He shoves the coins into his pants pocket; the chocolate and comic book go in his jacket. That's how he likes it. Won't look up in case she's still smiling. At the door he pauses a second before stepping out, so he can hear it. *Tinkerbell.*

Not too cold today, not too hot. *Just right, Goldilocks.* There's Buppy's, his favourite. After Gerald got lost, after the policeman found him, Buppy sent food down to them, a club sandwich and a hot chicken sandwich and stinky fish. Cans of pop. Mom said they didn't have to pay for it, it was a gift.

"See, Gerald?" Nana said. "Everybody loves you." He misses Nana so much.

He looks with yearning at the corner. He'll just stick around for a bit, see what kinds of cars go by. He saw a pink Cadillac the other day and told Barry about it. The people didn't wave back.

Danny and Mikey aren't around anymore to bug him. There was something on TV, about a boy falling off the bridge, and Jessie said it was mean Mikey. But Mom told him, don't be so foolish.

A bus pulls up to the stop, they always sound tired, and Gerald steps back until it leaves. Mom says never, ever get on one without her. He shakes his head. *Don't think about it, the scary nights in the cardboard teepee. The noise when the train went by.*

A long blue car stops at the light. Blue's his favourite colour and it's an Impala like Barry's.

Gerald waves, fast, before the light changes. *Look at me*. A little girl in the back seat waves back. She's missing a tooth. The light goes green and she pulls away, still waving.

He stays a few more minutes but no good cars today. He'll see what Mom and Barry are doing. Mom said they'll have "a family outing" this weekend. Sounds boring. On Monday he has stuff to do at the workshop, and Sally might bring more peanut butter cookies. With the criss-cross on top.

Acknowledgements

Many generous people helped get this book past the finish line. Thank you, Whitney Moran, managing editor at Nimbus Publishing and Vagrant Press, for your keen eye and for welcoming a first-time author. Freelance editor Penelope Jackson was wise and kind, and championed the manuscript. I might not be here without her.

Writer Becca Babcock, my mentor through the Alistair MacLeod Mentorship Program, asked all the right questions and was endlessly encouraging. Thank you, Becca. Through the Humber School for Writers, David Bergen gave invaluable advice on the story in its early stages. I enrolled in Carol Bruneau's class in revision, which inspired me to change—and I believe improve—the opening.

Sherry Hassanali, acting as sensitivity reader, eased my mind about using language that's inappropriate today but was nevertheless true to the time and key to this story. My friend and fellow writer Sue Murtagh pushed me to continue when I needed it. It's been a joy experiencing "first books" together. Marilyn Smulders urged me to try again. Members of a Halifax writers' group were among the first readers and kept me on my toes, especially Valerie Spencer, Susan Drain, Gwen Davies, Bretton Loney, Rosemary Drisdelle, Sheila Morrison, and Stacey Cornelius. Thank you, Elaine Flaherty, for your common sense.

My cousin Tanya Toner Cole showed me the path underneath the A. Murray MacKay Bridge, and I knew immediately I'd use it in the novel. Dr. Adva Barkai-Ronayne, veterinarian and friend, confirmed, yes, a hamster can die that way. Staff of the Killam Library at Dalhousie University brought in a book on Henry Morgentaler that was important in my research. Jackie Foster at Nova Scotia Power looked into the age of the utility towers near the bridge.

To my children, Rachel and Ben: Love you forever.

And to my husband, Rob, thank you for finding my sports errors, for cheering me on, and for tolerating a messy dining room table.